A Cowgirl's Stories

A Novel by T. P. Graf

Companion to The Life and Stories of Jaime Cruz Trilogy

Tumbleweed and Dreams (Book One)
Night Air Descending (Book Two)
Seeds in the Desert Wind (Book Three)

ISBN 978-1-7352332-4-6

Library of Congress Control Number: 2022908392

amazon.com/author/tpgraf
tpgraf@pm.me

A Note to the Reader

While this can be read as a stand-alone story, most of the
characters are introduced in the trilogy that precedes
this work. Getting to know each through "Jaime's stories"
will enhance "Sallie's stories" significantly.

This is a work of fiction. While some of the people, events, places,
and their context in relation to time may be real,
the story's characters are wholly imaginary.
The opinions expressed are those of the characters
and should not be confused with those of the author.

Dedicated in memory of
Tex Van Hoefen Harrison—neighbor and friend.
She always wore a smile and
extended a hand to any in need.

Acknowledgements

How can I begin to thank (again!)
Grace Chalon, Irene Checkovich and Veva Vonler
for their labors and support in telling my stories?
Friends in need—friends indeed!

Cover Cowgirl Image
Deborah Kolb
deborahkold.net

Other Notes of Gratitude

To the memory of the carpenter from Pettisville—
my humble, gentle grandfather,
Jacob H. Rupp (1886-1963)
for the poem, "The Monkey's Viewpoint"

For the prophets, living and dead—
Berry, Merton, MLK and Twain among them—
whose lives and words hold the key
to fulfilling the vision of heaven on this earth.
Ignore them to your peril!

Finally, to the creatures and people
who stitch together in one's imagination
that which brings forth characters and stories
to share with other travelers on the journey
on this, our beautiful, celestial orb.
Celebrate them to your delight!

T.P. Graf's Writings & Awards

As the Daisies Bloom - A Novel

PenCraft Awards - 2020 First Place, Cultural Fiction
Book Excellence Awards - 2021 Finalist
CIBA, 2020 First Place, Somerset Book Awards

A beautiful telling of life's trials and tribulations, always overcome by the love of family and of something greater than oneself. - Reader's Favorite

*Enchanting as it is charming ... intimately and poetically told ...
like a well-written symphony - Literary Titan*

*A powerfully written character-led novel; stark and unsettling but often funny too.
Highly recommended! - A 'Wishing Shelf' Book Review*

August Kibler's Stories for Tyler
Voices of Context from Eden to Patmos
(Companion to As the Daisies Bloom)

Firebird Award - 2021 Winner, Christian Poetry
American Book Awards - 2021 Finalist, Religious Poetry
Royal Dragonfly, 2021 Honorable Mention, Religion/Spirituality

A compelling and thought-provoking study of the bible and Christian history. The writing style is almost angelic! It's the sort of book you want to discuss; that stays with you for a long, long time. - A 'Wishing Shelf' Book Review

Graf has crafted a masterful work of modern literature that takes on some very complex topics...in a format that any reader can engage with and glean wisdom from ... entertaining ... highly recommend. - Reader's Favorite

The book offers fresh ideas ... absorbing ... thought-provoking and evokes a positive emotional connotation. - Literary Titan

Roots, Branches and Buzz Saws
More Stories of August Kibler

"Celebrate who you are, even if it is quietly...". That is what this book is, a celebration of August's life and a reminder to the reader to celebrate their life, who they are. - Literary Titan

*This book is a perfect example of how each life is valuable and is a story to tell...
important ... impactful ... perfect slice-of-life novel - Readers' Favorite*

*Insightful, powerful, a story of life and how it's changed by so many tiny
happenings. Highly recommended! - A 'Wishing Shelf' Book Review*

Looking Out onto Our World
Explorations of Power, Dogma and
a World Deserving of Contemplation

*Insightful, intelligent; the sort of poetry that will stay with you for a long time.
Highly recommended. - A 'Wishing Shelf' Book Review*

*Alive with sensory experience...refusing standard conventions
of storytelling...confident...each word in each verse deliberate ...
arranged for maximum impact...ripping and compelling ...
will engage even the most reluctant poetry reader. - Literary Titan*

*Introspective ... thoughtful and fascinating a realistic observation
of life's journey ... with an eye towards hope and celebration ...
full of emotive and intelligent wordplay ... highly recommended ...
a great pick me up and talking point to share with others. - Reader's Favorite*

The Life and Stories of Jaime Cruz (Trilogy)
*CIBA, 2021 Finalist, Laramie Book Awards -
TP Graf for a Series - Americana Western Fiction
International Impact Book Awards, Winner, TP Graf - Author for a Series*

Tumbleweed and Dreams (Book One)
From the Series - The Life and Stories of Jaime Cruz

*Firebird Award - 2021 Winner, Book in a Series
Firebird Award - 2021 Winner, Multicultural Fiction
American Fiction Awards - 2021 Finalist, Multicultural Fiction
Hollywood Book Festival - 2021 Honorable Mention, General Fiction*

*Graf manages to keep readers enthralled with Jaime's day-to-day experiences
chapter after chapter ... a beautifully penned tale of self-discovery and a strong
main character who stands out in a crowd. - Literary Titan*

A gripping story filled with colorful and often captivating characters.

An immersive journey of self-discovery and a sense of home … you find yourself invested in the lives of the people and the friendships that are made.
- Readers' Favorite

Night Air Descending (Book Two)
From the Series - The Life and Stories of Jaime Cruz

A cleverly-crafted, character-led family drama set in Texas. I got so immersed in it, I started to feel like one of the family too! - A 'Wishing Shelf' Book Review

Whether you're in the mood for a slice-of-life drama or a study of eclectic characters, Night Air Descending by T.P. Graf is a memorable read.
- Readers' Favorite

This is a beautifully written book that has a grounded and authentic feel so much that it feels like we are reading someone's diary … heartwarming … [with a] distinct literary aesthetic. - Literary Titan

Seeds in the Desert Wind (Book Three)
From the Series - The Life and Stories of Jaime Cruz

Every quirk, every nuance, and each daily challenge make this story relatable and enjoyable…a book that wraps around you like your favorite blanket and touches your heart in a unique way. - Literary Titan

Graf again delivers interesting, full-bodied characters that we can relate to and want to follow through to their conclusions… a story that will entertain and move you. - Readers' Favorite

A powerful, often thought-provoking end to this excellent trilogy. Highly recommended. - A 'Wishing Shelf' Book Review

A Cowgirl's Stories
Companion to The Life and Stories of Jaime Cruz Trilogy

Days in the Desert
Food for Body and Soul

Delicious and nutritious! - Reader Review

Momma's Creed

[Jesus said], "But I tell you who hear: love your enemies, do good to those who hate you, bless those who curse you, and pray for those who mistreat you. To him who strikes you on the cheek, offer also the other; and from him who takes away your cloak, don't withhold your coat also. Give to everyone who asks you, and don't ask him who takes away your goods to give them back again.

"As you would like people to do to you, do exactly so to them. If you love those who love you, what credit is that to you? For even sinners love those who love them. If you do good to those who do good to you, what credit is that to you? For even sinners do the same. If you lend to those from whom you hope to receive, what credit is that to you? Even sinners lend to sinners, to receive back as much. But love your enemies, and do good, and lend, expecting nothing back; and your reward will be great, and you will be children of the Most High; for he is kind toward the unthankful and evil.

"Therefore be merciful, even as your Father is also merciful. Don't judge, and you won't be judged. Don't condemn, and you won't be condemned. Set free, and you will be set free. Give, and it will be given to you: good measure, pressed down, shaken together, and running over, will be given to you. For with the same measure you measure it will be measured back to you."

Luke 6:27-38 (WEB - Public Domain)

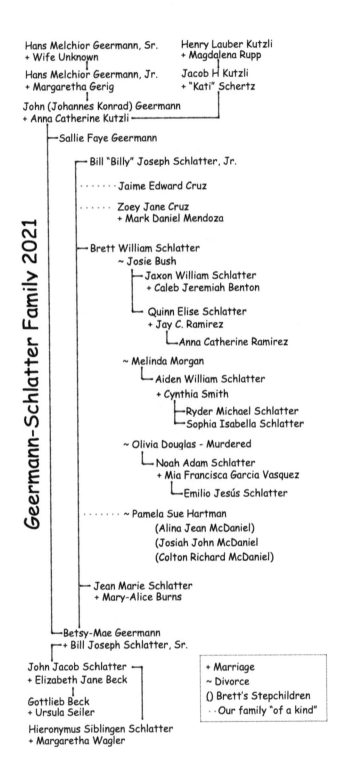

Geermann-Schlatter Family 2021

Hans Melchior Geermann, Sr.
+ Wife Unknown

Hans Melchior Geermann, Jr.
+ Margaretha Gerig

John (Johannes Konrad) Geermann
+ Anna Catherine Kutzli

Henry Lauber Kutzli
+ Magdalena Rupp

Jacob H Kutzli
+ "Kati" Schertz

Sallie Faye Geermann

Bill "Billy" Joseph Schlatter, Jr.

Jaime Edward Cruz

Zoey Jane Cruz
+ Mark Daniel Mendoza

Brett William Schlatter
~ Josie Bush
Jaxon William Schlatter
+ Caleb Jeremiah Benton

Quinn Elise Schlatter
+ Jay C. Ramirez
Anna Catherine Ramirez

~ Melinda Morgan
Aiden William Schlatter
+ Cynthia Smith
Ryder Michael Schlatter
Sophia Isabella Schlatter

~ Olivia Douglas - Murdered
Noah Adam Schlatter
+ Mia Francisca Garcia Vasquez
Emilio Jesús Schlatter

~ Pamela Sue Hartman
(Alina Jean McDaniel)
(Josiah John McDaniel)
(Colton Richard McDaniel)

Jean Marie Schlatter
+ Mary-Alice Burns

Betsy-Mae Geermann
+ Bill Joseph Schlatter, Sr.

John Jacob Schlatter
+ Elizabeth Jane Beck

Gottlieb Beck
+ Ursula Seiler

Hieronymus Siblingen Schlatter
+ Margaretha Wagler

+ Marriage
~ Divorce
() Brett's Stepchildren
· · Our family "of a kind"

When I "hung up my spurs," it didn't dawn on me that I might live a lot longer. It was Noah who first pronounced, after my old horse, Nellie, was in the ground, that I had a lot of years left. Up until then, it had never really occurred to me. I figured by the time this ol' cowgirl was in her seventies, the body would be worn out, and I would, hopefully, just not wake up one morning.

Death has not been somethin' I have ever feared, though I have no complaints about living. I don't even mind havin' to work out the mornin' kinks that come from too many years in the saddle. Reminds me I am alive, and I am *always* grateful for another day. As long as my hearin' holds out, I have the birds to sing to me. It would be a sad day for me if I lost both sight and hearing. Maybe, I'd have some new sense with which to appreciate all the creatures that make their home here, but I'd just as soon keep what senses I have. I have always been a lover of creatures, but I digress just a bit.

It has been a long established realization in this family that when Noah, Billy or I predict some future notion, however implausible it may seem at the time, such predictions are to be taken seriously. So, I had to assume Noah was right, and I had more years to go than I'd thought possible.

I had promised Nellie that when she was gone, I would not get another. When she went to her reward, I was already in my seventies, and so I figured that was an easy promise to make. It was one I honored, though I doubt Nellie would have really cared. She might have even wished, deep down, that some other horse would get to put up with my Swisher Sweets as she had done for those thirty-plus years—snorting more at the whiff of smoke going up her nostrils with every passin' year. In fact, snorting at me just lightin' one up. I suppose it was her way of disapproving of my unhealthy habit in fear that I might go up on the ridge before her. She certainly didn't want to break in another rider.

Soon after Billy was back home, he said he thought he'd try old Nellie out. I told him, "Good luck with that." I said it in jest, as I figured if Nellie would take to anyone it would be Billy. Over the years, she had hiked many a back leg, giving a good kick to any cowboy that got near her. She'd even kicked Bill, though Bill always described the kicks he received as "more of a love tap." It was enough of a tap for him to never try and ride her, and the other men always got a good bruise. In one case a *cabrón*, that rather deserved it after pokin' her with a hotshot, got two broken ribs. That was his last day ever helping us on the ranch. He threatened to sue me, but never did. I did have enough witnesses that saw what he did to provoke her, and she was in her prime in those days. She could put forth one *helluva kick!*

Well, Billy got her all saddled up and hopped on top. She just stood there. He shook the reins. "Giddy-up!" Billy shouted. She just stood there. He then asked me, "How do you get this damn horse to move?"

"She just goes when she knows she and I are both ready."

"Well, I'm ready," Billy asserted. "What's it take for her to get ready?"

"Probably for you to get off," I answered.

Again he shouted, "Giddy-up!" Adding this time, "You old nag!"

He *shouldn't* have said *that*, and Billy wasn't quite prepared for what happened next. She gave the biggest buck I'd ever seen from her with her back end goin' a good four feet off the ground. Billy found himself thrown off in the dirt.

He just got up laughin', patted Nellie on the neck and said, "Ol' gal, you take care of Sallie, and I'll take care of you. How's that for a deal? I won't ride you, and neither will anyone else on this ranch."

Nellie nudged him in the chest almost knocking him over on his backside, but he caught his balance. Billy concluded the exchange, "All right. It's a deal."

I suppose before I get too far into this story writin', I should explain what got it started in the first place. I was quietly minding my own business—deep in a book—and tucked in my usual corner of the couch, enjoying the small cracklin' fire in the skillfully laid-up, lovely rock fireplace that Ernesto and Jaime had built those years before, when Noah stopped by with no other apparent agenda than to see what I was up to.

"Aunt Sallie, how many books you gonna read before you get around to puttin' down for us all everything you ought to be passin' along?"

"I didn't think ol' cowgirls made much of a habit of writin' down their life," I replied. "Though I suppose a few write some poems."

The boy's answer to that was, "Grandpa writes the poems; you need to write the stories."

"Well, Noah," I replied, "I will give it due consideration since you asked. I don't know where I'd start. I guess I'll just have to get that laptop you and Billy and Jaime got me for Christmas and see if anything comes forth. I've had it a month and haven't done much with it. I guess the three of you had hittin' me up with this notion all along. I wondered what y'all were up to when I opened that box."

Noah explained, "I told Billy and Jaime that given how you scribbled back in my school days, if any of us had some hope of actually reading what you wrote, then we were going to have to get you on a computer. Billy thought maybe an old Smith Corona was more suitable. The only reason I knew what that was, was because of the old one Grandpa used to have in his office."

"Your grandpa, grandma and I shared that typewriter anytime we needed to have something typed up. It's probably still around here somewhere. Bill probably just stuck it in a closet. I could manage on it pretty good, but your grandpa definitely went about it with the hunt-and-peck mode. Your grandma could type as fast as she could think."

"Yeah, in addition to English lessons, she taught me to type, though I learned on a computer," Noah recalled.

I added, "You can assure those other two across the cattle guards that I'll *give* it a whirl. No guarantees. I at least owe to you three and Jaxon, Aiden and Quinn—hell, Brett and Jean for that matter—some of the things I remember about early life on the Geermann ranch. Not just *my* early life and your grandma and grandpa's, but your great-grandparents' especially. They were salt of the earth."

Then Noah said, "Now, we don't want some glorified version that makes everybody look like saints, though I can't think your stories would come out in that fashion."

I laughed at that. "You don't have to worry too much about that. You might have to worry more about puttin' an age restriction on 'em so they don't fall into impressionable young minds too soon. We wouldn't want Anna Catherine or that young'un of yours gettin' corrupted before their time."

"We'll risk it," he said, adding, "and we need to be humored a bit as we go along, so we can picture your little head-bobbin' chuckle as we read. You and Billy are our primary entertainment, after all."

I laughed at that too. "I guess my laugh is more of a chuckle, and I didn't realize it came with my head bobbin' along in rhythm with it. I don't know where that came from. I'm pretty sure I didn't do it as a girl. Must have come from all those years of bobbin' in the saddle. Hopefully, it's not from some undiagnosed nervous disorder. If I start bobbin' my head when I'm sittin' still, let me know."

"We'll let you know," he replied. "To date, it comes only with the chuckle, and it suits your cowgirl ways."

"I should warn you, too. I'm likely to write like I talk. When we were dividin' up who was gonna teach what when we started homeschoolin' you, your grandma said, 'I don't care if the Spanish he learns from you is rough compared to what would be used in the Mexican universities, but I don't want you teaching him English grammar. At best, your grammar and spelling are near approximations to the actual language.' At that I laughed and responded, 'That you even give me credit for a near approximation is more generous than I expected.'"

Noah assured me, "Who gives a rat's ass if it's proper English? It needs to sound like you! Grandma would say the same thing. As she put it in my school days, don't confuse what passes for conversation on this ranch as actual English."

"That's a good one," I chuckled.

As quickly as he had appeared he was gone. Like his Uncle Billy, Noah can't be away for very long from whatever real work needs doin'. Jaime can't be described as lazy in any form or

4

fashion, but he has always deferred to Foreman Billy to set the course and pace on any given day for the work that needs gettin' done. Noah's right there with 'em knowin' that when Billy wants to pass the foreman duties on, he, too, has to be ready just as Billy had been ready when Bill passed the duties to him.

Duty passin' in this family is an undramatic affair. My daddy was still healthy as a horse when he corralled Bill and I one morning and said, "I'll watch you two from now on. Don't screw it up." We had no idea he was even thinkin' of steppin' aside.

With that, Bill and I worked out how we best thought we could and should work together so as not to get on each other's nerves. As the years passed, it turned out getting on the other's nerves wasn't something we needed to be concerned about. I never did get irritated with him, and if he ever did with me, he kept it a well-guarded secret.

Like unto it, Billy and Jaime claim they never have had an argument with each other. We all laugh at that—well, I guess they laugh and I bob my head and chuckle—but it does appear to be true, and it must be said has been just as true for Bill and me.

Now, where my sister, Betsy, is concerned, that's another story. The only thing that saved me from never speaking to her again during her fundamentalist days was the fact that she'd never come out to the ranch. Those few miles kept me from ever tellin' her what I really thought—that is, with any frequency. She knew very well what I thought of her runnin' Billy off and ignoring her only daughter, who lived not more than twenty miles from Bill and Sis's house in town.

I've rambled on enough for now, I suppose. If some unsuspecting great-niece or great-nephew picks this up one day to read it, I thought I'd lay out what got me motivated to make a start.

I can't promise any strict adherence to chronology. Memories aren't stored in chronological order, and we are workin' from an old lady's memories. And for sure, memories often get all tangled up and refreshed by the present. That said, from here we'll have to forget the present and go back to 1937 and meander back from there to "prehistoric" times—pre-my history that is. I won't go back so far as to get to Adam blaming Eve for temping him. Then again, just writin' that reminded me of Daddy, so I guess I am gonna go back to Adam for just a bit, after all.

Anytime Daddy would do something he considered dumb after the fact, he'd look at Momma and say, "The woman made me do it!"

And she'd say back to him, "The only thing I've ever made you do is to take off your horseshit boots before you come in the house."

That was the one and only phrase my mother ever used that contained the word shit or any other "vulgarity," as they say. Daddy and I didn't have any high moral calling to avoid the frequent use of shit, damn and a few others that Momma and Sis worked to avoid for the sake of their Church of Christ souls.

It seemed the only reason Momma and Daddy landed with the Church of Christ crowd was it was the first protestant church going into town. Convenient stop I guess, not that gettin' across Fort Davis took more than a couple minutes even back in the horse-and-buggy days. Given how far the ranch was from town, they never made a habit of going any too often.

As a young'un I thought we were German. Daddy said we were mostly Swiss. When I asked what the difference was, Momma said the Swiss like quiet while the Germans like beer. Of course, bein' Church of Christ, she would look at it that way. Daddy wasn't all that quiet and did like beer well enough—Church of Christ or not. She always said some German must have gotten in there somewhere.

Once when I told this story to the family, Jaime said, "I'm pretty sure the Swiss like beer, too."

Sis had been married a year or two and still no children were in sight. Bill joked, it wasn't for lack of tryin'. I happened to ask Momma one day why it was our family was so small, when so many back in the day had a dozen kids. She told me, quite matter-of-factly, about how unprolific her family was. It was then she told me she'd had two miscarriages before I came along. When I asked if she'd ever told Sis about her problems, she said she had even before Bill and Sis married. She thought fair warning was in order, and wanted to ensure Sis felt free to talk about it should she have her own miscarriage.

As Momma put it, "It's one of the heartaches we women have to contend with, but with a loving husband, you get through it. We know Betsy has nothing to worry about when it comes to a supportive and understanding husband."

That night at supper she mentioned to Daddy me askin' about it. He just smiled and said, "What we lacked in quantity we made up for in quality."

Momma was better about keepin' tabs on who was who than Daddy ever was. She'd scribbled down what little she knew of the family tree, and I've kept that sheet folded up in the old German family Bible. I guess it's about time I pass that sheet with my additions along with the old Bible onto Noah. Sis and I agreed that he should have it, since he's the one that looks like he'll be on the ranch long after we're gone.

My great-grandfather, Hans Melchior Geermann, Sr., came from somewhere around Schaffhausen, Switzerland and settled this ranch in 1887. HM, Jr., as my daddy called him, was five years old. No one seemed to bother letting anyone know who Mrs. HM, Sr., was, or where she came from. We never even knew her name. I tried to find an obituary for the poor woman but never came up with one. I know she died giving birth to her second child. Even her headstone in town is just marked, "Beloved wife and mother." Damnedest thing I ever saw.

We did know HM, Jr.'s wife's name, my Grandma Margaretha. I tried calling her Maggie for short, but she corrected me in the German accent she never lost. She spoke more German than English, and I think that's why Sis and I assumed we were German. Having learned since then what I have about Swiss dialects, I'd guess even a German would have been hard-pressed to understand her. I learned after she was dead that her adherence to her native tongue probably had much to do with the fact she never learned to read any English, and so she stuck with the Swiss-German she knew. That "High German" Bible belonged to her. It wasn't exactly a handy size to deal with, but she read it pretty much every day, according to Daddy.

Daddy had a fiddle that he passed on to Billy when he was just a little tyke. Billy stuffed it in a garbage bag when he left the house seemingly for good that fateful day, and he had it with him in Van Horn, where he used his lonely hours to master it. He put it in the bag just so his mother wouldn't see him leaving with it. She couldn't have really stopped him from taking it, since it had been given directly to him without passing through Sis. As it was, she wouldn't even look at him, so he could have walked out carrying it and she'd have never known.

He was going to take it out of the bag when he began his hitchhiking, but decided he might look like Al Capone trying to hide a sawed-off shotgun in the case and, thus, hurt his chances of catchin' a ride. Probably a good idea, as you are more likely to see someone totin' a gun out here than a violin.

Daddy called it the Winzeler violin. We don't know to this day if that was a family line through which it made its way to us, or if it was the Swiss craftsman who made it. Not so long ago, Sis looked on the Internet to see if she could find any Winzelers around Schaffhausen. Indeed there are some. She even found one that makes violins and violas. It could be an enduring legacy. We like to think it might be both the craftsman and an ancestor rolled into one. It certainly is possible. I don't know why this persists in my mind, but for some reason, I operate from the notion that Grandma Margaretha had Winzeler ancestors. Maybe I heard her say it once and I just can't call the memory up with any clarity. Who knows?

I'm sure the violin has little monetary value as violins go, but it was crafted well enough to last for generations. Billy has cared for it well, and it remains something that will be passed on to someone in the family when Billy knows it's time.

I remember Granddad playin' it. I wouldn't say he was a fiddler. He knew some classical pieces and played them well. I couldn't tell you the name of any of the pieces he played, though I could still hum the tune for a couple of them. I asked Sis if she knew what they were, but she's no more cultured than I am in that regard. Our music history lessons were lacking from our formative years and have not been enhanced since.

I also remember Granddad and Grandma singin' together in the evenings. They would harmonize singin' old hymns, and they even knew a few in German that their folks had passed along to them. I wish I had a recording of both their singing and his playing. I also wish I could remember those German hymns, but I couldn't sing you a single line. Probably a good thing. Sis claims my singin' is closer to a squawk than a tune, but it sounds pretty good to me. I guess maybe it's only when I get a little too enthusiastic that it runs more towards the squawkin'.

Sis sings pretty good. She doesn't have a big voice, but it's clear as a bell. When she sings, you can understand every word. Billy likes to imitate a female opera singer with vibrato so wide you can't understand anything "she" sings. That's just for show. The boy has a very nice voice just like his momma. How did I get off on this tangent?

When I was a teenager, I went through a brief time when it seemed like any little thing irritated me. It mostly had to do with teachers irritating me and not wanting to be in school, but I went through a general period of impatience. I tried to hide it around Momma and Daddy, but I guess I didn't do that very well.

That reminds me how a few years back when I talked about "suffering in silence" after a bad reaction to a tetanus shot, Sis corrected the record, recalling how my teacher sent a note home with me to have Momma keep me home until I was feelin' better. Sis says I moaned and groaned for days. I admitted all those years later, I might have done a little moanin' and groanin'.'

Anyway, one Friday afternoon when were back from town for the weekend, I got right to my chores, but got to doin' them far more carelessly than usual. I was *really* in a grumpy mood.

Daddy stopped and stood with his pitchfork still in his right hand. "Sallie Faye, put down the pitchfork and come sit on this bale."

Of course, I did as ordered. I never felt him tower over me, ever before, like he did in that moment. He stood over me, leaning on his pitchfork with both hands, and he looked at me a moment or two. I think he just wanted to be sure he had my undivided attention. He did!

"I know you don't have many memories of your Granddad Geermann. HM, Jr. spent a lifetime dealing with, as he put it, his sin of impatience. His impatience drug him into real anger. I don't want you to think I or my brother or your grandma were abused. We weren't, but we did live in some fear and trepidation about makin' Dad mad. Usually, we didn't have to do anything. Anything gone wrong on the ranch would set it off. It wasn't until you girls were born that he finally worked through his problems.

"I'm telling you all this now because it is easy enough to let our impatience turn into anger and anger turn into impatience—one feeds on the other in a cycle. Your chore doin' these past few weeks suggests to me, you could well get in this habit if you make a little more effort. Is that something you want to do?"

"No, Daddy. I don't want to be angry, but that school *makes* me angry!"

Daddy replied, "I hope we're seein' the worst of it and not your teachers or classmates."

"I suppose if I'm not hiding it from you, they probably see it, too."

"Yeah, they probably do." He continued, "I know your granddad said, impatience was a lifetime habit that only got harder to break over the years. For him, seeing you girls persuaded him he never wanted you to see his anger. For me, I just took my mind to all the things I found beautiful around here, and I transported myself there. Maybe that will help you, too. If it doesn't, never hesitate to talk to me. We'll work through it. Whatever you do, don't let the school and your feelings toward it have power over you.

"How are you feelin' about that pitchfork now? Are you ready to take it up with a little less attitude and a little more care?"

"I can do that, Daddy," and we carried on with our chores.

My daddy, Johannes Konrad Geermann, was born January 1, 1914, and always went by the name of John. Momma, Anna Catherine Kutzli, was born January 3, 1914—two days apart. And they'd end up with two miscarriages and two daughters, thus eventually dividing the ranch into two, though since Bill and I worked together it was more of division on paper than in practice. That was all to the good as far as Momma and Daddy were concerned. Bill was the son they never had.

I'm grateful that neither thought I needed to bring a second "son" into the family. For reasons not known to myself, let alone anyone else, I never wanted to marry and have never regretted not marrying.

Momma's family was tied back to her grandfather that settled in East Texas. Her granddaddy had come over and opened a bank in Nacogdoches. Bill's family, Momma's family and Daddy's family all were connected back in the old country. They made it their mission to stay connected even though they settled in different parts of Texas. It wasn't much of a connection those first years, but in 1896 when the Fort Worth Livestock show started up, they all agreed they'd attend every year. Momma and Daddy met that way, and Daddy hit it off with Bill one year. Within days, Bill found himself on a West Texas ranch, and soon enough married to the youngest daughter.

For the one scribblin' down the family connections, Momma never did much more than write down her family's names. Even then, she didn't know or didn't bother to go past her own grandparents. Though in this regard, she did say her grandmother, Magdalena, was a Mennonite, to which she credited her own "tendency towards pacifism" as she put it, and where she acquired her love of quiet contemplation. If this is indeed where Momma got her inspiration, it is a trait that both Sis and I very much appreciated and emulated in our own way. It was that trait in Momma that Billy had appreciated so much—almost to our surprise. Billy truly inherited Daddy's crazy wit and Momma's reflective soul.

Here I go wandering off again.

As for the stock show reunions, they worked *muy bueno*. The Schlatters were there to sell, the Geermanns where there to buy, and the Kutzlis were there to oversee their investments in other cow-calf and sheep operations. In those days, the Schlatters were among the first (and were certainly at the top of the game) for breeding and selling Brangus bulls—red and black. They never left the stock show without awards and sales booked out for another year—sometimes two or three. Whenever Daddy bought one, he was always given "the family discount." Of course, the only family we were to the Schlatters then was the fact the families were all from Canton Schaffhausen, but Daddy never turned down the discount.

And it must be said, some of the "bulls and heifers" being traded included their own offspring. I guess it was good tradin' in those days. I don't know of any divorces or abusive marriages in the mix. Down the line, when the young'uns went lookin' on their own, there were plenty of both, including my own nephew's shenanigans for too many years.

By the time Momma's granddaddy was ready to retire and let Momma's daddy run the bank, they'd had enough of the hot East Texas summers. Henry and Magdalena moved back to Schaffhausen, which did not end well for them. They soon found themselves living next to a world war, which they didn't think would entangle their homeland. However, Schaffhausen was accidentally firebombed by the Americans on April 1, 1944. They, and about 500 others, were killed, and it left a lot of homes and businesses destroyed. They say people in town were just looking up at the planes overhead—never expecting to be blown to bits. After that, the towns up by the German border painted big Swiss flags on their roofs, but apparently, it didn't do any good. The Americans ended up bombing another town soon after that. So, the only bombs dropped in Switzerland during World War II were American.

I would share a lot more about those early generations, but I don't know any more. The questions we might have asked that Momma and Daddy perhaps could have been able to answer came to me and Sis after they were buried up on the ridge, not far from Noah's place on the ranch. Whatever they did know and could have passed along, I guess never occurred to them that such might be of interest to us. That chapter is closed for eternity.

Daddy always said he was educated the same way as Abe Lincoln. He was past school age before the ranch had a car or truck to run into town. He was "homeschooled" as every ranch kid was in those days, except for the few that bought a house in town and mostly sent the girls off with their mothers for schooling while the dads and sons worked the ranch.

He didn't seem any worse for having avoided public school. His mind was a human calculator, and he could add things in his head, that would take me far longer to do on paper. As has been noted by others in the family, Billy inherited his ability to formulate a plan in an instant with no apparent flaws. That gift skipped a generation. Sis and I can claim neither the gift of calculation nor the gift of formulating plans. Beyond that, his two main gifts seemed to be amusing others and working like a son of a gun. I'd say every member of the family got a dose of that last gift, and of the crowd, Billy got the biggest dose of amusing others. It's only fitting since he is the spittin' image of Daddy—looks which carry along just as much as he ages.

I didn't see the resemblance that much when Billy was a boy, but then, we really didn't have but a picture or two of Daddy when he was a young'un. When Billy came home after those twenty years of being up in Van Horn, me, his momma and the whole town thought ol' John Geermann had been resurrected from the dead.

Momma attended public school in Nacogdoches. At seventeen she started college at Stephen F. Austin. After a year she decided she'd rather be a rancher's wife than a schoolteacher, and as Daddy said, "Your momma didn't figure she could do any better than me." To that, Momma would add, "Maybe I should have made a little more effort to find out for sure."

Talkin' about their education reminds me of something my great-nephew, Jaxon, talked about. When he was at Sul Ross he said they talked a lot about "lifelong learning." Apparently, this was some new idea or something. I said, "It is true enough, plenty haven't learned a thing in years, but we've been practicin' lifelong learnin' ever since the ranch's founding." Bill says it's a nice soft sell for the colleges to keep you comin' back to pay more tuition. I'm sure that's right. I guess that's enough on lifelong learning. If you aren't learnin' all your life, you do so to your peril.

Momma was quiet and soft spoken, but she loved to sing. She always thought the best thing about the Church of Christ was the four-part congregational singing. There was never a piano or organ —it was just voices makin' music together. She really liked that. I didn't think about this until I started writin' just now, but maybe this was another throwback to her Mennonite grandmother. They too used no instruments. I don't know if the Church of Christ in Fort Davis has adopted instruments or not. I haven't been in that church since Momma's funeral. I bet if there'd been a Mennonite church in town, Momma and Daddy would have gone there.

Quite a few years ago some cousin of Momma's, who I'd never met, but with whom Momma corresponded off and on over the years, sent her a poem from some Mennonite relative of theirs who lived somewhere in Ohio—some little place called Pettisville. We found the poem pretty humorous. Daddy said the monkey summed things up pretty well.

The Monkey's Viewpoint
by Jacob H. Rupp

Three monkeys sat in a coconut tree,
Discussing things as they're said to be.
Said one to the others, now listen, you two,
There's a certain rumor that can't be true;
That man descended from our noble race;
The very idea is a disgrace.

No monkey ever deserted his wife,
Starved her babies and ruined her life.
And you've never known a mother monk
To leave her babies with others to bunk;
Or to pass them on from one to another
Till they scarcely know who is their mother.

And another thing you'll never see—
A monk build a fence around a coconut tree,
And let the coconuts go to waste
Forbidding all other monks a taste;
Why if I'd put a fence around a tree,
Starvation would force you to steal from me.

Here's another thing a monk won't do—
go out at night and get on a stew;
Or use a gun or club or knife
To take some other monkey's life.
Another thing, friend, please tell me why
You never heard of a monk telling another monkey a lie.

Did you ever hear of a monkey pretending to be
Something he was not in a coconut tree?
Did you ever hear of a monk wrecking another monkey's life
When he should have been home with his children and wife?
I know we look queer and make lots of fuss,
But we want you to know, man didn't spring from us.

Daddy's favorite stanza was,

And another thing you'll never see—
A monk build a fence around a coconut tree,
And let the coconuts go to waste
Forbidding all other monks a taste;
Why if I'd put a fence around a tree,
Starvation would force you to steal from me.

That was why Daddy said the prophets preached that some grain should always be left in the field for the needy to glean. "The greed-driven don't want to leave a single grain unsold. They've got to have it all!"

Daddy died when, having fallen off his horse, he fell into rocks. I guess rememberin' that set me to mind that when Nellie died, I figured I should probably quit ridin' too. I didn't quit altogether, but I never did ride alone after Nellie was gone.

Momma died soon after Daddy. I'm pretty sure she had leukemia or cancer of some kind, though she never went to the doctor to find out. She had to be in a lot of pain, but Vera, our faithful housekeeper, and I did our best to take care of her as her only wish was to "die in peace and at home." Sis came out about every day towards the end, but she was still in her fundamentalist days. One day after Sis had left, Momma said, "When she told me she was still praying that I'd be healed, I felt like punchin' her. I certainly don't want to go through this again. I'm ready, and she needs to accept that."

I asked Momma if she told her that. She said, "I left out the punchin' part, but I've said the other part six ways to Sunday. I think it's more about her trying to prove to that church crowd of hers that she's got the faith to heal me more than it has to do with my welfare and wishes."

That was the one and only time I ever heard Momma rail on about my sister's fundamentalism. I never knew what she might have said to her over the years after Billy left home at age sixteen having been driven away by her fundy ways.

Not wanting to relive the past once my sister came to her senses, I never talked about what Momma had said until I went to writin' this down. Then I thought I'd better come clean.

When I laid it out to her, she said, "I was a fool, and Momma knew it. And she still loved me. Yes, you need to tell her part of the story, if you're going to tell the truth—warts and all. My family has redeemed this prodigal mother from her prideful ways. Some from this side of the grave and maybe Momma and Daddy from the other side. At any rate, I am redeemed."

I put my arm around Sis as I replied, "I'm grateful every day that we *all* have been healed."

I've now been on this earth just shy of four score and four. Bill is a good three years younger than me, and Betsy would like to think she's more than the four actual years younger than me that she is. So, all three of us have officially made it to old age.

I'm not going to pretend to understand genetics or nurturing instincts. All I know is in the few pictures we have of our earliest childhood, I was always in little bib overalls and cowgirl boots, and Betsy was always in a dress. When Betsy and I were going through old pictures not long ago, we both had to laugh at the fact that neither one of us ever asked about our contrasting attire. We would both acknowledge that whatever brought it about was fitting for each of us. I never wanted to be a frilly-girl any more than she wanted to be a cowgirl.

As long as I can remember, I'd be up in the saddle on Daddy's lap with the reins in my hands. And as far back as my sister can remember, she doesn't recall ever ridin' up in the saddle with Daddy. Momma, the banker's daughter, never did ride, and I know she was glad to have Sis's company with her up at the house.

When it was time to decide if we were going to be homeschooled or go into Fort Davis, Momma and Daddy decided to buy a little house in town where we could stay during the week. They had a little-bitty rock house built next to the Baptist church where we could walk to school. Momma had a car, but she didn't drive it any more than she had to. That little rock house is still there, though it looked better in our day than it does now.

Momma thought about puttin' in a little garden, but what lay around that house couldn't be described as ground. It was one big layer of rubble rock with some grama and Bermuda growing up through it. We mowed it, and that was it. Since we weren't there in the summer anyway, puttin' in a garden would have only been good for the few things you could overwinter or get quick in the spring.

One year, a skunk family decided our place was *the* place to be. We kept smellin' 'em close by, but it took a trip into town by Daddy to figure out that the small family had moved in under the house with us and where they were gettin' in and out. While he managed to get 'em flushed out by spraying a hose at 'em, it wasn't without their full defenses stinkin' up the place which lingered for weeks. Daddy laughed and said he guessed he'd have better waited for the end of the school year to get 'em out, so the place would air out over the summer. Momma said it was convenient that he could go back to the ranch and not have to smell it all week like the rest of us. It was bad for days.

Momma sprayed *"eau de toilette"* all over Sis and me everyday before school, just to be sure we didn't smell like skunk. When I saw the name on that bottle, I said to Momma I wasn't sure somethin' out of the toilet was much better than skunk.

I bet I hadn't thought about those skunks in forty or fifty years. It's the only time I can remember Daddy laughin' when I thought Momma might take a broom to him!

Each passin' school year seemed like an eternity to me. (Given that, I'd have never guessed I could have enjoyed teaching Noah with my co-teachers as much as I did.) Girls my age just called me a tomboy as though I was supposed to be offended. I wasn't. The only boy that paid me any attention was Norman.

Norman was the class clown, and he did entertain me of a kind. He persuaded me to go on a date or two in high school, but I wasn't any more interested in him then than I would be later, as far as any deep romantic feeling towards him. As it was, he was off to the big city as soon as he graduated—off to make his fortune. I never did hear from him again until Sis and I ran into him in Alpine several years back. He never did find his fortune, and what he might have hung on to was taken by his ex-wife. By the time he arrived back in Alpine, he was living as modestly as one can.

I suppose Sis has better and fonder memories of her school days than I can pass along. The only thing I ever looked forward to was the weekend when we could get back to the ranch. Sis would have stayed in town on her own if Momma had let her. That was a notion she would ultimately prevail upon once she was married— much to her new husband's disappointment. She and Bill lived in the little rock house. Patience would be Bill and Sis's virtue. It would take ten years before Billy came along. By the time Brett was on his way, they decided they needed a little more room.

Momma midwifed Sis's never-ending labor when Billy came into the world. That was one *hell* of a labor. After that, Momma told Sis she needed to get a proper doctor for any others that might come along. When that big bundle of joy finally was born, all you could do was look on in amusement. I haven't seen all that many newborn babies in my life, but that boy was pure delight. He had a head full of black hair, eyes the size of quarters (and just as dark as that hair), puffy-rosy cheeks that looked like some chipmunk had told him how to pack in provisions, and a hind end that looked like someone had split a Pecos canteloupe and put one in each cheek.

Daddy took one look and said, "Bill, you're gonna have to find some other way than spankin' this boy. With that hind end he's never gonna feel a thing. I don't know where he got it, but it ain't from me and it *sure* ain't from you!"

And up until those teenage years, when Billy and his mother got into it, it must be said, Jesus himself couldn't have had a more pleasant disposition than that boy had.

Brett and Jean weren't far behind, and Momma could have easily midwifed both of them as they were easy labors as labors go. Both were more typical of what one expects. As a baby, Brett took forever before he'd sleep through the night. Jean was a little better, but they each went through the "terrible twos." Or as Bill had said to Daddy and me, "The terrible twos seem to be stretchin' mighty far into the threes."

As Brett would acknowledge now, his oblivion to other people's feelings stemmed from his envy as the middle child lined up against Billy's natural charms with people. In true confessions, he told me that he was glad Billy had left when he did, even though after that, the house was devoid of much joy for a *long* time.

I need to back up some. When Daddy offered Bill the job to leave San Angelo to come work on the ranch, Bill was thrilled. His family owned just over 10,000 acres and had run cattle for a long time. As Bill's dad would tell people, "The only problem with this ranch is every time I try to drill a well for water, I hit oil." Bill confirmed such was the case, as their ranch turned into a landscape full of pump jacks. As the cattle were thinned out, the scrub moved in until it was 10,000 acres of pump jacks, prickly pear and mesquite.

Bill said he learned early on that if you don't keep ruminants on the grass you're gonna get desert, scrub or both. He and Daddy were of one mind on this point, and Daddy and Granddaddy had used some sheep and goats over the years to "mow down" what the cattle wouldn't eat. He called it nature's symbiosis, and as he would add, "Ignore it to your peril." And a lot of ranchers, either too lazy or too unobservant of nature's ways did ignore it— overgrazing or simply not keeping the cattle numbers up sufficiently and moving them often enough to keep healthy stands of grass.

When it came to land stewardship, Daddy and Bill were masters. I just followed their wise counsel and observed how many people didn't bother to notice how much healthier our ranch and our cattle were than most. Of course, we were well off the beaten track.

Bill had only worked for Daddy about six months when my googly-eyed sister snagged him in the marriage net. Bill had been stayin' at the bunkhouse but soon found himself moving to town and comin' out during the week to work on the ranch. Sometimes he would stay overnight if work demanded it, but mostly he drove back and forth to town for the next forty-some years.

When Sis moved out, Vera moved in. Vera had been born in *Ojinaga,* and her folks moved back and forth across the Rio Grande before finally settling permanently in Fort Davis. Vera never married, though she had a couple of older, married siblings who stayed around.

At about the same time Vera moved in, Daddy and Bill built a greenhouse so Momma and Vera would have a place to grow some tomatoes and other produce. Momma finally got her garden, of a kind (as we've all adopted Jaime's "of a kind" descriptor for anywhere it seems to fit, as it does here). She already had her orchard, planted by Grandma Margaretha and now mature, which included half a dozen pecan trees, three apple trees and three cherry trees.

Momma, Vera, Daddy and I had our own division of labor. Momma was seamstress, chief gardener, general bookkeeper and tax accountant. Vera was chief cook and bottle washer as well as backup gardener and ranch hand attendant. I was chief stable mucker, horseshoer and general ranch hand. Daddy was head cowboy, foreman, master planner and entertainer. And as he would say so many times, bringing Bill into the ranch works "was all to the good." With Bill there it cut down significantly on havin' to hire the sometimes unreliable ranch hands.

It was all to the good in more ways than one. Not only did Bill bring his shared gifts of stewardship and hard work to the ranch, he also brought an ever-growing income from all those San Angelo pump jacks. Every year his folks would send Bill and his only other sibling, a brother, a share of the oil revenues. When his dad died, the mother moved off the ranch and into town, and the brother moved onto the ranch. When she died a couple years later, the ranch officially became property of the brother, though as per the will, any oil, gas and mineral rights from the ranch were split 60/40 with Bill getting the larger share.

I jokingly asked Bill once if he was jealous with his brother gettin' that ranch for a mere 10% gain on the oil revenue. He said he'd have given up that 10% and 10% more not to have to look at "that pump-jack-mesquite ranch." I think we all knew Bill got the extra share for his stewardship—and the "ranch gift" to the brother was to conceal that fact to the highest degree possible.

Once it was deeded to him, the brother wasted no time tearing down the modest ranch house the boys had grown up in, and constructing what Bill referred to as *"the* monstrosity." Bill was never in it, but from then on, every Christmas card featured that house in one way or another. As Bill would say, "He seems to think he has to outdo William Randolph Hearst." There was no real love lost between the two brothers. Bill never went to San Angelo once his parents were both gone, and the brother never once bothered to come out to the ranch. For what we knew of it, he never came out to the Big Bend except for his brother's wedding. For that event, he stayed at the Indian Lodge with the others, and then skipped town as soon as the wedding was over.

He died just last year. Word came to Bill after the fact, and only as a matter of paperwork from the lawyer attending to the proper passing of the brother's oil, gas and mineral rights on to the brother's heirs.

Bill said, "At least I don't have to feel guilty about not wantin' to go to his funeral. No one bothered to tell me what I was missin'."

At the time, he had shared with Jaime and Zoey, "The estrangement from your family is certainly different from my own, but estrangement is estrangement in whatever form it comes. I have certainly been estranged of a kind from my brother for as long as I can remember, and I am pretty well estranged from whatever constitutes his family. I couldn't tell you one grandchild's name.

"Truth be told, it was only the online obituary I looked at after the fact that confirmed I did at least know all his children's names. It didn't list their children, but just stated he left behind numerous grandchildren. I couldn't help but notice it left out the usual 'departing of our beloved father and grandfather.' Maybe they weren't any more fond of him than I was."

I couldn't have been more than five—comin' up on six—when I first heard Daddy use the word, "symbiosis." I'm nearly certain it was before I was in school. Daddy and I were in town, and he was talking to some other rancher when he mentioned nature's symbiosis. When we were back in the truck on the way home, I repeated the word, correctly I might add, wonderin' what it meant. I liked the sound of the word, which is why it stuck.

Daddy glanced over at me with a rather surprised look, and before answering my question said, "If you can pick up on that kind of word at your age, I'd better watch what I say from now on."

I could see he was amused by it rather than expressing any actual concern. He framed the answer in terms of what he thought a young'un like me could comprehend. "It means workin' as God intended."

That made enough sense to me at the time that I didn't ask anymore about it, but I never did forget that word. I used it a few times with my teachers in Fort Davis, when, whatever they were doin' or teachin' was going against the workin' as God intended. While they didn't necessarily agree with my use of the term, any time I used it on the ranch, I was never corrected. I heard it from Daddy often enough over the years to reinforce I probably was using it in its proper context—at least of a kind.

To me, it summed up how Momma and Daddy lived in the world. If either's faith existed as some insurance policy for the afterlife, it was never apparent to me. I suspect both believed in some afterlife though neither ever confirmed that one way or the other with any absolute notion of what it might be. They did talk of a heaven, but I heard very little about them having any fear of a hell. It was only during Sis's fundamentalist days that Hell, as a place, came into the family conversations. Of course, Sis determined who was goin' there and who wasn't.

Once, when I asked Momma after Sunday school, who goes to Hell she said, "Only those who put themselves there, or are put in a hell in this life by those same people through their evil ways. Too much suffering in this world is manmade."

I suspect Daddy would have given much the same answer. Her answer seemed logical to me, and I never bothered to get a second opinion. It didn't occur to me then, that her answer didn't really tell me if she believed there was an "eternal Hell" or not. For sure, she believed in hell on this earth.

When I was just eight or nine years old, I asked Daddy what Heaven was like. "In Sunday school they said the Bible said it was streets of gold and gates of pearl," I recalled to him.

He asked me, "How's that sound to you?"

"It don't sound like any ranch. I guess we'd have to live in town," I answered, "but it doesn't sound anything like Fort Davis or even Alpine."

I didn't think my answer shed any insight as to my view of the Heaven I'd been told about, but I thought it answered his question as best I could at that age.

Daddy replied, "John Geermann and John of Patmos have very different views from each other toward the goodness of this world. I can't buy into his visions.

"They say God's essence is pure light—no darkness. Seems an odd characteristic to me when you look at the slice of the cosmos we see with its vast darkness where giant suns look like specks of light. You know how much I love to stare off at those specks of light, but it's the vast darkness they are set in that makes it all extraordinary.

"Sallie Faye, I have no idea what Heaven is. I can't even prove there is one. No one has ever come back to tell me all about it, and even Jesus seemed to just offer some generalities as to what he would compare it to.

"If I have to sing unending hymns in the bright lights or strum a harp for all eternity, I'd just as soon rest quietly in the ground and let my bones go back to the one earth we have and that I love deeply.

"What do you make of that, Sallie Faye?"

"I'd be good laying someplace close to you and Momma. That would be enough for me."

So it was from Daddy's nature-symbiosis views and the goodness of this earth that I believe I began my lifelong love of, and connection to, nature and its creatures. Much has been made by others of my "Dr. Doolittle" talent for conversing with the birds, with Noah's dogs, Kola and Koala—who used to be Billy and Jaime's dogs before they left the nest to be with Noah—with Nellie, of course, when she was living, and with any other critter that happens to have the patience to put up with my inquisition of their day.

It is one of those unprovable gifts, but whatever it might lack in scientific validation, it does not lack in the mystical connection so many have felt at one level or another through much of human history. If Billy, Noah and I have an extra measure of that mystical connection, I am not one to argue against it. I will again attribute this gift of contemplation—which I believe it falls under—to Momma. I certainly got my love of birds from her, while my love of horses and cattle came from Daddy. I never heard Daddy carry on much of a conversation with his horse or any cattle. Any words used generally came out of some frustration towards a particular animal's non-cooperation. That often came out as an "'od dammit!"

I once asked him if his leavin' the "G" off kept it from takin' the Lord's name in vain, or if he just didn't like the letter "G" since he left it off the end of most words, too. He said he just didn't see what the "G" added to those words, and so he didn't bother with it —a habit, once my school days were done, I fully adopted myself. I told him, maybe I'd start going by Sallie 'eermann then, but he laughed and said that would cause all kinds of trouble as people always insist on legal names, adding, "To my good fortune, they all assume John *is* my legal name, and I can skirt around having to sign everything 'Johannes Konrad.' But they would wonder about that missin' 'G' on 'eermann."

As to takin' the Lord's name in vain, he said he didn't think God really cared about a little cussin' as long as we weren't cussin' someone to belittle and hurt them.

He added, "Now, the prophets, and Jesus himself, had no problem cursin' the hypocrites in power. And as far as taking the Lord's name it vain, it seems to me we do that when we print 'In God We Trust' on our money, when it is clearly our money, our weapons and our might that we trust. Like unto it, when we say, 'God bless America' as we justify war. Those *are* usin' the Lord's name in vain to my mind, and we do it with national fervor endorsed by too many preachers."

He didn't want to cause a problem for me in school, so he waited till I was probably about twenty to tell me he didn't like that they had added "under God" to the pledge. "Sallie Faye, I have had enough trouble reciting that pledge to a nation that so clearly mocks liberty and justice for all. Then they had to, once again, use the Lord's name in vain. Be forewarned, mine is a minority opinion. Espouse it to your peril."

Momma heard him use his "'od dammit!" every now and then, and she never offered any chastisement. Of course, she never used it—at least so far as I knew. I doubt she ever even mumbled it to herself. It just wasn't in her nature to use words to express her frustrations. Hers was more a countermeasure informed by her taking *very* seriously the Sermon on the Mount, and I think she was perfectly aligned with Daddy's view towards what constituted taking God's name in vain.

I remember her telling me when I was teenager, "If you can master Luke 6:27-38, then, Sallie Faye, you'll be way ahead of me— as I am persuaded that is the instruction from our Lord for us all."

She is right. I never have mastered that or have come even close, but when she thought of the Sermon on the Mount, that was the summary instruction that stuck in her mind—and it must be said, has forever stuck in mine as well. She recited it aloud every night before going to bed. Kneeling by my bed, I too recite it these days, as I also add my gratitude for another day. Sis goes into her chapel every night at 8:00 sharp—rain, sleet or snow—and does the same.

Momma's credo truly included loving your enemy, judging not and being merciful. She also considered "the lilies of the field, how they grow." As that last one suggests, Jesus taught nature's symbiosis as well. Ignore him to your peril.

Luke was definitely Momma and Daddy's favorite New Testament writer and for much the same reason. As Daddy put it, "He's the best storyteller of the bunch, and we need stories."

Momma would add, "Every life has a story to tell. When you're old like me, you'll see how all the ordinary adds up to the extraordinary and becomes *your* story to tell."

She wasn't all that old when she said that. I hadn't thought about her sayin' it in years. Here I am, an old woman, addin' up the ordinary. She was right—I find it all extraordinary!

Momma talked to any bird that happened to be within earshot. Any day the windows could be opened, even if a bit chilly, they were opened to allow the birdsong in. She never reported back to me what they might have said to her, but I'd still give her credit for allowing my very active imagination to carry on any number of conversations with her feathered friends. She would even tell Daddy at the dinner table whatever conversation I might have had in her presence. Neither ever seemed to suggest I was getting carried away. To the contrary, Daddy would often respond, simply saying, "Nature's symbiosis at work."

Sis never seemed to be envious of my "gift." Somehow, we were able to avoid the too-typical sibling rivalry or disquiet that infects many homes—including Brett towards Billy back in the day. She had her frilly interests, and I had my symbiosis interests. Neither seemed to conflict with the other. We wanted very different lives despite our mutual, deep admiration for our parents. Momma and Daddy let us be what it seemed we were born to be.

I was always of the mind to let others be what they, too, were born to be—that is, so long as it was not in contradiction with nature's symbiosis and the wise words from Luke. Murder, hate, greed, pride and other such sins are not symbiotic with God's intentions.

Some were quick to judge my niece, Jean, when she first started dating Mary-Alice. Of course, the usual "abomination" and "against nature" judgments were brought forth from those commanded not to judge—including Jean's own mother. I just couldn't see it that way. Just as I was all cowgirl and Betsy all frilly-girl, it seemed to me that Jean was then what she had always been. I know for a fact, it was not a thing she went looking for, and she was indeed frightened by it for a time, thanks to the good Christians and the homophobic world around her. She was the first to hear my now oft quoted line, "I've never been one to think love only comes in one way—prescribed by somebody else."

When I said that to her, she said it was like a giant weight lifted from her shoulders. I added, "'Come to me, all you who are weary and burdened.' I don't think that invitation had restrictions based on who you love."

Jean, Mary-Alice and I spent the next twenty years stayin' connected, while estrangement infected the Schlatter household. I held out hope it wouldn't be forever, and I prayed to God not to let those girls move away where the miles alone would foster a permanent estrangement. That bit of investment on my part, in compassion and prayer, would one day pay off, finally—too long overdue. It was pure joy seeing Jean's reconciliation with my sister and my sister's acceptance of Mary-Alice as a member of the family in good standing.

Jaime once shared with me his view of his own life's problems. As he put it, "I was the problem plain and simple, and I and the rest of the world seemed to know it."

To my sister's credit, once she shed the burden of her certitude, the love and generosity that came forth thereafter could indeed be summed up by saying it was grace upon grace for any and all she met. She had been the problem and she knew it. And like Jaime she was healed by the love around her. All she had to do was open herself to it.

I lament for all the children of the world whose parents, like Jaime's and like my own sister, for too many years, can't see they are the problem plain and simple, while the rest of the world knows it and stands idly—helplessly by.

There were many animals I would have liked to converse with that nature's symbiosis seemed to mostly deny me. Among these were deer and antelope—of which there were many on the ranch— jackrabbits, aoudad up on the mountain side, the occasional mountain lion and even rattlesnakes, to name a few.

There were brief times when the deer would come near the house—only if there was some flowers blooming or some grain to be had. But they didn't seem to be big conversationalists—only sayin' somethin' about too many venison sausage recipes goin' around. They contended the cattle, like me, were dumb, and so I should talk to them—keeping things on an even playin' field. I think they are right that cattle are dumber, but both are beautiful in my mind. Whether I'm as dumb as an ol' heifer is for others to decide.

I can see how the antelope just sorta stand there when hunters come along. We don't have hunters on our land. Huntin' them is about like shooting a pet dog. I don't call that huntin' when there's no challenge to it. The antelope don't seem to know they should fear us, but as conversationalists, I think they are mute. They never come up by the house, but you can trot right by them on the ranch, and they just carry on grazin' or staring off across the range. They like to stare off. I guess they like contemplation too.

I've never trusted javelinas enough to make conversation. Their poor vision and propensity to tear flesh to pieces suggested to me a proper distance was in order.

I had to have the same distancing respect for the mountain lions. There is *no* problem with their vision, and a little inquisitive girl or old cowgal might look a bit too temptin' for dinner.

Of all the critters, rattlesnakes are the most feared by most people. I'll grant we have a lot more of them than we do mountain lions, so their ubiquity doesn't help 'em. They are feared firstly for just being who they are, sadly, and secondly, because if you do get bit, it won't be pretty and might well be deadly. That said, I never have been bit nor any horse I ever had, either. (Knock on my wooden head.) Their one language is the rattle which means, "Get the hell away from me!" And they do mean it! They will also respect you for doin' so. They don't come lookin' for you, and the few people I've known that have been bitten were always doing somethin' dumb they shouldn't have been doin'.

Kola and Koala stood back from one once, barkin' their heads off. They seemed to know to leave it alone, but wanted us to know it was around. I'm just glad the snake was patient with their display, and when the dogs came running back to us, the old rattler slithered off in the opposite direction. I suppose the rattler figured if he struck one dog, the other dog would have his head snapped off in one good chomp. Best to leave 'em be.

Nature may be violent in its ends often enough, but it is hard to say that it lets the books get out of balance in the long haul. And amidst that violence is the symbiosis that keeps it all going in the wheel of life. It is a beautiful thing in its context—amazing in fact. Sadly, it is our one "superior" species that seems to be clueless more than not to the mystical connection that should be a part of how we live our lives and how we fit into nature's symbiosis.

I've only had three horses in my lifetime. Daddy never bought a pony for me to ride. Until I could manage ridin' on my own, I rode with him on his horse. I was six when I got my first filly. She was quite young, and we sorta grew up together. I never told Nellie, but this first horse, who I named Honey—a flaxen-chestnut Morgan—was, I would hold to this day, the most beautiful horse we ever had on the ranch. Her long, silky-silver-gray mane and tail with the same shadings shimmered in the sunlight. Her light chestnut coat was like the color of honey, thus the name.

I might have thought it was just a young girl's infatuation with her first horse, but even Momma said, "Oh, my! What a beautiful creature!"

Daddy, to his death, would say there never was a finer horse than Honey on this ranch, that she was extraordinary, and how we had lucked out that the breeder didn't seem to realize what he had.

When Bill moved to the ranch, he brought his own horse with him. He took one look at Honey and asked if I'd trade even up. Honey was getting up in years by then but still holdin' her own. I told him I thought it would hurt his horse's feelings if we did.

There are some animals that just know they look a cut above the rest, and she was one. With her noble gait and her head cocked up, I'm sure she would have won any competition she was in. The Geermanns weren't much for going after ribbons and trophies, and I certainly didn't mind. Such activities require frequent road trips and days away from the ranch. I wasn't any more interested in being away than Daddy was. And takin' a horse out on the highways going sixty to seventy miles an hour, with people flying around you faster than that, never seemed like best equine practices to me. Even as a girl, it would have worried me. My feelings on this point have only gotten stronger with age.

Anything I could do for her care, I did without ever feeling like it was any kind of a chore. She was my first true responsibility, and I embraced it. Honey and I developed our routines, one of which was our Sunday afternoon ride—weather permitting—with Daddy and his horse, Buckle. Buckle came to the ranch at the same time as Honey, when Daddy's older horse, Bandit, went into retirement. He would take Bandit out on occasion, but felt like he was getting too far up in years to be a reliable workhorse. With our younger horses, we always gave both a good run while on our ride. I suppose it was a pretty slow run when I first began riding, but it seemed like we flew across the flatlands. Certainly, by the time I grew into her, Daddy and I would really let them haul ass as we came *"down the stretch!"* towards home.

As long as I can remember, I was Daddy's little right-hand-cowgirl helper for the regular shoeing of our small pack of horses—herd seems like too big a term. You know I had to be much more of a hindrance than a help, when all I could do was stand there and get in Daddy's way, but I never got shushed aside. As long as I can remember, he would explain to me what he did and why he did it. That applied not only to shoeing, but to every aspect of life on the ranch. He was a teacher *par excellence*, and I was his enthralled student.

One of the things that must be taught, and had better be learned early on for any child growin' up on a ranch, is dealin' with death. Even by age six, I was under no illusion that Honey was gonna live forever. Death was never shielded from me or Sis. Both Momma and Daddy's inherent instinct was to approach it head-on and with a heart always towards dignity for whatever creature had met its end.

Momma would give a good "Christian burial" to any little bird that happened to die around the house or barns. Not only did she find this hers to do, but we were expected to be in attendance. That included Daddy. Her Christian burial consisted of digging the small hole, gently laying the bird in and quoting Jesus—"Are not five sparrows sold for two pennies? And not one of them is forgotten before God." And with that, she would have Sis and I take our hands and gently cover the bird with the earth to which the small creature was thus returned.

Daddy, too, treated every animal with all the dignity one could muster. Of cattle and every other ruminant, he would say, "Sallie, we could chew on that grass all day long, and we'd starve to death. They work it in their gut and turn it into protein."

I remember saying, "Nature's symbiosis, I guess."

And he replied, "Nature's symbiosis—respect it, and be grateful for it."

He chuckled when I then added, "Ignore it to your peril!"

One night at supper, Sis asked, "Daddy, is it a sin to eat meat?"

I'm not sure what put that in her mind to even ask a rancher, and a few years back I asked her about it. She didn't remember ever askin' the question. I think she was only about six.

Daddy said, "Well, Isaiah said that one day 'the wolf and the lamb shall graze together, and the lion shall eat straw like the ox.' They call that the peaceable kingdom. It sounds nice, and it does call us to ponder how we live in this world. But at the practical level, the lion isn't a ruminant and lives on meat. Thus it shall be for all time—at least far as I can see into the future. Like unto it, every man, woman and child needs protein. Dense protein our bodies can easily absorb is most readily available from meat—or fish if you live where there are fish. You've probably noticed, we don't have any fish out here.

"When I look at the land given us and the two-thirds of what we call agricultural land across the globe, I don't see another way than making our symbiosis with the ruminant. Our calling is to care for them as best we can, and say our prayer of gratitude when their relatively short, simple life comes to its end."

When I recalled this to Sis, she said, "I remember him saying that. I just didn't remember it was my question that prompted it. You sound like Daddy saying it. Your memory always was better than mine. That steel trap of a brain can remember everything—I'd say pretty close to word for word."

"I don't know about everything, but I'm grateful it remembers the important stuff." I then asked her, "How many little girls do you think knew what a ruminant was at our age?"

Sis laughed, saying, "I doubt there are that many adults in the city that could properly tell you what a ruminant is or what animals are indeed ruminants."

"Too true—too true!" I exclaimed.

34

We never really went anywhere except that one annual trip to the stock show in Fort Worth. Even then, we made it as quick a turn-around trip as possible. This never going anywhere even extended to not attending weddings and funerals of Momma's relatives in East Texas—including her own folks' funerals. Such trips were viewed as too far and too long away from our responsibilities, though it must be said in her folks' case, neither wanted to be embalmed, and they were put in the ground in short order. She couldn't have gotten there in time even if she'd wanted to. She felt no compunction to make the trip to stand over their graves after the fact.

I don't know if Momma ever received any criticism from her family for never going back or not. If she did, she kept that and how they reacted to herself. I suppose it helped that in those days "runnin' the roads" wasn't nearly so common. Once you moved across the country—where moving across Texas is about the same thing—you were considered "pioneer stock" and were pretty much left alone to make your own way.

Momma would write a letter just about every month to her momma, and her momma did the same. I don't know what happened to all those letters. The few I read were always tellin' Momma about who died or got married or divorced or what child was doing what, of relatives I never met. Still, I'd like to reread them now, and see what I might have missed the first time around.

Of course, Daddy's kin died on the ranch, though they were all buried in town. His one older brother, Huldreich Rudolph, "Rudy," decided to be career military, which Grandma Margaretha was none too happy about. Daddy was the natural-born rancher, and Rudy wasn't all that interested in ranching. He died in World War II in the drive against the Germans in Metz, France. What was left of him was buried over there in the Lorraine American Cemetery along with 10,000 others. "The glory of war," as Daddy would say.

I remember Momma saying once, "War is the antithesis of your Daddy's notion of nature's symbiosis."

I guess she didn't think God intended us to destroy each other, even though plenty of that happened in the Old Testament. When I asked her, "Aren't we supposed to believe everything the Bible says? Weren't they doing just as God had commanded?"

She replied, "Don't believe everything you read. I've read the entire Bible, and the best I can discern, people in power, or the people who want power, can justify anything. That does not make them right."

That was all she really said on the subject. What I did come to learn from her was this—if somethin' didn't fit with the Sermon on the Mount, then we, and all others before us, got it wrong. I'd say that is profound wisdom, too easily dismissed by the prideful and powerful. And certainly dismissed by hard-shell "literalists" who like to take every verse in the Bible literally that applies against someone else, and ignore every verse that demands something of them. "In God we trust," as I've seen it practiced, does not carry over to living as Jesus taught.

Daddy never had to worry about being drafted. He was too young for World War I. By World War II, he had a ranch to run, and so he had an ag exemption. As Grandma Margaretha noted, one dead son from the war was one too many.

Like unto it, Bill was too young for the Korean War and escaped by the skin of his teeth from getting drafted in the Vietnam War. That war, as Bill would put it, made you ask, "What the *hell* were we doing—dropping napalm on farms and villages? For God's sake!" The same question he's asked of every war since.

Bill said if he'd 've had to go to Vietnam, he hoped he could have been in the Coast Guard. "At least their mission is search and rescue and not bomb and destroy. I suspect my chances of dying or being maimed wouldn't have been much different, but my chances of not having to kill and destroy would have been better."

Sorry, I got carried away there and strayed some from my account of our stayin' mostly at home, though I did circle back in explaining why Daddy never was in the military and thus was never taken off to some foreign land.

Back to the point, vacation and travel were not words we talked about. I never felt deprived of the good life. I was pretty sure we had it already, and I certainly didn't need to go anywhere lookin' for a better one. Sis's idea of a better life was to live in town, but even she never had any hankerin' for big city life.

As she put it, "As far as the commandment for loving my neighbor goes, I'm challenged enough in Fort Davis. I don't think I could do too well with more people."

To that I answered, "Runnin' into the few I do at the grocery store, post office and the Slo Poke Cafe gives me more than adequate opportunities in that regard. And my sin is, I love most of them the further I am from them."

The one thing that did appeal to me was ridin' the Sunset Limited. There was somethin' about the train that I thought I'd really like. Where it went didn't seem to matter to me. It was just the thought of ridin' the rails. I guess I'd do all right on an ocean cruise, too, though I've never been on one. The thought of sittin' and lookin' out as the miles pass was enough in my mind. All about the journey and not the destination, as they say.

I did finally get to take that train ride with Billy and Jaime when we went from Alpine to New Orleans. That trip confirmed three things. I liked the train—as traveling goes, it's the way to go. New Orleans was interesting, but I don't need to go back. And lastly, I was glad to be back home in my own bed with my birds singin' to me.

One of the highlights of the trip would be quickly dismissed by most. When we were waitin' to board the train in New Orleans for the trip home, Jaime and Billy were wrapped up in some conversation that, unlike me, I was ignoring. There were two Amish couples and two small Amish boys clearly traveling together who had piqued my interest. I've always wanted to spend some time around the Amish. As fellow agrarians, I figured we were bound to have common ground for an interesting conversation. They won't drive, but they'll ride along with someone who has a car, and these Amish were talkin' to the ticket agent about how much they loved to ride the train. We already had that in common. They were in no hurry to get home—all right, we *didn't* have that in common. They had been down in Louisiana multiple times since

Katrina hit to help with the cleanup and rebuilding. They were going on the Sunset Limited all the way to Los Angeles before going back east to get to their home places in Missouri. This was their fourth trip to help the non-Amish. Free labor. No reward except knowing you helped someone else. You don't see that often!

When they settled in their seats in the station, I went over to introduce myself to see if I couldn't strike up a conversation. I needn't have wondered if they would talk to an ol' cowgirl or not. The same man that had talked to the ticket agent struck up the conversation wantin' to know all about our ranch. He was *really* interested when he found out that our ancestors had come from Switzerland and that at least one of my great-grandparents was a Mennonite. He laughed when I said being Church of Christ, we'd strayed far from the straight and narrow since then.

He explained how a lot of the Mennonites that came to this country, about the time the Kutzlis would have come over, were often called Amish-Mennonite. He contended there wasn't much difference in those days, and he explained that now you have dozens of flavors of Amish and Mennonites to where, on one end of the spectrum, you have the minimal technology group while at the other end, the totally technology adapted. He said his group were of the kind that had no problem "going out into the world and using a good power saw," though he didn't own one himself.

I had to chuckle at that, and hoped I didn't offend him in doin' so. I clearly didn't as he grinned back at me, adding, "I wouldn't want to broadcast this, but the Mrs. here has been known to use the coffee maker in the motel room when there is one."

She gave her husband a little jab in the side, though I could see she didn't really mind him tattlin' on her.

He claimed that by the hats and beards of men and the head coverings and dresses of the women, Amish can slice and dice who's who from one group to the next. I'll take his word for that. I was amused that the boys' fedora hats looked more like they'd be Mafia sidekicks than Amish boys, while the men had the straw hats I expected. He pointed out he had to have a new hat for this trip. On their last trip, the father of one family they helped commented how much he liked his hat. "They'd fed us nearly every meal, and they were so thankful for our help, what could I do but sign my name in that hat and hand it to him." He laughed and added, "I just had to pray I wouldn't die and go to Hell for traveling home without my hat."

His wife gave him a harder jab than before—without the accompanying smile.

He continued, "When we were back this time, they had us over for dinner one evening, and there was that hat, hanging on a hook in their kitchen."

I asked him who tends to things while they are off on these missions to help with such disasters. His answer didn't surprise me —I just wanted to hear him confirm it. "An Amish community doesn't have to go looking for help. Everybody takes care of everybody else."

The train rolled in, and our conversation ended. I'd soon be comfortably settled into my roomette for the overnight trip home. They'd be in their coach seats for their long journey back to the community that defines them.

There is no question, I would have "theological issues" on many fronts with the Amish. But my one and only direct encounter with them satisfied to my mind, once and for all, their first instinct is to be kind and whatever they might get wrong—they get a lot right!

Pondering on how this group won't even wear a button so as to not appear "vain and prideful" got me to thinkin' about pride on the train ride home.

Our family never has been one to try and turn pride into a virtue. Of the "seven deadly sins" I (and Bill, it must be said) believe it rightly belongs at the top of the list, followed by greed. I'd say all seven continue to infect us badly, but the sin of pride is unique to how highly laudable it has become as a virtue. Even to the point where we assign *our* pride to someone else's life. Parents are notorious for this—I don't suppose that takes any evidence beyond the obvious.

I would hate to hear someone say to me, "You must be so proud of Billy." Why should I claim pride for Billy's life? When he was (according to Sis at the time) "given over to the Devil," I'd have dared to have one of Sis's gossipin' church crowd say to me, "You must be so ashamed of Billy." My nonviolent ethos would likely have given way to a good punch in their "wagging lips."

And for that matter, as wonderful as Billy is, I would hope I never hear him say how proud he is of me or even some accomplishment of his own. We are formulations of time, circumstance and chance. When our good fortune is mostly an accident of birth, it is hardly a matter of pride when compared to someone else who was born in some abusive family or destitution in this or some foreign land. As Jaime can attest, love, rightly placed, can overcome a dark past. If love isn't the key to a life well lived, then I would contend you've been fooled as to what a good life is. It is remarkable how much love you can pour out on those around you, pride free.

Are pride and shame the continuum upon which we are to measure our relationship to "our children?" (I have to put it in quotes since I don't have any of my own.) That doesn't seem too healthy to me. When a parent is ashamed of their child, as Sis was during her dark ages, has that parent really done the self-examination required to understand their own role alongside time and circumstance, or to take into account even the mental health and well-being of the child? More times than not, I'd say, "No." Yet, when they screw up, "I'm so ashamed." When they win a game, "Oh, I'm so proud!"

When some Fort Davis man recently received national attention for what was a truly noble act of service, I overheard someone in town—who I knew for a fact didn't even know the man who's been gone since before she arrived—say, "I couldn't be prouder of this deeply humble, brilliant, good man."

He is all those things, but what the *hell* did she have to do with it? Proud of his humility? What an odd statement in and of itself. I guess she's probably proud of her own humility, too. I assume it was now some "braggin' right" 'cause he was from Fort Davis. Maybe that's it, or maybe it's just a reflection of how poor we are at knowing how to view the world from any vantage point other than the ego —illuminated with its spotlight, pride.

Someone who had learned that Jaime designed the ranch house and chapel said to him at Quiet Day, "You must be so proud." I was eager to hear what Jaime might say in reply. He told the woman, "I can't take credit for a gift I can't explain." I thought that was a good answer. I feel exactly the same way.

I have learned that humility and humiliation are not derivatives —one from the other. Humiliation has a lot more to do with the ego gettin' a good beatdown. Jaime pointed out that he found it odd to read about Jesus's "humiliation" on the cross as he'd heard that referenced on more than one occasion in his reading. He couldn't see how that was even a possibility. As he put it, "He hung there dying—forgiving those who put him there. Absolution for all. Hardly an act of humiliation. That's pure strength!"

I told Jaime, "And like unto it, he didn't go to his disciples after the resurrection and say to them, 'I am so ashamed of you— abandoning me in my hour of need!'"

Billy added, "Nor did he say, 'You can take pride in what I've accomplished—overcoming death.' 'Peace to you,' that was the message."

If I can pass along to those who follow the notion to park over in the dump heap of life the ego-pride/shame-humiliation system that seems to define our world, and instead, base our relationship with others on Paul's fine list he called the gifts of the spirit—love, joy, peace, patience, kindness, generosity, faithfulness, gentleness, and self-control—I do believe we could come *mighty close* to heaven in the here and now.

I do get off on tangents.

When I got back from the train trip, I discovered Ol' Nellie thought I'd abandoned her or croaked and no one had bothered to tell her. I guess I forgot to say goodbye before I left. She said I did anyhow. She might just have been absentminded in her old age and forgot I told her. One of us was absentminded anyhow. Since I couldn't remember tellin' her, I guess it was probably me. She gave me all kinds of hell when I got back, but she never could stay mad for long.

In his later years, Daddy said he'd kinda like to go to Switzerland. "It looks pretty good to me. I'd like to see if I could figure out why they all left."

I asked him why he and Momma didn't go since Bill and I could see to everything. His answer was, "If we could be transported without long flights, we might be more inclined. Your mother isn't any more excited about what it takes to get there than I am. Then there's the risk that the grass being greener when it *really is* greener might make this old rancher covet all that grass and water."

I don't think Daddy was any more covetous than I've ever been, but it was like him to give due consideration to life's temptations. I suspect if they had gone, he'd have come back sayin', "It's real purdy, but I'll take the wide-open range any day!"

There certainly were countless times on a ride, he'd stop and just stare off across the grasslands and mountains. If the cattle, deer and antelope were all three in the frame, it for sure would make him stop to look. We'd sit there a long time. He never spoke at those times, and neither did I. Soon enough, I understood how those silent moments fed his soul, as they fed mine, too.

When we'd start the trot again, he'd say, "Now that was all to the good. All to the good."

Huh—I guess I got my propensity to repeat a phrase from Daddy. Never thought about that before. It's amazing what works its way into an ol' cowgirl's mind.

There were also moonless nights when he'd announce, "I'm gonna go sit and look at the Milky Way. Anybody gonna join me?"

We didn't have to answer. We just had to follow, and we all did.

I remember one time, he'd settled in his chaise lounge, looked up and said, "Girls—that includes you, Anna—look at that little slice of the cosmos. Somethin,' isn't it?"

I asked, "Daddy, kinda more than a slice, isn't it?"

His answer to that was, "As the cosmos as a whole goes, it's a slice. Oughta humble us, don't you think?"

I decided he was right, and I didn't need to answer. We just stared up into the night skies some city people never see in their entire life—which was there any clear night we had a mind to pause and look up. Lord, have mercy—it's beautiful.... It's beautiful!

Not only did our beloved isolation and responsibilities limit our travels, but every bit as much the news of the world getting to us. My childhood was long before satellite TV. We had no "broadcast channels" any antenna could have picked up. We could on occasion pick up the AM radio station in Alpine but almost never tried, I suppose in part because the signal coming over the mountains wasn't all that dependable, and what we did catch wasn't all that inspiring—a lot of advertising and not-too-good music. Daddy would try to catch the noon ag reports every once in a while.

That was about the extent of our efforts except for the few nights Daddy liked to see what far-off station we could pick up. It had something to do with the reflection off the ionosphere, he said, and we could pick up stations hundreds of miles away. Sometimes they'd be crystal clear for a time. I still try to tune in just to find a station every now and then. I just turn the dial to see what I can find. Generally, I don't even tune into what they are actually broadcasting. Too often it's a preacher I just have to shake my head at for the little I pick up during my brief encounter. A station from Mexico is more interesting to me. I love to hear how fast they can rattle off their Spanish. I can speak it, and I can write it, but they lose me quick. I'm a slow thinker and a slow talker and, apparently, a slow listener as well.

Any other news came by post, and since we only got to town about once a month in the summer to get groceries and the mail, our weekly or monthly journals meant that most news was old news by the time we got it. During the school year, Momma would stop for the mail on the way back to the ranch—when she thought about it. Clearly, it wasn't much of a priority as she only thought about it every third week or so. It didn't seem to bother Daddy, and since Sis and I never got any mail, it certainly wasn't something we thought worth remembering either.

I knew there had been something called a depression before my time. I didn't really know what it was, and I didn't see how it had

had anything to do with us. I'm sure it did. Plenty of people, who, out necessity or greed or both, had "leveraged" themselves, found they were broke and lost their farms and ranches. Even my lessons in that were well after the fact. In the double-whammy, as Daddy called it, some of the "sod busters" found their farms reduced to dust. Daddy said for those poor folks, despair was the order of the day, adding, "They got to see how much this country cares when their farmers and ranchers are suffering."

When I asked why their farms went to dust, and why they were called sod busters, he explained how they had taken grass prairies and turned the sod into fields for croppin', adding, "They learned the hard way some land needs to be grass—nature's symbiosis. The first drought, and all they had was dust."

That made sense to me.

Roosevelt had been the president all my life at this point, and what little I knew about his programs consisted of the CCC, which had built the state park just outside Fort Davis. Momma and Daddy had driven down there to see the men at work a couple times while it was being built. It all was finished by the time I was old enough to remember. I thought the lodge was beautiful. I still think it's beautiful. Roosevelt was all right by me.

But the building of state parks soon enough moved into the war machine of World War II. We went from building beautiful structures to joining the world in blowin' them up! I'm not offering a judgment on all those who fought and died.

I was only eight when the second president of my life dropped the atomic bombs on Japan. We couldn't believe the images that came in our news magazines. I remember it like it was yesterday. Momma literally cried when she saw them. Daddy exclaimed, "'od Damn! Are we going to unleash any technology just because we can? Just keep doing it until we've destroyed everything—everything!?"

Momma never had much to say about politicians, but she made it pretty clear what she thought of Truman. Daddy's politics changed then, too. He'd said the first two votes he ever cast were for FDR. During the next election I asked him, "So are we Democrats still or Republicans?"

Daddy responded, "Are these my options? I'll never give my loyalty to either party. Best I can tell, if these politicians' lips are moving they are braggin' or lyin' or both. As ol' man Cardona would say, "*Todos cabrónes*—every last one of them."

I didn't know what a *cabrón* was then, but I figured if Daddy agreed with ol' man Cardona on the subject, I would, too.

I'm gonna diverge from my history tellin' for a minute to mention our long connection to the Cardonas of Fort Davis. The two generations after me know well enough all about badass Ernesto, who certainly livens up any gathering. Thanks to Jaime's connection to Chuy and Lupe, we also got to know them as well, and along with Chuy and Lupe, the beloved Elma—Lupe's mother. Sis and Elma had their own special relationship the last years of Elma's life. She sure loved Jaime, Billy and Noah, confessing that she was, except for Lupe, closer to them than to her own children. In particular, she had a real heart for Jaime, and all he'd overcome.

Chuy was just a year older than me, and Ernesto several years younger. Lupe was a year or two younger, and she ran with a bunch of her cousins, so growin' up I never got to know her. Of the Cardonas, Mando and I were the same age, but I never really got to know him all that well either. We'd visit for a time when he'd bring out the occasional load of gravel to the ranch. Same with his wife, Tanya. She bought her own dump truck when she won a scratch-off, and she took over the run to the ranch once she had her truck. She certainly livened up the Fort Davis hauling business. She looked like she was born to drive a truck, same as I was born to ride a horse. I got a real kick out of her the few times we had a chance to visit.

Rogelio, the fourth Cardona brother, would bring his backhoe out anytime we needed a hole dug to bury something or someone. In case that sounds like we're killin' people off and burying 'em to hide the evidence, the only burials of people thus far have been Momma and Daddy—and the sheriff knows all about them. Now that Jaxon and Caleb have their own backhoe, compliments of their granddad and Ernesto, I reckon they'll dig my hole when the time comes.

Ol' man Cardona, who was actually a bit younger than Daddy, did any construction work we needed on the ranch. With some other Cardonas' help, he built the little rock house in town as well. He'd also help Daddy with the cattle whenever he needed one extra hand. He was always given "right of first refusal."

I guess writin' about the Cardonas isn't really diverging from our history when taken in context to local history. Of all the Fort Davis families, gringo or Hispanic, it must be said, our years have forged the strongest connection with the Cardonas.

It always humored Billy and Jaime that, as different as Bill and Ernesto were, they were such good friends. Their mutual respect and admiration for each other inspired Billy to suggest that Bill needed to take Ernesto up on the big outcropping and ask for Ernesto's intentions. When Billy told his dad this, Bill just said, "Good lord." Of course, Billy had to say it in front of Ernesto and Rosalina. Ernesto thought it was a good idea, to which Rosalinda just shook her head and said, "I guess if you're going to leave me, it might as well be for Bill. He can take you from here on."

I never thought of Momma or Daddy as being great students of history. Comin' along in time when they did, they were mostly focused on surviving and thriving in their splendid but sometimes harsh isolation. Bill, on the other hand, was an historian to his core. He wasn't interested in someone else's acceptance of the "facts." He dug and ascertained for himself what he believed and why he believed it. Propaganda was wasted on him. It was Vietnam that really made him dig into America's war history. And as he would put it, the more he dug the more he could see how—going all the way back to our first wars—one connected to the next and the next.

He also studied the "McCarthy era" and the hearings that captivated America for too long when we were just kids. I remember he and Daddy talking about them not long before Daddy died. I'd never heard Daddy say anything about them before, but clearly, he had followed the news reports.

I remember what Daddy said to Bill and Bill agreeing with him. "There are a lot of people in this world that look at those shameful chapters as one-offs—'Oh, it will never happen again! Never again!' they cry. You and I both know that's *bullshit*! The victims of the witch hunt might change, but the lust for a scapegoat *never* dies."

When Watergate was nonstop news, Bill said, "Nixon must have pissed off all the wrong people. It's not like he's the first president to lie and try to cover it up, and he certainly isn't the first to be an asshole."

By the time the Iraq War of Bush II came along, Daddy had gone up onto the ridge for his final rest. When the bombs started dropping, Bill lamented, "We are hopeless and lost. There is no lie this nation will not tell; no treaty we will not break; no pain we will not inflict; no child we will not kill."

I replied, "Bill, that's a mighty bleak outlook."

But I'll be damned if I could say anything against it. It was too true—too true. *Hell!* Another generation later, it's still true.

We always said Daddy was crazy, and that Billy inherited his crazy gene. Neither were of a kind to ever try to demean anyone—or make fun of them unless they were part of the play. Ernesto is the best example of that—always playful and glad to be part of the story, and Jaime, always the good sport for all Billy's "lovin' on him" at the Slo Poke.

Daddy never told any kind of ethnic or aggie or lawyer jokes. Once when I was along and someone in town told an ethnic "joke" (well, racist is the more accurate term, I suppose), I noticed Daddy didn't laugh—or even pretend to smile. In the truck on the way home, he said, "If you can't find humor from your own life and have to stereotype some group, then you're not funny." That was the end of the lesson—short, sweet and to the point. He figured I got it, and I did.

The first time Daddy and I went riding on a Sunday—the first Sunday when I was just startin' to ride Honey—Daddy helped me saddle up my horse and then proceeded to do the same with Buckle except somethin' was wrong. I said, "Daddy, you slung the saddle on backwards."

He just kept right on—not sayin' a word. When he was done, he said, "Well let's saddle up. I need to be able to keep an eye on you ridin' that horse for the first time."

"Daddy, you're crazy!" I thought for sure he'd redo the saddle, but no, he hopped right up and proceeded to ride backward during the first half of the ride. Then he said, "I'll have to redo this saddle if we're gonna find our way home."

When I told Momma what Daddy had done, she just laughed.

I never did tell Billy about this, and always wondered if Daddy would pull the same stunt on him. When Billy got his first horse, Billy, Daddy, Bill and I headed to the barn for that first Sunday ride. Bill watched just smiling. I don't think he knew exactly what Daddy had in mind, but he figured it was worth the free entertainment.

Billy hadn't paid any attention until we were all ready to saddle up. When Daddy got up on the horse, the six-year-old boy exclaimed, "What the Sam Hill you doin'?"

Just like he'd told me, Daddy responded, "I need to be able to keep an eye on you ridin' that horse for the first time."

And same as before, halfway through he reversed, so we could find our way home. But as Daddy reworked his saddle, Bill turned his around, saying, "Since your Grandpa's leadin' the way home, *I'll* have to keep an eye on you."

I sat in the saddle that afternoon tickled from head to toe.

Momma and Sis were standin' there watchin,' grinnin' from ear to ear when we all trotted in. They had watched from the window when we left, so as not to give anything away. When Momma saw Bill coming in facing the ass end of that horse, she laughed, saying to Sis, "I'm afraid *my* husband has corrupted *yours.*"

Billy thought for years that the two had worked it out ahead of time, but Bill's addition was pure spontaneity—Daddy inspired.

Daddy and ol' man Cardona also shared a mutual playful streak. I never wondered where Ernesto got it. He just took his *papá's* playful nature and ratcheted it up several degrees.

Any joint task involved threats about castrating the other one if only they had anything to castrate. Ol' man Cardona would say, "You know with all my kids there's something down there," and Daddy would answer, "With all your kids they've dried up and fallen off." Fortunately, so far as I ever knew, neither pulled down their drawers to prove what was intact or not.

Momma, quiet as she was, was no stick in the mud. She enjoyed Daddy's playful nature even when she was the object of his "affections." The busier she was, the more inclined he was to come up behind her and start nibblin' on her neck. She'd shake her head, gigglin', "Must you?" And Daddy'd say, "I'm just your little shnookums, and you're my little heifer!"

Momma'd respond, "I'm an old cow and you're an old ornery bull. Both past our prime. Don't you have some work to do?"

"Nothin' near so important as lovin' on you!"

And she'd say, "I got work to do. Go find some work almost as important, then."

"If I must," Daddy'd say, on his way out the door.

Once when some people from church came out for supper, Momma looked over and saw Daddy had unbuttoned his jeans and had lowered the zipper more than half way. Momma saw, too, that one of the guests had noticed it. "Dear, you seem to be getting rather comfortable."

He answered, "If you didn't feed me so well, I wouldn't have to undo my pants!" Everybody just laughed and Daddy sat there with his jeans half undone.

As I write these memories, I wonder if I do Daddy's good humor justice. So much of what made Daddy crazy in our eyes was his everyday good nature and those big, expressive, dark eyes. Every time I look at Billy, I'm staring right back at that same twinkle that defined Daddy's disposition.

Daddy almost never showed any real anger. Certainly, never any towards us. Other than the occasional aggravation with an uncooperative animal, I can't recall him getting upset at much. His condemnation of the atomic bombs where the most forthright display of anger I ever saw from him.

If he slipped and fell in a shitty mud hole, he'd just get up and say, "Ain't I purdy now?" Once when we ran out of gas on the way back to the ranch, he said, "I guess I'll be walkin' back to town. I meant to fill up while I was there." Of course, he didn't need to walk back to town. He always kept a gallon can in the back of the truck in case we, or any other stranded motorist, needed it. Part of his good plannin'. Besides, we were already back to where we could see our own cattle guard. We had our own tanks on the ranch and could fill up when we drove the last remaining mile on his one-gallon spare.

When you are kind to the core the way he was, and able to find joy in the everyday happenings that most don't register as something to be joyful about, I guess you *are* crazy by the world's standard. All I know is Momma, Sis, Bill, Billy and I were crazy about him. I can't speak for Brett or Jean. I don't think either ever spent enough time at the ranch to get the full measure of who Daddy was. I do know that both, now that the Schlatter family has healed, cherish every minute they get to spend with their own momma and daddy. I'm lucky to have lived long enough to see the divided made whole again.

When I was in tenth grade, even though I do believe that my daddy knew such was a lost cause, he thought I ought to check out the college in Alpine. It was called Sul Ross State College then. (I guess they figure it's upgraded since, as it is now called a university.) We didn't go to the "big city" of Alpine any more than we had to, and Daddy had a habit of saying as soon as we'd hit the "city limits," "Ain't lookin' like much so far." Of course, he didn't really mind Alpine. He just liked to say what he did as his endorsement for ranch life over living in town. Our annual trek to Fort Worth got nearly the same line on entering, only with added emphasis. "Fort Worth *sure* ain't lookin' like much so far." Upon our exit, he'd declare, "There! *That's* done for another year!"

Our college excursion included attending a rodeo while there. It was a family affair. You will note, since I'm jumpin' to the rodeo, that I don't have much to say about the college visit. I was ready to get out of the classroom—not get into another one.

Daddy laid out that while he was taking us to the rodeo, we could decide for ourselves what we liked or not about it. The only thing mentioned beforehand were the barrel races, and of those, how he liked seeing the younger riders. He appreciated the skill and agility of the animal to "tear it up" and thought any boy or girl that could ride like that was "all to the good."

That was all he said before the rodeo. We never did applaud once while there. The parts Daddy did enjoy you could see easy enough just by lookin' at him, and the same with the parts he didn't like.

On the ride home he wanted to get our reactions. Sis didn't like any of it—to no one's surprise. I wasn't sure what I thought. Not much of it looked like real life ranchin' to me, and I said so, adding, "Looks to me like ridin' them broncs and bulls is tryin' to tell your body you don't care much about it."

Daddy then explained his view of it all. He didn't like the calf ropin' or ridin' bulls. He hated seeing those calves thrown down "like a sack of feed," and to keep a bull just to make 'em "pure-dee-mean" wasn't right either.

He elaborated, "I have to rope calves on a regular basis, as you well know. I've never had to see how fast I can do it. Care requires patience, and with speed come carelessness and injury."

I couldn't argue with that, and I knew Momma would have shouted, "Amen," if she were the amen shoutin' kind.

With the bulls he added, "I guess the only thing I'd be good for is the clown trying to steer the bull back into the pen. I can flap my arms and look silly easy enough. Safety engineers and no trophy."

I've already noted that the Geermanns weren't much interested in ribbons and trophies, but it must be said, neither were they for competition in any form. This was expressed in numerous ways. The fundamental flaw as expressed by Daddy was the need for a winner and a loser. "I can't clap for some boy or girl who got first place to every other child not 'winnin'.' And I *ain't* gonna clap for grown-up men who measure their manhood by their trophies—including their trophy wives."

I didn't understand the reference to wives at the time, but I did finally figure it out. I'm not sure what inspired that thought on that particular day, but he must have seen someone who brought it to mind.

We were taught a simple lesson from our earliest memories. You have to do things simply for the joy or the necessity of them. And more than not, one could find joy in the necessity as well. That was the John Geermann creed, as best I could tell.

Muckin' out the stables was one of the necessities, but when we'd do it together, Daddy and I could always find something to make it not seem like drudgery.

He taught me to enjoy shoeing horses, and I've passed on my skills in that area to the boys on the ranch, who, I would contend, do it as much for the joy of a job well done as for the necessity of it.

Daddy and I liked to get the bat and glove out and hit balls to each other. It was never a competition. We just liked doin' it on a summer evening when the work was all done. It wasn't Sis's thing or Momma's thing, and it wasn't some competition between me and

Sis for gettin' Daddy's attention. He enjoyed it, and I enjoyed it. That was enough.

Momma taught Sis to sew. Momma enjoyed it. Sis enjoyed it. That was enough, too.

Of course, I can't count the number of times we went ridin' just to ride. I believe our horses enjoyed it every bit as much as we did. The bond between horse and rider, when forged from care, is undeniable.

I've seen it every bit as much, too, with those dogs and that boy. And before Kola and Koala knew the good Lord had called them to minister to Noah, they were every bit as much bonded to Billy and Jaime. When they let the dogs go with Noah to his new house on the ranch—young man that he was—I said to Billy and Jaime, "You sure know how to raise dogs and boys. And the fact that you know when to let 'em all go proves just how well I must have taught you." I had to add my little chuckle to that last part.

Billy and Jaime said in unison, "Too true—too true."

I told 'em, "I don't know if you're sayin' that to my good teaching or to your good raisin'."

Billy replied, "Cause and effect, Aunt Sallie. Cause and effect."

I never did go off to that Sul Ross college, and I never did go to another rodeo. Momma and Daddy's general attitude toward competition was clearly passed onto me. On occasion, I went to the six-man football games in Fort Davis, which I found more humorous than competitive. Even then, enough screaming parents put me off from makin' a habit of it. Some people take a game just too seriously while not taking real problems seriously enough. As I looked at one father in particular, I couldn't help but lament for his poor son on the field, as the town got just a glimpse of what went on at home.

I never acquired any interest in professional sports of any kind. The older I got, the more vulgar I thought it all was. Multimillion dollar contracts to "entertain." People out here in the boondocks obsessing over "their team" and the latest "scores." I've even seen obituaries where it says how the deceased was a great fan of this or that team. I just don't get it.

It must be said, I am easily entertained and feel truly blessed. All I need is some bird song and the beautiful world around me. That is enough. No ribbons, no trophies, no winners, no losers. Not a dollar changing hands. Not a parent in my life to scream at the ref *or* at me.

There is no better way to begin to understand life on a high-desert-mountain ranch than to delve into the "stationary parts" and the "moving parts" that define the Geermann-Schlatter ranch—and certainly most others in the area. While ranch life across the globe would share certain characteristics, it is the unique aspects of every section of land—for any wondering a section is a square mile, of which we have many—that define the place and how we must live to be in symbiosis with it.

I should note, to dissuade any notion of my ignorance on the matter, the stationary parts are relatively stationary in our generational life spans for the most part, but even those parts are in constant motion over geologic time.

It is the land's unique aspects that represent why most programs for land conservation and preservation by the government are only marginally effective as a general rule—some downright, fundamentally flawed. You can't dictate one way for all things. Nature doesn't operate that way. In fact, nature is always seeking to thrive and not just survive. "Conservation" too often seeks to maintain an already degraded place. When it comes to regeneration, too many people have no clue where to begin, and so they just accept that trying to keep it from degrading more is an okay standard. As has been seen, more than not, that approach over time may slow the degrading, but it doesn't stop it, let alone reverse it. Stewardship and not conservation is the way to regeneration.

I guess I'm done with my political posturing on that topic for the moment. I am not anti-government, but I am anti-ill-informed bureaucrat and like unto it, its oft-associated driver, the bought-off politician.

Until a big flood destroys something or lack of rain causes water rationing, it seems fair to say that most city folk see rain as a general nuisance—particularly those slow drizzlin' rains that last two or three days. Now, don't get me wrong, I do like sunshine, and we have no lack of that here. However, there is no better moisture for the soil than those slow drizzlin' rains, and when we get them you can almost hear the grass, as well as every animal that nibbles on its new growth, proclaimin', "Hallelujah!" A few good snows and drizzly-winter days bring spring wildflowers to life that can lay dormant for years. The desert turns from brown to bright blues, yellows, oranges, reds, purples—practically overnight. We'll take the microburst, gully washers over nothin', but you can't beat those slow rains and snows for bringin' life to the land.

One good summer shower can bring the cenizo into full bloom, and when that happens, bees, who are generally hard to spot, suddenly cover the bush in their productive hum to extract what must be a favorite nectar for their home place. I never have figured out where home is, but they waste no time getting started on the bright pink cenizo blooms. You can walk right up to the bush and watch 'em at work. It's an amazing sight.

Daddy had a beekeeper in Marfa bring us a hive once, but the bees soon took off. He said, he guessed we'd have to buy any honey we wanted. He wasn't inclined to spend money twice to find out if a second bunch would stay put. He joked, "Must be the bees didn't find our place to their likin', and a second bunch might not take to us, either. I couldn't take the rejection a second time."

A rancher a couple years older than Daddy lived down south and didn't fare nearly as well as we did up north in the Davis Mountains. When the summer rains commenced, if Daddy ran into him, he'd ask if they'd seen any rain yet. By then, we might have had two or three inches and sometimes more—the ranch green as Ireland. (I have to trust pictures for that comparison. Never been there, of course.) The old rancher, somehow never despairing, would have to answer all too often, "Not a drop, but we are one day closer to rain."

One day closer to rain. That was his mantra—well, prayer of a kind, for sure.

Our particular land, with its surrounding mountains, has a knack for spinnin' up a good afternoon thunderstorm in July and August, and a heavy shower might pass over us two or three times, as it bounces back and forth between the peaks before peterin' out. Often, between the showers, we'd get brilliant double rainbows.

I can recall some years where we didn't get nearly as much as we'da liked, but I can't think of a single year where we went without a drop. I know some down south saw long dry spells, more times than they should have had to see.

So, some years, we had grass that didn't even make it to seed— or barely so—and some years when it looked like wheat fields ready for harvest. The only problem with those wheat-field years was all that extra tall grass, once dormant for the winter, made for a mighty powerful combustible by spring at the slightest spark.

Over the years we had our share o' fires from lightnin' strikes. If we were lucky, the rain put them out about as soon as they started. If we weren't so lucky, then we had to be mindful about what to do next to protect the animals and ourselves. I was only three or four when the University of Texas built the McDonald Observatory, which to the good fortune of this area, has brought with it over the years a lot better gear for dealin' with wildfires than we would have probably ever mustered otherwise. Crews are pretty well johnny-on-the-spot when it looks like some fire isn't going to burn itself out quickly. It's all hands on deck in those cases, and I've done my share over the years not to just address a fire on our land, but on any ranch up this direction.

Billy and Ernesto got a big taste of that back in 2011 with the Rockhouse Fire that burned for weeks and covered well over 310,000 acres—that's pushing upwards of 500 square miles. We fretted for the three weeks Billy and Ernesto were off workin' with the crews to keep that fire in the mountains and off the ranches and away from homes. Still, some homes were lost (all in the first day), and plenty of cattle and other wildlife died in the fire. The crew did a helluva job as far as the Geermann-Schlatters were concerned. With the fuel from the exceptional grass from the year before and sixty-mile-an-hour April winds, all the blaze could do was rip across the land.

There is no question, water and fire are the two main determinants to the health of all the stationary parts of the ranch— that is, the land. Furthermore, both elements have their cascading effect on all those movin' parts contained therein—every blade of grass, every creature, and I guess, you'd even have to put some of the land in that category. It was easy enough to do damage to the stationary parts by diggin' somewhere you shouldn't have or by overgrazing causin' the earth to wash away in those gully washers. The long habit of stewardship of our land meant these damages were minimal. I can't think of anywhere we harmed the land to cause one, but we had our own natural gullys that dug that little bit deeper into the mountains and the *arroyos* across the flatlands with every passin' gully-washin' rain.

I don't know how anyone can feel anything but joy when you look at the beautiful landscape and know that not only you, but the generations before you, have done their utmost to be in symbiosis with it. Daddy viewed such alignment with nature as an act of humility. How could pride come into it? Pride suggests we have some superior way. My observations over the years, which I know align with Daddy's observations in his lifetime, suggest our so-called superiority may lead to great damage by a deliberate act, crude carelessness, or simply from the best intentions goin' awry.

Beyond the slowest moving parts of the ranch—the grass, prickly pear, cholla, yucca, cenizo, piñon, and oaks—there is the vast array of swifter moving parts.

Wildlife is such a part of our life in the desert mountains. It is a constant reminder that we are just one more species among many. Applying that same humility, we should never interpret our role as dominator. Carelessness in this regard can certainly lead the self-appointed dominators being dominated against their will. A good rattlesnake bite comes to mind, when you think you can fool around with 'em tryin' to show off for someone.

Then, there are the unsuspecting times for even those who respect nature's order. Once, when Bill and I were out workin' cattle, we broke for a sack lunch we'd brought along. We hitched our horses to a tree and headed up for what we knew to be a good sittin' rock, a bit higher up, and in the shade of a larger oak. After enjoying our leisurely lunch, we headed down the hill just as we heard somethin' hit the ground behind us. We turned to see a mountain lion runnin' higher up into the hills.

"Holy shit!" Bill exclaimed. "That lion was sittin' right over our heads. Good thing we're both lean. She musta thought we weren't worth the effort."

I chuckled, "Could be her daddy told her to leave folks be on this ranch. He probably told her, 'They don't bother us. We don't bother them.' I'm pretty sure I heard her mutter somethin' to that effect as she slinked away."

"That would explain it better than my 'being lean' hypothesis," he reckoned. "Though I'd guess it had to do more with still digestin' a jackrabbit or two."

There were plenty of times after that we'd go for rest stops on those sittin' rocks, but we never did so again without a close examination of that oak tree and what might be restin' in it.

We certainly have never assumed that we are done learnin' as to how to see to the ruminants on the land. These included all our cattle, of course, and the shorter stays of sheep and goats when we needed a good brush scrubbin'. We are also just as mindful of the deer and antelope. They don't require much from us other than our respect for their migratory patterns. There never have been game fences on our ranch to confine them for easy pickin's for some city-boy hunters. We've never made a fence any higher than necessary to get the cattle moved around for the best health of the grass. Any section that doesn't have cattle always has any and every gate opened for their convenience. Any place with a water tank is maintained whether it has cattle at that time or not. We have a salt block near every water tank. As Daddy always said, "The little bit of work required is all to the good."

Some years, we have a steady visitation from roadrunners and jackrabbits. Some years pass when they seem to all but disappear.

Momma and I always enjoyed looking at big anthills. That is to say, we enjoyed the big harvester ants. Momma didn't appreciate "their little cousins" who would sneak through invisible passages and into her kitchen. Daddy didn't like "the little suckers" either, and for good reason. They could easily cause a fire. For reasons beyond our knowing, they like to build their ant nests inside any electrical box, which could then lead to a short circuit—suicide ants, as Daddy called them—generating sparks that could set off a grassfire or burn down a house or barn. Part of our semiannual maintenance runs included making sure all our electrical panels were ant free and covered with about the only toxin on the place to keep them away.

Momma said the big harvester ants did all their good work "out in the open," and we weren't to pour anything on their mound to kill 'em. She did her best to never step on one. "They were here before us, and will be here longer after us," she would say. Of course, that would apply to the little ants as well, but it was far more enjoyable watching the harvester ants at work bringing a load on their back two or three times the size of them. According to Daddy, they could sting a grasshopper and kill it. That was all right by him—all to the good.

We have a lot of the desert-adapted kangaroo rats all around the ranch. Momma liked them as they had no interest in calling our house their home. They live in burrows near any cactus or *agarita* bush. Daddy said they can survive without ever drinking any water because they don't sweat, and can get all the needed moisture from their diet of seeds and nibbles of grass. He said they could detect the sound of an owl approaching.

I've seen their long back legs catapult them a good nine feet in one leap—handy when a rattlesnake is on your tail. They have large heads with big eyes and small ears. In addition to their long back legs, they also have pouches in their cheeks to stock up.

Anytime Kola or Koala would spot one, they would leap straight up on all fours—repeatedly popping up a good foot off the ground. It was quite entertaining. I only saw the dogs catch one or two—then they didn't know what to do with it but bring it to us. As soon as they'd let it loose, the critter would take off. I'd guess any other rat around them would pretty quickly have an inferiority complex. Cute is not a name I'd apply to any other rat, nor can I think of anything some other rat could do to amuse me.

Well, I guess there is one exception to that. We assumed it was a pack rat or two that got into a little shed we hardly ever went into. All we kept in there was something we didn't need but on rare occasions. They'd chewed a sizable hole in the siding on the backside, out of our sight—and didn't stop there. Daddy made the mistake of putting Momma's White Mountain ice cream freezer in there at the end of one summer. When he went to get it for her many months later, the rats had literally chewed the entire bottom off the tub. He thought it was pretty funny. Momma said, "Well, you can't say the woman made you do it. You picked that dumb shed to store my freezer in all on your own." The rodent or rodents had also left buckets of cholla cactus on every single flat surface. Daddy thought it might be easier to burn down the shed than clean it all out, but he and I got on heavy leather gloves and did our best.

The night air is, more often than not, filled with the cries of the coyotes. They are, I must confess, our love-hate critters. I love to hear them and respect their right to be here since we are the invasive species not they—but we lose newborn calves to them, and back in the day, we lost our share of sheep and goats to their carnivorous ways. They seem to multiply more prolifically than mountain lions, which is better than the other way around, I suppose. The coyotes' natural symbiosis is to feast more on rabbit than beef. Thus, there has been no ranch eradication program. I'm just glad rabbits breed as fast as they do. And their death is pretty instantaneous—certainly in comparison to takin' a calf down. I never witnessed it, but I have a pretty good notion that baby javelina is a regular favorite. Something keeps the javelina population down, and having once witnessed a coyote pack takin' down a full-grown javelina, I know they aren't afraid of 'em.

Anytime I think I'm smart, all I have to do is ponder the instincts and habits of the smallest creatures and look at life with complete amazement—even at spiders with their elaborate webs shimmering in the sunlight. Spiders and I are live-and-let-live as long as they stay out of my bed and shoes—yes, even tarantulas. I never have seen a tarantula in the house. They just saunter slowly across the desert floor and don't seem intent on botherin' me any more than I am interested in botherin' them. I wouldn't say they're cute, but they are fascinating. However, if a scorpion gets in the house, he's gonna find a boot on top of him at the first sighting. He should have stayed outside where he belongs!

It is no secret that my favorite wild moving parts are the birds. I got my reverence for them from Momma, and of all the creatures I carry on a conversation with, I find the birds' views the most interesting. Unlike Nellie, they never fuss at me. Top of the list are those that like to hang around the house and barns. The more they sing the better. That is not to say, I don't like some of the more elusive. Some stay year round and some head south for the winter.

Hummingbirds are among the seasonal. Momma always tried to have things blooming for their arrival and throughout their stay. Sis and I continue her good work.

The swallows fly around all summer in and out of their mud-packed huts usually erected over a door, but they head deep into Mexico, and further, before any cold weather arrives. I always rather hope ours migrate to the mountains in El Salvador and spend the winter with *Padre Jesús,* Ernesto and Rosalinda's youngest son—the Franciscan friar—whose work our family has followed all these years. He has confirmed they have swallows, and he figures they summer on our ranch.

The swallows always find their way back to their summer home in hopes we haven't knocked it down. If it does get knocked down or falls off, they get busy puttin' up a new hut right in the same spot. After Momma realized they weren't gonna find some location better suited to where she wanted it, we quit knocking 'em down, and put up with a little bird shit by the doors. They have a soft-spoken little chirp and provide plenty of acrobatic entertainment. Is there a happier bird? They sure look happy dartin' about.

Turtle doves—I guess technically, mourning doves—are year rounders, and come around cooin' to tell me when they think it is gonna rain. They are most always right, but I might go several days without seeing them—generally in pairs when I do. Fidelity to each other, I guess.

Sparrows like the barns and seem to know better than most how to thrive in any setting—town birds, city birds, ranch birds—they seem to be content anywhere. Saint Paul must have gotten inspiration from the sparrows for his lines, "I have learned to be content with whatever I have. I know what it is to have little, and I know what it is to have plenty." They are underappreciated in my book, and of course, they are always given a good Christian burial when we spot one dead.

There are always scaled quail around the ranch, but without some seed to lure 'em close, they keep their distance from the house. Still, when a covey of twenty or thirty come trottin' along on the ground, I just have to chuckle at their little legs goin' as fast as they can. One little spook, and they give up on the ground run, and take to the air. Tryin' to get those fat breasts off the ground is as amusing as their runnin'. Those wings give it all they got to get 'em airborne.

On occasion, we see a flock of wild turkeys, spot a golden eagle, hawk or falcon, or are amazed by the rare spotting of a beautiful painted bunting. The owls that nest in mountains hoot their night's approval at our leaving a few mice around for their nourishment. As must needs, we set a trap or two in the house, but poison is never on the menu.

I always keep an eye out for any bird that seems to have gone off course and is out in the desert far from where they are supposed to be accordin' to the Audubon Society. If they land long enough and close enough, I try to find out how they ended up here. Most don't seem to speak West Texas *Gringa* so I never really find out much.

My steadiest friends are the cactus wren and the curve-billed thrasher.

You gotta respect any bird that could make a nest in the cholla. I get near one, and I'm stuck with a needle, and dadgum, they hurt! But that's where the cactus wrens call home. Curve-billed thrashers will sometimes nest in one as well, though ours seem more inclined to find an *agarita* bush. When Bill put in his solar panels, they decided they liked the underside with its aluminum frame where they could tuck in out of the rain. We were amazed how quickly they decided that was *the* place to be.

As for cholla nests, they have explained, it's not easy on the front end to nest there, but the rewards are what it keeps away. Ain't no snake gonna climb up and have a wren or thrasher omelette or a newborn for breakfast. The snakes can't get up the steel column that supports the solar panels either, so they seem to have another snake-proof nesting arrangement. Damn smart, if you ask me!

I love the curious nature of the cactus wren and their little chirpin'. Leave a door or window open, and they'll come take a closer look. They are particularly good conversationalists.

I suppose with so many colorful birds, these desert birds— whose males are indistinguishable from the females, unlike some of the showier species—wouldn't be at the top of most people's list, but they are at the top of mine. They are my most faithful, feathered companions.

My thrashers love to perch up on some wall or post or chimney and have a look around. They remind me of my contemplative momma—particularly since their favorite place for their morning and evening hymns and prayers here at the new house are on the parapet wall of Sis's chapel—always sittin' where I have a clear view of them. I listen intently for their invocation and benediction each blessed day. They just make me happy.

With high school over and done with, I was back at the ranch year around and happy for it. Momma and Daddy accepted easily enough my disinterest in Sul Ross—or goin' to any other school. Neither could have imagined me going off for a career in some city, though Daddy was easily amused by the notion of me walking into Neiman Marcus in Dallas in my bib overalls with a Swisher Sweet in my ear. He said next time we were in Fort Worth, he might drive me over there just to get a picture of it.

My smokin' Swisher Sweets is a bit of a mystery. I took 'em up right upon graduation. Sis had a fit. Honey didn't care. Momma said they stunk, and if I was gonna smoke 'em, it had to be outside. Daddy never smoked, so I don't know where I even got the notion, but I did take up that lifelong habit—easin' up some in recent years.

Now that I was an "adult" and full-time cowgirl, Daddy and I worked out our daily routines and division of labor. I volunteered to take on all the stable muckin' as mine to do, but he insisted that was a joint chore, and I wasn't to deprive him of the pleasure.

He'd say, "I got to keep a little horseshit on my boots to keep your Momma happy. You know how she comes after me with a broom if I try to sneak in the house with 'em on."

So, we stuck to our joint muckin', which generally did inspire him to tell one story or another. He seemed to get inspiration from horseshit. He'd even recite an improvised poem every once in a while, though he never wrote 'em down—and if he had, I think Momma would have seen to it they got lost somehow.

One I remember went like this.

There was an old horse named Honey
whose piles of shit were all runny.
The dung beetles thought they were yummy
and ate till they filled their small tummy.

I told that to Momma at supper, who declared, "Such poetry can stay in the barn," though you could see she was fightin' off a smile.

Another was—

My dear little cowgirl, Sallie,
a day don't go by when you dally.
Work comes right up your alley—
puts to shame any man in the valley.

Momma liked that one a lot better. Sis wanted her own, so right there at the supper table, he rattled off—

My dear little Betsy-Mae,
you brighten my every day.
There's much more I could say—
for a fine happy life, I pray.

Momma said, "I guess you need to compose one for me now so I don't feel left out."

Not so long ago, a girl named Anna
left her family from near Louisiana
had her heart set on a ranch in Montana
and ended up on the Texas savanna.

Daddy laughed, "I had no idea when I started on that one that Anna was such a hard word to rhyme! Couldn't figure out any good lovin' words to work in there." Which prompted him to try again.

The wife of ol' John is a keeper.
Every year his love grows deeper.
There might be some kept cheaper
But by golly, he's gonna keep her.

Momma declared, "Ol' John isn't going to find one he can keep cheaper! I think that's enough for one evening."

I sure strayed off the path of ranch chores, there. Daddy's crazy poppin' up again!

I moved from apprentice to head shoer, a role I would maintain until I passed it on to Jaime and Noah. Billy, who had shoed many a horse in Van Horn those twenty years he was up there, didn't mind that chore going to one of "his hands," but he'd still shoe his own horse more than not just to keep in practice.

By the time I came along, we weren't drivin' cattle across the country to get them to rail cars, and while we technically had a registered brand, we never branded our cattle. Daddy figured even if a steer escaped through the mountains to another ranch, then probably they could keep him, as we must have not been givin' him the attention he wanted. "Maybe they'll do better by him," he'd say.

We were both good ropers and handy with a whip.

Whip—that makes me think of something our certified heathen, Jaime, brought up once after he'd become a gen-u-ine cowboy. He saw some copy of a religious painting in the Bible story book Lupe gave him. That book caused Jaime all kinds of trouble tryin' to reconcile those stories with what was actually recorded in the Bible. He certainly opened Sis's eyes more than once. At first, she said he must be readin' from a Catholic Bible, since Chuy and Lupe were Catholic and had given him his Bible. But when he'd quote word for word what it said, she found her good old King James said the same thing.

I know—I'm veering off track. In the painting it showed Jesus taking a whip to the money changers and showed some of the animals in the background. Proof positive Jesus was no pacifist! Well, there was a problem with that as Jaime discovered in his due-diligence search of the scriptures. It says Jesus turned over the money changers' tables, and using a cord, he drove out the animals from the portico of the temple. If you've ever moved cattle, you don't get them started by saying, "Here, cowie, cowie!" A good crack on the ass might get 'em moving as much from the sound of the crack as the actual contact to their thick hides. They feel it—the same as we feel a thump on our backside, but it's a long way from animal cruelty. It seemed, Jesus wasn't as violent as that artist tried to make him out to be. I guess it was a reflection of how the artist would have gone about it, or maybe his rich patron steered him in that direction. It wasn't Jesus's violence that got him in trouble big time with Caiaphas and his buddies that day. It was disrupting their indulgence-for-sale scheme.

We've always done more movin' around of cattle in smaller pens than most. According to Daddy, that was something he and Granddad worked on over the years as they tried to figure the best way for the cattle to keep on good grass. Their general conclusion was the animals moved in herds for a reason and the millions of buffalo that roamed across the plains regenerated the vast seas of grass as they moved. That was the pattern to try to imitate. I helped Bill as he did more on that front, and Billy and Jaime moved it further still with even smaller pens and near-daily moving when we launched the GS Ranches meats.

While we certainly did everything needed for the day-to-day runnin' of the ranch, Daddy never thought we needed to take on periodic work to then take work away from someone else. That was best exemplified with his long-standing patronage of a butcher who handled all the meat we kept for ourselves, and his hiring a Cardona cousin to haul our cattle.

Daddy said, "I don't want a semi-trailer sittin' here unused months on end. 'The laborer is worthy of his hire,' to quote Luke."

That pretty much covered the truck, the butchering and anything else he'd rather not take on. He was always one who worked damn hard to make a livin', but had no need to try kill and himself to make a killin'.

Our duo had only lasted about three years when Bill came along to substantially add to the full-time workforce. He was an instant fit.

Once Bill started gettin' some of that annual oil revenue, Daddy told him, "Bill, I admire that you work as hard as you do for this family and these cattle. You could be like some who get an income and don't think any work is required of them ever again. They indulge themselves on a daily basis. And then there are some—

even worse I suppose in my book—who get the benefit of good fortune and are never satisfied. They have to have more and more and more, and they don't care what it takes to get it."

Bill, ever the gentleman, replied, "Sir, I appreciate that. It's the lazy ones in the first group who will complain the loudest about their taxes and what's going to the poor. And it's the other group, the more and more and more crowd, that bring about the wars and suffering of this world."

Daddy put his arm around his son-in-law. "You're a wise young man, Bill Schlatter. A wise young man."

It was clear from the start that marriage was the inevitable outcome, and Bill and Betsy didn't wait long before marrying. Bill would have liked to have been married on the ranch. Sis preferred a church wedding in town. Bill would have liked to have lived on the ranch. Sis preferred in town. We know who won on both accounts.

Some of Bill's family came over from San Angelo and stayed at the Indian Lodge. (I'm surprised they haven't renamed that by now.) Sis invited more people in town than Momma thought necessary, and she ended up having to talk to the Baptists, so she could use their bigger church.

Now, I'm not going to blame the good Baptists of Fort Davis for Sis's fundamentalism streak. The biggest bunch of her group came from that church, but there were others from the Presbyterian and Church of Christ who longed to have their own Church of Self-Righteous Anger and Gossip. I never told Sis (until this writing) that that is what I called her group. Bill knew. I never even told Momma or Daddy, as I kept my mouth shut for their sake. I didn't want to cause them any more grief than they were goin' to bear as a result of their daughter's new-found religion, but I'm gettin' ahead of the story.

They had their big church wedding and moved into the little rock house Momma and Daddy owned right next to the church. The Baptist minister wanted to make it clear that all the bride's wedding party needed to be in dresses. That was, of course, intended for me. He certainly knew from seeing me around town that I never wore a dress. Sis had asked me to be her bridesmaid. When she told me what the preacher said, I told her, "I guess I'll have to stand with Bill, then. That side'll have pants on. I assume he doesn't want Bill and his groomsmen in dresses."

Bill smiled and suggested, "We men could wear kilts. I wonder what he'd think of that?"

Daddy couldn't help but laugh.   Momma, who always wore a dress, really surprised me. Addressing Sis, she said, "Daughter, you asked your sister to stand with you. You need to decide if you are going to honor who you know your sister is or if it's more important to please the preacher. If it's to please the preacher, you should ask someone else to be your bridesmaid."

I was shocked, and I could see so was my sister. If Daddy had said it, neither of us would have been surprised.   Comin' from Momma, it did catch us off guard.

Daddy added, "The woman of the house has set the terms. The man of the house concurs."

I wore my slacks to the horror of the Baptists and most other churchgoers. The preacher asked Bill, "Do you know what you are gettin' into?"

Bill told me this several years later.   I asked him how he responded. "I walked away. I didn't think it deserved a response."

Bill had been livin' in the bunkhouse since movin' to the ranch. Now, it would become only his home away from home. Up until the wedding, he ate supper with us every evening—eatin' breakfast at the bunkhouse and skippin' lunch more often than not. With Sis and Bill both gone from the supper table, the three remaining just kinda stared at each other the first couple evenings.

On the third night Daddy asked, "Did Betsy-Mae do all the talkin'? We sure have gotten quiet."

I relayed that message to Sis as him saying, now that she's not there, we can finally get a word in edgewise.

She protested, "I hardly ever said anything! You and Daddy did all the talking."

I chuckled and acknowledged that was mostly true—that I wasn't sure why her absence had brought on our new quiet mood.

It didn't last into a fourth night. The three of us found our new groove, and any one of us that had any news to share from Sis or Bill, shared it with the others.

Before Billy came along, Bill often stayed out at the ranch two or three nights a week. When Sis was due to deliver, he made sure he was home every night. That was a pattern that would continue as long as the kids were home with few exceptions. I would contend

72

that his concern for Billy and Jaime driving the mountain roads at night goes back to those long years of "commuting." He hit a deer about once a year, which he hated. He was never hurt, but killing the helpless animals with his truck was a burden to him; in his mind, a burden too easily dismissed by too many. He thought some of these people who claim they are against killing any animal to eat need to take a fuller measure of their lifestyle. "I wonder if they take into account that just in this country alone, a million and a half deer are killed every year by vehicles. That's just the deer! 'Oh, I live in the city and don't drive a car!' Do they even ponder for a second all the wildlife killed by cars, trucks and trains? Pile on top of that the 'pest control' to keep critters out of the fields and orchards. We have a lot of people that put on blinders to see only part of the equation."

Bill also saw his share of swerving vehicles of obviously intoxicated or drugged-up drivers. He had more than one close call, and he never wanted his children on the roads at night.

I suppose simply due to the family's history with its propensity for small families, it was ten years before Sis was "great with child." That soon became an understatement. She got bigger and bigger. When she and Bill were out for Sunday dinner in her ninth month, Momma announced, "I'm coming back into town with you to stay until whatever it is that's on its way comes to pass."

Daddy added, "You will either deliver or blow up. Momma better be there either way."

For unto us a child was born. Unto Sis and Bill, a son was given. And they put a diaper on that big hind end, and called the boy Billy. Our lives would change forever!

We had no idea what lay in store for us in the 1960s. By 1963, the nation dealt with the shock of the assassination of its president —and assassinated in Texas! Betsy called us from town to tell us the news. Now we had a Texan as president. Daddy, not inclined to conspiracy theories, did joke once well past the shock of the event, "I doubt ol' LBJ did any mournin' for his boss. He's the big man now."

He may have been the big man, but it seemed he let himself get sucked into another war halfway around the world, which he only escalated with every passing year. Unrest was the order of the day. While we were certainly isolated from it, we weren't ignorant as to the strife at home and abroad.

A year later, I was dealin' with my own grief. Honey dropped dead—quite literally. I wasn't ridin' her at the time, but one minute she was standin' there, and the next she was on the ground—dead. She was just over twenty-five by then. A good life, but certainly on the lower side of average. We accept life as it comes on this ranch and aren't inclined to pay some vet to cut dead animals open to see what killed 'em.

As Daddy would say, "I don't want my body carved up when I'm dead, and won't do it to an animal unless absolutely necessary."

Rogelio Cardona came out to dig the hole with his backhoe, and we put her in ground near all the other horses who had died on the ranch. Daddy said a few words as to how beautiful and extraordinary she was, and Momma said a nice prayer. I laid her blanket over her body, and Daddy, Bill and I covered her up. I spent the night crying. It was the first real grief I'd ever known.

I knew out of necessity we weren't going to dally getting another. We always kept an older horse, whose well-earned retirement allowed them to live with minimal ridin'. The horse Bill had brought with him from San Angelo had "gone out to pasture" the year before, and so for the couple months before we got another horse for me, I rode Bill's retiree.

Soon enough, Bill and I went horse shopping and came home with an overo brown and white paint horse with blue eyes. I named her Stormy—after those eyes. We all had said how beautiful Honey was. Stormy was pretty, but I was always more inclined to say that rather than beautiful, she was kinda funny lookin'. And while Honey strutted around like the show horse she was, Stormy was playful and kinda silly. We hit it off right away, and I was glad to have a totally different kind of horse.

It ain't right to try to duplicate the experience with one to the next. My general observation in life—don't put on a child or an animal the characteristics *you* want. Let them be who they are. Everyone will be the happier for it. That's not to say you don't guide 'em when you see they're goin' wrong. But you have to be damn careful you know what is right and what is wrong. From what I've observed, too many depend on someone else deciding for them what that is—usually someone pullin' a scripture verse they like over dozens of others. It makes for a lot of grief in a family, as my sister learned to her and our family's detriment.

Billy was born in that tumultuous year of 1968. By the time he came into the world, The Rev. Martin Luther King, Jr. was dead. Robert F. Kennedy was dead. We were totally engulfed in the war. We had declared absolute strangers to be our enemies. We did not know the people's history, their language or their culture. Most Americans couldn't have found the tiny country on a map. Yet we were good, and they were evil. We needed to kill them to protect our goodness and ourselves.

As Bill rightly asked, "Can anyone tell me what these people ever did to us? It's our noses in their business—not the other way around."

The year was taking its toll on all our spirits. Upon the news of RFK's death, Daddy lamented, "I could easily despair from the violence of our nation. It seems if a man speaks for peace, he's a dead man. If he speaks for justice, he's a dead man. If he speaks for love, he's a dead man."

75

Daddy had to bury Buckle shortly thereafter. He outlived Honey by about four years but wasn't as old as some horses get. Still he'd had a good run and received a good Geermann Christian burial in the horse cemetery. When Daddy got his next horse, he speculated that this new horse—he named Starshine—would likely be his last. "I think she'll probably see me out."

I didn't want to think it, but I guessed he was probably right. I think the name was inspired by his love of the Milky Way and filled him with the notion of his soul drifting toward it to be one with the cosmos in some new way.

When Billy was born later that November, Daddy picked up the bright-eyed boy into his arms and declared, "War and riots and death are the order of the day, but God's gift of life and love goes on. The innocence and beauty of this child renews my hope for what can be."

That certainly summed it up for me. I don't claim any maternal instincts. I certainly never wanted to have a child any more than I ever wanted to marry. With Billy in my arms, that was always enough for me. Instinctually, I was drawn to this stout, chubby little bundle of joy. I had no idea why that bond was there, or why it was so strong. It certainly wasn't any kind of envy of Sis having the child. It seemed to me (my overactive imagination at work, no doubt) that as the boy looked up at me, his happy disposition said, "I love you, Aunt Sallie." That such proved to be the case when he came to talkin' "was all to the good" for this cowgirl.

My God, I loved that child! I couldn't have loved my own any more. By the time he could walk, one of us was hikin' him onto our lap for a ride around the ranch. Daddy and I always gave Bill first dibs, but Bill, considerate enough to know how much Daddy and I wanted the boy close to us, yielded a lot more than he wanted to, no doubt.

From his second birthday on, Billy and Sis would come to the ranch for supper on Fridays—Bill still there, of course, from the day's work. Billy would then spend Friday and Saturday night with us on the ranch. Momma and Daddy would drop him off at home on Sunday if they happened to be going into town for church. Otherwise, Bill would show up for our frequent Sunday afternoon rides and take Billy back home with him. That was the more frequent pattern of the two. His weekend stays would persist right up until his departure from our lives at age sixteen.

Billy never seemed much interested in anything but being a little cowboy. Like me, he was eager for his first horse, and he loved ridin'.

On his sixth birthday, he got that horse. Bill asked him what he wanted to name him. Billy responded, "I know he's a boy horse, but do you think it's okay to a call a boy horse Sal?"

Bill smiled, looked at me and then at Daddy. "Son, I think Sal is a fine name for your horse."

And so Sal it was.

Billy and Sal were made for each other. The young gelding quarter horse had a jet-black coat, a big, stocky hind end and big black eyes, just like his rider. Like me and Honey, Billy and Sal grew up together. Sal even seemed to have the same personality as Billy. You couldn't do anything to aggravate either one of them. A happy boy and a happy horse. Billy tended to the care of Sal as much as he could, livin' in town as he did. I tended to the horse otherwise and was glad to do so. Besides, I needed to make sure Sal understood the precious cargo he was carryin'.

During the week, we'd often have the horse tag along riderless, just to give him some exercise and have him grow accustomed to us and his surroundings.

As soon as Sis was pregnant with her second, Bill and Betsy bought their house on Front Street, and Daddy and Momma sold the little rock house.

Momma, knowing the answer already, asked Daddy, tryin' to act all serious, "Don't you think we might want to keep it so when you are ready to retire, we can live in town?"

That was when he set the terms for his own burial. "Not only am I *not* going to retire to town, I'd better be buried out here on this ranch. I never did understand why the Geermanns before me let themselves be buried in town. Have a church service if you must, but don't bother on my account."

I should probably mention before going on that right after Billy came along, Daddy announced that he thought we'd give up our annual trips to Fort Worth unless anyone objected.

He said, "Now that we captured the best Schlatter bull for our daughter and can get any Brangus we might want directly through him, I don't see the point of making the long trip, which always requires leaving things in the hands of hired help."

No one objected, so that was the end of that. Bill joked that he could now blame Daddy for not being able to go see his brother.

Since that time, none of us has ever been back to the stock show—a family tradition parted with for practicality more than anything.

When Brett came along, it wasn't like we didn't make an effort to give him the attention he was due. But as for his comin' to the ranch, it never took. The few times we'd try to hike the youngster up on our lap for a ride around the ranch, you'd have thought we were torturing the poor boy. He'd scream until he was handed back down to his momma. Later, when he could have had his own horse, he expressed absolutely no interest in gettin' one. The few times he might ride with us, he looked as uncomfortable on a horse as Billy looked comfortable—Billy lookin' like he was one with the animal. Brett had the look of near dread.

As I have already stated—don't put on a child the characteristics *you* want. Proverbs postulates, "Train up a child in the way he should go, and when he is old, he will not depart from it." I've long seen parental disappointment spring from this. The problem on the one hand is I've never been convinced most parents know the way the child *should* go, and largely for reasons I've already stated. And then there's the fact that I don't think parents realize the proverb is telling them they are highly unlikely to live long enough to see "their way" come to fruition. Parents want to see results! The proverb certainly doesn't suggest, "Bring them up as you would have them go, and your teenager will be your delight."

We accepted that Brett would rather be in the house or in town, and we let him be. He much preferred a good set of Legos over playin' cowboy. He would show us his latest "floor plans." He rarely ever put a roof on any of this house creations. I guess that was our first clue that real estate was as good a fit as any for his natural interests—that or workin' as a builder—but there again, he wasn't any more inclined to pick up a hammer and saw than he was a saddle.

About the only time I ever saw Brett was when we'd all have Sunday dinner together—sometimes on the ranch, sometimes in town.

Jean was the last to come from the union of Bill and Betsy. Sis laughed at the thought of knowin' how to raise a girl. "You would think it would be easier, but you and I are so different. I'm not at all sure how I go about letting her be a frilly-girl, as you always called me, or a cowgirl like you."

"Or somethin' in between—I don't know either," I responded. "Momma acts like she doesn't know what she did to get one in bib overalls and the other in a dress."

Betsy reasoned, "Obviously, she had both garments on hand. I guess I'll do the same, and see what the child picks out to wear when the time comes."

She almost did that. Sis never did like my bib overalls, and so she opted for blue jeans instead. From the time she could point, Sis let Jean pick out her outfit for the day. Most of the time, it was a pair of jeans; sometimes a dress, but only on a Sunday. I guess Jean saw all the girls at church in dresses and matched them to fit in. Momma's chastisement from the Baptist preacher insisting that I had to wear a dress at the wedding set Sis to laying out jeans as an option on Sunday, just as well as any school day.

Jean was somewhere in between frilly-girl and cowgirl. Until the religious day of reckoning in the Schlatter household, little Jean was left to be whoever she would be. She liked to ride, and she liked to sew. We could see right away she liked numbers and structure. If she ever colored, she was of the kind to be precise— always inside the lines. If you gave her a blank page to color on, she really had no clue what to do with it. When you'd suggest maybe she draw a horse or her momma and daddy, everything was stick figures. People started with a line going up and down with any animal's line goin' side to side and every head, a circle.

She just didn't have a creative bone in her body, but she could organize anything—a trait that over time was more of a help than a hindrance to her mother. As Sis explained, "Every time I come into this kitchen it's a new day as to where something is going to be. I hope she gets her system perfected soon. Though I will grant, it is a steady progression towards the perfectly organized space—as is her own room."

The mid-eighties brought about my own grief of losing my second horse—too soon. Stormy had struggled off and on with colic over the years, and it finally did her in. As was par for the course, we didn't do an autopsy and gave Stormy her good Christian burial in the horse cemetery.

Daddy ran into the sheriff soon thereafter who told him about a bad situation with a horse he'd intervened to save. He wondered if Daddy would take it. We'd never had a rescue horse before, but he wasn't going to turn away a suffering and neglected animal. I rode with Daddy to go pick up the horse, who was being kept at the vet's clinic trying to nurse her back to health. She was quite a sight! I doubt her hide had ever felt a brush before the vet tried to clean her up. Even then, she still had dried shit-mud cakes stuck to her. Her ribs were sticking out. She didn't seem to like any man around her, which, no doubt, reflected her previous treatment from her owner. To the vet's amazement, she did let me handle her without any fuss.

Yes, this was my much loved and long-lived Nellie. Part of the reason I never knew for sure how old she was stems from not knowing exactly how old she was when we brought her home. I contend that once her strength was renewed, she adopted that helluva kick of hers for any man that got too close, out of a long-harbored resentment over her ill treatment as a young filly. She never would talk about her dark days.

She certainly didn't lack personality! I chuckle just at the thought of how our symbiosis so quickly flourished and so easily amused everyone around us. She said she could see I was a tough gal, which is why I was okay in her book. It was her notion that any lesser horse wouldn't have made it—that she, too, was a tough gal.

I still miss her. I promised her that if she went first, I wouldn't put her in the horse cemetery—she'd be on the ridge where'd I'd be buried, but upwind a bit from my Swisher Sweets. That was a promise I kept. So even now, she's only the second horse in the Geermann cemetery—Starshine bein' the first. We put her right next to where she stood that day lettin' us know where Daddy went down. I'll leave it to Billy and Noah to decide if some other horse belongs there in the future. I'm sure Nellie would be okay with some more company, as long as it was a horse or horses the boys thought would respect her standing in the horse history of the ranch.

81

In that regard, she stands alone in havin' survived gross mistreatment but recognizing immediately that she and I could forge together a new and vigorous life for her with a bond that could only be explained as some mystical union—or as Daddy viewed it, nature's symbiosis in its perfected form. She may not have been the most beautiful horse I ever had. Any outsider would have said the buckskin Morgan was pretty ordinary, but that ol' gal had a heart like no other horse I've ever known!

From Billy's birth to his fourteenth year, the Geermann-Schlatter family was filled with joyous normality. I can't think of much of anything to write down that stands out from those years, other than all the things you might expect from three growing children.

Bill was more Methodist than Church of Christ, and since he thought the Methodists did a nicer Christmas Eve service, we all, including this ol' cowgirl, would go in for the service. Bill and Betsy would then come to the ranch with the kids following the service and spend the night for our Christmas Day together. Daddy always had a nice piñon from the mountains on the ranch. We had presents under the tree and Geermann-Schlatter prime rib on the table. There was no visit from Santa. Somehow commercial Santa granting children's wishes never took with Momma and Daddy.

That's one of those things I'd like to ask them about now, that I never thought to do while they were living. I suppose it helped that we didn't have TV all those years, and maybe it wasn't any more than that. But, I'd have to add what I do know, which is, while unspoken, neither ever showed the slightest interest in fantasy characters of any kind. (Yes, I can hear the atheist say that God is a fantasy character. To declare so with certainty, seems to me, is equal to the fundamentalist of every religion.) Both looked to the natural world for their entertainment and enrichment. That was enough for them.

Throughout the year, we had many wonderful Sundays with everyone at the ranch for Sunday dinner and a relaxing afternoon. After dinner, some were off for a ride around the ranch, while the others enjoyed the patio or sitting next to the fire, if it was a little chilly out. A little cool air never kept us from ridin,' though there were plenty of Sundays in the winter when Daddy would declare, "I gotta go out in the cold on Monday, but I don't have to on Sunday." On those days we'd all play Chinese Checkers, a card game or some board game—as Billy liked to call them "bored" games. The only one that ever seemed to really like any of that was Brett. He did not inherit the non-competitive gene the rest of us had. He liked to play to win.

Jean did like card games, as she was good at keeping track of what was played. However, in that department, when up against Daddy and Billy, she had no real advantage. Momma's notion was if it was a four-hand game, then it would be Daddy, Billy, Brett and Jean that played together. What Brett would lack in keepin' track of cards was offset to a degree by his more competitive nature. That left Momma, Sis, Bill and I to go off quietly into another room and read.

And when it came to appreciating quiet, the four of us were of one mind.

Oh, dear! Now I have to begin the tellin' of the most painful years of our family's history. You already know the full account of its redemption, but the account of the twenty years of estrangement has only been a high-level recounting of some of its impacts.

I want it known up front, not only has Sis discussed my take on those years, but she has added to it, so that our account is of "one mind" as to all that went on during that epoch. One has to commend her for facing what she calls her prodigal years—dark years, as she looks back on them now—and facin' 'em head-on. It is even more important to her than to me to tell it as unvarnished as possible in some hope, and her prayer, that those who follow will learn from our family's history.

It ended in her Damascus Road moment when, thanks to Mr. Benson's book *The Body Broken*, "The scales fell from my eyes," as Sis puts it. The beginning was far less dramatic as she slowly moved from the sister I had known all my life to an unrecognizable zealot. Billy affectionately referred after the fact to this period as, "The time the body snatchers took my mother away."

Bill, too, has "added to the record" for recording the most honest account of both the pain and redemption we went through as a family.

Gradualism has become a disease of a kind, and I would say in our lifetime it has infected unsuspecting millions or, given the population these days, more likely billions. It is certainly endemic in the good old US of A. Our politicians count on it! And too many of the self-righteous have found it useful to spread *their* ideology as well.

Jaime says there's a good reason ideology and idiot sound so related. I can't argue with that.

Nature uses gradualism in its inherent cycle to adapt and thrive. Too often "we" (men and women) use it to soft-sell all manner of evils and ever-narrowing ways of seeing the world. In nature's gradualism, life is transformed in amazing ways. In the diseased version, man (who I'll single out here for the historical burden of the disease they rightly own) uses gradualism to tighten control and reduce the spectrum of what is possible. The only amazement is their absolute obsession with wealth, power and control.

Now, if you think I'm getting carried away here, just ponder with me for a bit. How do we justify every war? We have to start plantin' one seed at a time about why this or that country through this or that leader is going to be a threat to us. Sometimes they speed up the timeline as it progresses, but the sales pitch is the same. Identify the villain. Slowly manufacture consent. Desensitize people to the cost, both human and monetary that the impacts of war will bring. Sell our readiness as the sure path to victory. (Larger spending on arms is required to ensure that readiness, of course.) Display any image that stirs emotion and, even better, outrage, of the villain's evil deeds—which may be true, but doesn't need to be true to be just as effective. Any suffering child will do. Of course, we may be just as guilty of such evil deeds, but man's gradualism doesn't care about nuance or truth, however glaringly hypocritical it might be.

That in a nutshell defines the gradualism of political theatre. The dumb part, it seems to me, and certainly to our historian, Bill, is how endlessly we recycle the same stupidity war after war.

But enough about politics. I just wanted to show that the gradualism that infected Sis is not some phenomenon unique to the religious nuts of the world.

As best I can tell, the world has never wanted for lack of zealots. The Bible talks about them enough, and the only people that ever seemed to really work Jesus's last nerve were the many hypocritical zealots of his day. One might have thought "good Christians" would have brought an end to such, once and for all. It would be nice if we *could* do it *for all*, but if anything, in my lifetime it is only gettin' worse.

While color and culture were once the big dividers on a Sunday morning as to where you might worship, now all too often, it is the ideology you adhere to that defines where you show up on Sunday. Rightly, it seems to me, a good many have said to hell with all of it and quit going anywhere. "The church" has only itself to blame for this.

Just to be clear, I am not endorsing after the fact the evil made manifest by signs for "whites only" or "colored only" as though segregation by color is better than segregation by ideology. Such is the same evil! But there are natural associations that are not evil, and celebratin' such cultural expressions is a wonderful thing in my book. Whether it is a simple, four-part, unaccompanied singing of hymns in a Church of Christ or a lively, all-instruments-and-hands-on-deck, foot-stomping, hands-a-clapping, Black congregation—both are beautiful to me! I lean a lot more toward the quieter, but I'd like to think my brothers and sisters in the African American congregation would welcome an old cowgirl to shout a hallelujah or two right along with 'em. Such is the body of Christ healed—not the body broken.

For Sis, it took one preacher to plant the seed. He split a small church, taking a few members with him since the old church "wasn't growing in the Spirit" as defined by him. This preacher had to be sure his religion aligned with his politics, though that was somewhat hidden in his own gradualism when he first assembled his little flock. I do think they need to align, but in his case (and many others) it was politics that trumped any conflict with Jesus's teaching. In fact, Sis says that it was his emphasis on "loving Jesus" as a "born again Christian" that somehow made it a whole lot easier to begin to ignore how Jesus lived and how truly radical his teachings were. "We had our happy-clappy Jesus we could praise all day long. It didn't cost us anything," as Sis explained.

One of Sis's friends was a founding member of this little offshoot, and given her prominence in the community, rallied too many others to her new cause. Sis was persuaded to visit. Bill went a couple times and just said it was not his cup of tea. He thought their happy-clappy-Jesus preacher made a few too many promises of prosperity if you were giving your money to him. You have to give to get, it seemed, or God wouldn't "bless you."

Once they had their happy-clappy clan, then the preacher began his gradualism in earnest of who wasn't "worthy." First it was just those stuck in "dead churches." All that required was an evangelical spirit to try to recruit a few new "worthy" members.

The sermons became long litanies of family types who would end up in Hell for all eternity, if they didn't come to church every Sunday. Since Sis didn't want her family going to Hell, Bill finally relented and started going most Sundays, and the kids were drug there every Sunday. Billy, who was fourteen by then, had already been baptized in the Church of Christ, but I'll come back to that in a bit.

Then the sermons turned from families in general to individuals, who were not only going to Hell, but as best Billy could tell—and Bill wasn't blind to it either—were so abominable they couldn't be saved no matter what. The preacher's gradualism eased into that more than I feel the need to spell out. It was the means to his ends that led to where the good-natured-all-his-life Billy started to rebel. If you were a Baptist, or any other "Christian," then all you had to do was be "born again" again, baptized again (to be sure this time both were the real thing), pay your tithe to the new preacher and your soul was good to go.

But if you were an abomination, then by god, you were goin' to burn for eternity. At first, the abominations were nobody that lived in Fort Davis, so far as anyone knew. Top of the list were communists. (Like I said, politics trumped Jesus.) Soon enough the list included Muslims, Hindus, Buddhists—any other religion—and of course atheists, though I'm sure there were some of those in Fort Davis. In those days, such views were kept to oneself. Then soon enough, the list included the "secularists." Those consisted of anyone who voted for the "wrong" candidate, mostly—especially if they had any "socialist leanings"—but could apply equally to any number of people who didn't take the Bible "literally."

As he ratcheted down on exactly what was acceptable to be taken literally from his "inerrant" Bible, and what was to be ignored at all costs that would challenge both his literalism and inerrancy, virtually all of Momma's beloved Sermon on the Mount was chucked aside. Select verses dominated—many from Leviticus and Joshua. Paul's words were sliced and diced to the preacher's convenience as well. I recalled Momma's wise counsel regarding the Bible, "Don't believe everything you read." Or as I added back then—"or everything preached at ya."

I don't even need to spell out the list of who can never be born again because "God hates them." "They are given over to the Devil!" We all know the list too well. Sadly, it is alive and well and being preached across the country every Sunday and on TV and radio seven days a week. Jean was on it even though her mother was still clueless at that time. I was not so clueless, though Jean was too young to know for sure herself.

I did say to Sis back then, "All this castigatin' to Hell might put one or more of your own children into eternal damnation. I hope you're ready for that."

"None of *my* children will ever go over to the Devil!" was her reply.

I feared for her as much as for her children. In retrospect, maybe if Momma and Daddy had attended Sis's church just enough to really see what was going on, they could have intervened somehow. I knew there was no way I was darkening their door for all the aforementioned reasons. And yes, dresses were required attire for women. Sis never insisted Momma and Daddy attend, as at least she seemed to accept their faith was sufficient. She didn't need to save them from Hell, even if they were giving their money to the wrong church.

Bill and I couldn't make a dent in the newfound armor the preacher liked to pile on his followers—bastardizing Paul's more noble image of putting on the armor of Christ. However burdensome the weight, Sis wore it with great pride and conviction.

Oh, and of course, the preacher *loved* Betsy—not only for her zeal, but all the more for her large gifts in the offering plate. Bill wasn't any too thrilled with his oil revenues funding "the snake oil salesman," as he referred to the preacher.

All hell finally broke loose when, by Billy's sixteenth birthday, the preacher *demanded* that Betsy get Billy baptized into the church.

"Billy needs to make his profession as Brett did last year. Why is he holding out? Clearly, the Devil is trying to take hold of his soul. You've got to act *fast*."

I'd like to say that is my hyperbole of the situation, but Sis says those were the exact words the preacher used. As he became evermore unrelenting towards Sis gettin' Billy "saved," she became evermore unrelenting in her pursuit to snatch Billy out of the

Devil's grasp. Bill was helpless to stop it. I was helpless to stop it. *Momma and Daddy* were helpless to stop it. Sis was fully indoctrinated into the who-is-in-and-who-is-out Church of Self-Righteous Anger and Gossip.

And gossip that group did. They knew the sins of everybody in town, and castigated them left and right to the eternal flames. I know Bill felt the eternal flame on his own ass from all the self-righteousness the group dished out. He never bought into it at all, but he tried to be the faithful husband, which was no easy task— then, or for the next twenty years.

Bill said up until Billy's departure, he'd go enough to keep Sis off his back and would check his mind at the door. "I never did so much daydreamin' in a church in my life as I did those two years before Billy left."

Lord have mercy. What I have to say next is the hardest part. It pains me to relive all this. I may short out this keyboard with my tears. They just won't stop.

Now that I've composed myself a bit—the tears gone for the moment—I continue the saga.

For what came next, I was glad Vera wasn't there. She was never under foot, even though she lived in the house with us. She would typically make breakfast for us, put whatever she made in a tortilla for herself, and then she would go work in the greenhouse while it was cool in the warm months. In winter, she preferred to take her burrito back to her room. It wasn't like she wasn't welcome to sit down with us, which she did every evening. It was just one of her peculiarities.

When we'd have help staying in the bunkhouse, then Momma would cook our breakfast and dinner. Vera would be up early to go over to the bunkhouse and cook a hearty breakfast for the hands, put together a small sack lunch for them, and have a big supper waiting at the end of the day. Usually, the help was only there for a few days, but if we had a big project, then they might be there several weeks or even months. Such was the case when they'd work the next layout of fencing, water lines and tanks for the smaller pens that was part of the plan to move the cattle around more frequently.

There was no help around the ranch at this time. In early December 1984, Vera had requested some leave to go care for her *mamá* who was convinced she wasn't "going to see another Christmas." Her *mamá* wanted to die in the town where she had grown up and married in Mexico, *Pedro Meoqui*, and be buried there. Vera's siblings had their own families. It was logical for Vera to be the one to care for her, and I don't believe Vera would have had it any other way. Both mother and daughter still had their Mexican citizenship, so going back was no problem. Vera and her siblings were all born in *Ojinaga* where their *papá* had driven semi-trucks between the countries. Mother and daughter had permanent residency in the US as well, so Vera didn't have to worry about coming back across the Rio Grande.

They made their trip, but as it turned out, her mamá saw that Christmas after all, then the New Year, then Easter, then *Cinco de Mayo*. Being "home" gave her a bit of a new lease on life. We told Vera we'd manage, and she should stay with her *mamá* as long as she wanted. She lived almost up until the next Christmas.

Enough about Vera. I just wanted to explain why she is absent from any tellin' of what came next.

It was the first Thursday in January, 1985. Billy had turned sixteen just a few weeks earlier, on the 15th of November. The strain between Sis and Billy had been burdening Bill for a long time. We knew that well enough, of course. However, when Bill arrived at the ranch, and as per his routine each morning, came into the kitchen where we were still seated, one look revealed a Bill I'd never seen before. I knew something terrible had happened. Daddy and Momma could see it as well.

Momma immediately asked, "What's the matter, Son?"

Bill broke into tears, sobbing like I'd never seen or imagined possible from him. He sat down at the table with us, and Daddy rose to go stand behind him with his hands on Bill's shoulders. We all remained silent, givin' him the space to speak when he could.

Haltingly, he finally eked out the words kinda one phrase at a time, "Billy's run away…. I have no idea where he's gone…. Oh, my Lord!"

Daddy said, "Oh, *shit!*"

I said the only words of comfort I could think of with such a shock. "Bill, he loves you. He'll come home."

Momma said, "That's right, Bill, he loves you *deeply*. He can't stay separated from you."

Bill regathered his composure from those words of comfort, but he knew the truth of the situation well enough. He reminded us just how real it was for him and for Billy. "Reconciling Betsy's hard line with anything that resembles the Billy we love is an impossibility. *God damn it!* I wish my wife could see that!"

I looked right at Momma when he said that. I thought she'd be shocked to hear him use "GD" in front of her, but it looked more like she was ready to say the same thing about her own daughter.

Daddy said, "Anna, I'm going in to have a talk with our daughter. Are you comin' along?"

I don't think she could have said anything without breakin' down. She just stood, put on her coat and the two drove off, leaving Bill and me to sit and stare at each other.

A few minutes passed when Bill stood up. "Sallie Faye, the only thing for us to do at this moment is to tend to our horses and cattle. Let's get to it."

I stood, put on my coat, and as we were out the door and on the way to the stables, I walked beside him with my hand on his shoulder.

As we saddled up for the day, I couldn't help but look at Sal as though the boy should be there saddling him up with us. Bill obviously knew what I was thinking and lamented, "That horse is gonna wonder if he's been abandoned.

"Sallie, I know my love for Billy isn't an iota stronger than yours. I sure hope you and Anna are right that love will lead him home."

I thought what a beautiful line that was and repeated it. "Love will lead him home. Bill, it's just got to.... It's just *got* to!"

We tended to the day's labors, and figured Momma and Daddy would be back by lunchtime. We headed back to the house and saw Daddy's truck. As we walked into the house, one look told us all we needed to know. We sat down at the kitchen table with them.

Momma stated what she already knew, "I could make a lunch if anyone thought they could eat something."

We just sat silently and shook our heads—food had no appeal in that moment.

Daddy then started. "We knew that preacher had brainwashed our daughter, but *good Lord*, the extent of the damage is even more severe than we'd dreamed possible. She is persuaded that the events in the kitchen yesterday after school confirm Billy has been given over to the Devil. In her words, 'I ordered him out before he corrupts the other two.'

"I asked her how in the *hell* could she possibly believe that a boy as mature and kind as Billy can be damned forever? Her answer to that was, 'Around you, he's a sheep in wolf's clothing. I've seen the real Billy, and he has lost his soul.' At that Anna burst into tears, and I felt like slappin' the shit out of my daughter for the first time in my life. Maybe I should have."

We were all feelin' the full measure of our grief. After a long silence Bill said, "I walked into this last evening with no clue as to what had happened that afternoon. Betsy told me what she'd done, and I couldn't even talk to her. I just turned back around and went lookin' for Billy. When you wanna look for someone, all of a sudden, Fort Davis has about six too many highways going off in opposite directions. I had no idea where he would head. Of course, he'd be hoofin' it wherever it was.

"As I was drivin' around, I thought maybe I should have called the sheriff, but then I thought I don't want the sheriff draggin' him back home like some juvenile delinquent. Right now, I'm more inclined to report my wife for child abuse than I am to callin' the law on Billy.

"Then I thought, well maybe he called out here, and I'm drivin' around when you might already know where he is. But that thought was soon replaced by the realization that he'd have called here as soon as he left if he was going to do that."

I said, "We know Billy's got good sense. We don't have to worry about him wandering into the desert and gettin' lost."

Bill replied, "I know that's right, and I was thinkin' the same thing. Wherever he is or is headed to, he'll be careful doin' it."

"That's exactly right, Son. *Exactly* right!" Daddy exclaimed.

As days turned into weeks, Momma, Daddy, Bill and I comforted each other with a few things we took as articles of faith. We believed that no news from law enforcement meant that wherever he was, we was alive. We trusted Billy's judgment for managing his own life—even though he was only sixteen years old. He had long been grown up. With his work ethic, he could find a situation wherever he landed, and he would take good care of himself. Lastly, when he healed enough from the shock of his mother's disregard of him, he would somehow get in touch with us.

I may need to clue in the younger readers that all this was well before cell phones or internet or GPS. It wasn't always easy to get to a phone, and certainly tracking down someone was no easy task. And if that someone didn't want to be tracked down, it could be impossible. For all we knew he was in Mexico. We even speculated such was probably the case.

Six weeks to the day had passed since Billy left, when perfectly timed for Bill's normal arrival at the ranch, the phone rang. Momma answered.

"Hi, Grandma. It's Billy. Is Dad there?"

All we heard was Momma's answer, "Yes, Billy," as she handed Bill the phone.

"Oh, *Billy*, we're so glad to hear from you! How are you?"

"Dad, I'm fine, and I have a job. I'm not ready to say where or what I'm doing, but I had to let you, Grandma, Grandpa and Aunt Sallie know I'm alive and well.

"I'm sorry I took this long to do it. Mostly, I just couldn't get the words out. I'd get to the phone, and I just couldn't do it."

Bill interjected, "We're sorry all the way around. I just don't know what to do with your mother. She was wrong to say what she said to you and to tell you to leave. You can always come here to the ranch—you *know* that."

"I do know that, Dad. I just don't think I can be around there as long as Mom is tied to that church of hers. I am not going to be estranged from my own mother living under my grandparents' roof. That just ain't right for me or for them."

"I understand, Son."

"I'd better go, Dad.... I will be in touch later on.... Don't worry about me.... I'm safe and well."

"We love you, Billy."

"I love y'all."

With that Billy hung up, and Bill relayed their conversation for us, adding, "I think he had to hang up before he started cryin', which I was about to do. Anna, I saw you were doing the same."

Momma said, "Just the sound of his voice saying 'Hi, Grandma' was like music to my ears, but it broke my heart all over again."

"He sure isn't givin' anything away as to where he is or what he's doing. I understand it though. I'd probably do the same thing," Daddy added.

Then Bill noted, "All our articles of faith pertaining to the boy seem solid enough."

He let out a long, loud exhalation as though he could take a deep breath in and let it out again for the first time in weeks. "I'm going to start worryin' less and hopin' more."

The Schlatter house turned as cold and silent as a mausoleum. In so many respects, it was dead. The life and energy Billy had always brought to the home was gone, and his siblings didn't understand what was goin' on to any meanin'ful measure. Sis doubled down on dragging them to church any time the doors were open. They were thumped over the head with the narrow ideology of the preacher and now trumpeted through their own mother.

With Billy gone, Bill never once darkened that church door again. Goin' hadn't stopped the train wreck with Billy and his momma, and the only thing Bill could feel towards that preacher now was genuine hatred for the damage he'd done to his family.

Furthermore, in the back of Bill's mind was—in one way or another—losing all three of his children. Whatever confidence he had in Billy managing his own life, he lacked that confidence in the other two. He feared for them in a very different way. The only thing that kept him from too much worry on that front was that both Brett and Jean seemed to be goin' along to get along. Brett had already "made his profession," and Jean made hers soon after Billy was gone. It wasn't all that clear that they had taken the preacher's bait the way their mother had, but at least both preacher and mother were placated for the time being. Only time would tell if Bill ended up with one or two more zealots in the family or some other version of estrangement.

It was four months since Billy's phone call to the ranch before the next communication arrived. It was a letter addressed to Bill, but sent to the PO box belonging to the ranch. With Bill's daily trips to town, we got our mail a lot more frequently.

He came into the kitchen with the letter. "I'm a few minutes late gettin' here this morning. When I saw this letter from Billy, I tore it open the second I got in the truck. I want to read it to y'all. I've already read it four times—I hope I can get through it."

He glanced at us for a second, as though he awaited our approval. Deciding, I guess, that was a silly notion, he started the letter.

Dear Dad,

I'm not all that far from home. I'm working on a ranch up near Van Horn. I'm happy to report that it only took me about five minutes to hitch a ride that brought me this far. I guess it was fate. The driver was coming right to this ranch. In fact, he's the foreman. He, too, left home when he was sixteen, and I think that's what secured the job for me. It's quite an operation—huge in comparison to the Geermann-Schlatter ranch, but it has had nowhere near the stewardship that defines your work or the work of the Geermann generations, past and present. If I'm to make a difference here, I've got my work cut out for me. The foreman put me to work the next day, and I've been working like a son of a gun ever since.

They like me well enough. We have quite a few ranch hands, and we all live in little bunkhousettes for lack of a better term. That is to say, I have my own single bed, a bathroom with shower and a kitchenette. They do feed us breakfast and lunch, so the only meal I have to prepare is anything I want for supper or on Sundays. Otherwise, we work six days a week and take turns for whatever needs tending to on a Sunday. I spend my open Sundays riding in solitude so long as the wind isn't blowin' to beat me silly. I remember Grandpa saying, "I have to be in the cold on Monday. I don't have to be in the cold on Sunday." I want the solitude of bein' in the saddle more than bein' warm in my little room. It can't be too cold. I get out even if there's some snow on the ground. Of course, we're past snows now until next winter.

Bill stopped for a minute. "Doesn't that sound just like Billy?"
We just smiled, and he carried on with the letter.

Some of these ranch hands might curl even Ernesto's ears with their language. Grandma would be wondering what to do with them to keep to her peaceful ways.

Momma interjected, "I'm not opposed to washing mouths out with soap."

We all laughed, and Bill continued reading.

... She'll be glad to know I've not been corrupted by them! "Shit" is the only word I use, and she's heard all of us use that often enough!

Then we all really laughed through our tears.

I know you will respect this. As long as Mom doesn't ask where I am or even if you've heard from me, I don't want her to know where I am or what I'm doing. If I thought I could repair that bridge, I would try, but it would take some mighty powerful persuading from you, Dad, to convince me such is even a possibility. As long as she has me cast off to the Devil, I plan to stay here for the long haul.

I am glad to report my soul is alive and well and thriving in the Sierra Diablo. I don't get many days off, but I've never minded workin', and workin' a ranch as big as this takes some doin'—that's for sure! Anyway, I wouldn't ever suggest a Sunday, because I don't want Mom catching wind of anything we're up to, but if you can sneak off long enough to meet me in Van Horn once or twice a year, we can catch up on our lives.

You know how much I love Grandma, Grandpa and Aunt Sallie, but I don't think they should come to see me if you do.

Knowing the next lines to be read, Bill couldn't go on. He just sobbed until he could finally make an effort to get out the rest of the letter. He repeated the last line he'd read, before going on.

You know how much I love Grandma, Grandpa and Aunt Sallie, but I don't think they should come to see me if you do. I think that is more heartbreak than I want to risk for them, and I <u>know</u> it's more heartbreak than I could take.

I love y'all with all my heart and soul.

Your son,

Billy

Well, the next order of business was a good long cry. Those words echoed in our minds, "I <u>know</u> it's more heartbreak than I could take."

The first thing Daddy said was, "That boy—he can make you laugh one minute and cry the next. I don't know where he gets it from."

I did and said so, "He's you, Daddy, and he's you, Momma. The laughter and tenderness come from you both."

Bill stood and paced around the room, and he poured himself some coffee. He took a sip and stood lookin' out the kitchen window. "The boy has set the terms, and while I'm not crazy about them, I know he's right. Is it safe to say we will do as he requested and respect them?"

Daddy responded, "Now you're just askin' a question you already know the answer to. All this has taken a lot of wind out of our sails, but sail on we must. The young captain in Van Horn has set the course he believes he can live with."

Momma added, "Until he says otherwise or our daughter softens up, we have to respect his wishes. I don't like it either, but I can imagine how hard it would be on him to see us all."

I added, "I could hug him, but I couldn't ever let him go!"

It hit me, then. "Bill, you need to get that boy's horse to him."

Bill responded, "I hadn't even thought about that. You are right, of course. I'm going to drive Sal up there first chance I get."

Daddy assured him, "You can do it today if you've a mind to."

"Well, all right then. Let's go get Sal loaded up, and I'll be on my way."

I reflect now on our calling Billy "the boy." We certainly used the term for that affection we held for him, but we all knew it was the man who made the request of us. It was out of respect for the man the boy had become that we faced our now-fractured lives together.

Eager doesn't begin to describe our waitin' for Bill to return. He pulled into the ranch about three in the afternoon.

"I'd have liked to stayed up there longer, but I knew I needed to get back, so I'd be home by my normal time. Besides, droppin' in unannounced as I did, I didn't want to cause any problem for Billy. His boss seems a fine enough fellow, but I learned from Billy that further up the food chain, a couple are more temperamental."

I asked, "Further up the food chain from the foreman? What kinda pyramid do they have up there?"

"Oh, they have CFO and CEO and COO and I don't know how many other C-something-Os. Billy couldn't say if any of them actually did anything or not. We laughed and agreed that they probably didn't do much but no doubt get paid well for it.

"When I got to the ranch Billy was out workin' on some fence row. The ranch foreman sent another hand off to fetch him, and he helped me get Sal and all his gear into the stables.

"While we stabled Sal, he said, 'Billy told me he had a fine horse back home. I suspected the boy can't tell a lie, and I see such is the case as pertains to his horse. This is a fine animal.

'Your son is a helluva worker, by god, I'll say that. I haven't seen a youngster work as hard as he does. He outworks just about every other hand on the ranch.'

"Then he laughed saying, '*I'm* not going to try to outwork him!'

"That's the cleaned-up version. I have to say Billy's comment about the language in use was no exaggeration.

"When he saw me, Billy came runnin' and shoutin', 'Look what the cat drug in!'

"I couldn't have said anything if I'd wanted to, but I did hug the boy. Sallie, so you know, I did have to let go, though it wasn't easy. He was sure surprised to see I'd brought Sal, and he gave him a big hug, too.

"I ate with him in the mess hall, and we talked awhile after all the others had headed back to work. His good nature is alive and well, and that was a delight to confirm. I will say he has opportunity there, and if this drags on any length of time, he may find it hard to come back to our little spread."

Daddy reckoned, "What we lack in C-something-Os, we make up for with long hours and low pay."

I chuckled, "That's a good one, Daddy."

"Just knowing you saw him and held him, Bill, lifts all our spirits," Momma said.

She was right, of course. We knew where he was. We knew he had his horse now—his only real piece of home, except what he carried in his heart. Bill had confirmed, firsthand, his well-being. Indeed our spirits were lifted, and through the days and months ahead, although we were forever homesick for Billy, we carried on towards some hopeful notion that all would be well—even if it required a long, long, long period of patience and a lot of prayin'.

Sis's devotion to the Church of Self-Righteous Anger and Gossip never wavered. Billy's resolve to stay away never wavered either. So one year turned into two, and then three and then four— and on and on it went. Bill visited with Billy about three times a year. He would call the ranch on the day he planned to go, and if whoever answered thought it would work for Billy to meet for lunch, then Bill would head that way. Of course, Bill would have willingly gone with much greater frequency. Billy never asked him to, and so Bill never imposed his will on Billy's.

We all understood, without havin' to ever ask Billy, that as hard as the infrequent visits were for both father and son, gettin' over each one was a burden for Billy, as he relived in his mind that day when the family was torn apart as he was "cast out." Truth be told, each visit carried that same burden for Bill and the rest of us. When you know you're going to be estranged with no end in sight, miles and infrequent contact are the little bit of defense one has from the dark and lonely days of separation.

The go-along-get-along siblings did just that, and at the first opportunity, they flew the coop. Even before his graduation, I'd heard from Mando Cardona that it seemed to be common knowledge in town that Brett was regularly trippin' down to Alpine for back-seat sex with two or three different girls. I'm sure if Ernesto had told the story, it might have gotten exaggerated to two or three at once. So far as we know, none ever got pregnant from him. So far as we know!

Once graduated, Brett went to Midland to study real estate and finance. As soon as Jean graduated, she signed up for summer school at Sul Ross. Bill rented her an apartment close to the college so, as he told me, "She could escape further influence from the snake oil salesman." She went full time, year round until she got her accounting degree.

Both Brett and Jean found love of a kind.

Brett married wife number one, Josie, at the end of his freshman year and was soon a daddy. He never did graduate, but he got a good enough job to support his family with a real estate firm in Odessa. Baby number two came two years after baby number one.

I set my purpose to get down to Alpine every couple months to see Jean. I didn't want to see another Schlatter skip town. In the spring term of her second year, she brought a friend with her to lunch. I was introduced to Mary-Alice. We exchanged all the customary pleasantries one does upon meeting for the first time— where her family lived (Midland), what her parents did for a living (which I confess I can't recall any longer), how many siblings (I'm pretty sure it was three brothers and two sisters though I've never met most of them), and so forth.

Then Jean added, "Aunt Sallie, Mary-Alice is a little more than a friend from school. We are dating. I hope you're not too shocked."

I figured the best thing to say was what I truly felt. "Mary-Alice, she's a good one. You might not want to let her get away, but know this, her momma's church would rather castigate their own children to Hell than to entertain the notion they might be wrong and show some compassion. And I'm sorry to report that my sister is one of the hook-line-and-sinker zealots of the place—as I suspect you may well already know. We still can't figure out how it happened. Does your family know who you really are?"

"No, and while they are not as fundamentalist as Betsy, they are plenty judgmental when it comes to gays," Mary-Alice replied.

I shook my head in disappointment. Given they knew I wasn't going to judge them for their love, they made it quite clear they wanted me to expound a bit on my views, and it must be said, a thumbnail version of my life that might help them understand their own. So, they got the whole load which basically went something like this.

We sure make a lot of unnecessary heartache for people. Oh, I know, the first thing some would say to me is that it's those children who cause the parents' heartache. When it comes to inflicting unnecessary heartache, it can run both ways, that's for *damn* sure, but the first reaction is to blame any number of "corrupting influences."

All you have to do is look at any number of children and see one of two things. Parents tryin' like *hell* to mold their children to fit the perfect social image they think of as "their group." This is *exactly* what Sis tried to do with Billy. We know how that ended.

Then there are the oblivious parents that refuse to see their child doesn't fit the macho-male/feminine-female identities that have been perpetuated all my life and well before—I suppose going back to Adam and Eve, though the Bible has plenty of eunuchs that didn't seem to be abused the way a trans child does in our day. One eunuch gets baptized by Philip without any reservation. Isaiah even says when Jerusalem is rebuilt they should be right in the mix —full members of the society, along with immigrants. A few Christians need to ponder those inclusions a bit, it seems to me. Of course, those are some verses they don't really like, and so they are chucked aside, despite how much they like to drag Isaiah out for provin' Jesus was the Messiah. Ezra said, oh no, we've got to maintain purity. Of course, purity is always defined by those who think they've got it, and Ezra, not Isaiah, won in the end.

I never lacked the self-assurance of who I was. Had I lacked that self-assurance, it mostly likely would have instilled fear of what someone else thought of me. It was a great blessing in my life, bestowed upon me by a momma and daddy that always celebrated who I was. I never wanted to be a man, but plenty of kids in school and no few adults gave me the look and made the off-hand comment that, had I been sensitive to it, could have—and no doubt I believe, would have—escalated into full fledged bullying. Yes, even in little old Fort Davis.

I figured they would like to ask, but probably were hesitant to do so, so I told them that I wasn't willing to be labeled straight or gay. I was who I was and never wanted to marry. I had a solitary life and preferred it that way. However, that was *my* life, and I didn't think anyone needed to emulate it for some perceived virtue. As I reminded them, Saint Paul said there ain't nothing wrong with bein' passionate for another. Go for it.

I shared the time Bill joked that with my bib overalls on, my breasts are hidden sufficiently that all I needed was a good mustache, and I could pass as a man easy enough. When he showed up for work the next day, all my hair was tucked up inside my cowgirl hat, and I had taken some horse hair and taped it over my top lip.

I asked, "Well, what do you think?"

He laughed, saying, "I think the hair looked better on the horse."

"I guess I'll stay a woman then."

When I was finally done with my discourse, I asked them if they were serious enough to think about making a life together. Each looked at the other and then just nodded their heads in the affirmative.

"Well, your Aunt Sallie will do all she can to help you make your way in the world. Don't ever feel alone. Jean, I know your daddy will accept you for who you are. Your momma may never come around, but I hope she does. That shouldn't stop you from finding happiness. That's about her—not about you.

"I gotta be gettin' back to the ranch before your daddy and grandpa think I've abandoned 'em."

As Jean hugged me goodbye, she whispered, "Thank you, Aunt Sallie. I just had to tell someone and felt safe telling you."

Unlike Jean, who would seek my support and counsel on a regular basis, Brett never once came to me with anything. I'm not so arrogant as to think I have some great gift of wisdom, and therefore he should have bowed at my feet to receive my gift. All I've ever thought I possessed was the distillation of common sense, kindness and gratitude passed along to me from parents and grandparents who knew their place in the world, and did their utmost to be goodly stewards of it.

Had his momma not gone off the deep end, I suspect Brett's life might have been a little less convoluted. He was never very close to Bill, just like he was never interested in the ranch. Finding common interests was never easy for either one of them. Sis got so wound up with the church crowd, she focused more on "redeeming" souls in Fort Davis not already given over to the Devil, than on seeing she was ignoring her own children.

It wasn't too many years before the grass was greener, apparently, in El Paso as Brett went looking for a new job and a new wife. Josie stayed in Odessa, as all her family was there. They were well on their way to divorce and were "separated" for the first year Brett was in El Paso. Little Jaxon and Quinn rarely saw their dad once he was settled there.

By now, Jean was out of college and livin' in Marfa with Mary-Alice, where the two accountants set up their own shop with Bill's financial assistance. Like me, he accepted the girls, and he didn't want to see them slip out of his life.

Brett, he felt, had already slipped away. Brett made little to no effort to connect his children with their grandparents. It's hard to know if that had to do with not wanting them to get indoctrinated by his mother, or his lack of natural connection with his father. Who knows? I don't think to this day he could fully answer that himself.

As he would freely admit now, and what we all said as his marriages proceeded from one to the next, Brett was in his oblivion stage. Head up his ass, as he once confessed. Oblivious to just about everyone in his life—including his own children, and absolutely, his own wives.

With divorce number one finalized, Brett moved on to wife number two, Melinda. Then along came their son, Aiden. As we would learn after we got to know his children, Brett admitted that Melinda suffered the worst of his neglect which was pretty bad all the way around. Soon after Aiden was born, he started having an affair with Olivia, Noah's mother. That carried on awhile until divorce number two was finalized, and Brett then married Olivia.

Once married to her, he had his last child, our Noah, but he didn't have his last wife. Brett, being too oblivious to know for sure, doesn't know why the marriage ended, but Noah says his mother felt neglected. Noah, little tyke that he was, had the Geermann gift for astute observation. Olivia demanded a divorce, and Brett granted it without a fuss.

He married his last, Pamela, who had her own three children. I guess Brett finally made some progress in that at least he admitted, after it was too late to save the marriage, that Pamela was the first wife he could honestly say he actually loved. Having been divorced herself, she vowed she would not remarry after the divorce from Brett, and she has stuck to that. Still, she and Brett forged the best kind of friendship, and he is now as much a dad to her three kids as their own father.

I wasn't a very good great-aunt to any of Brett's children when they were small. Bill and Betsy didn't do much better as grandparents, though for them it wasn't for lack of trying. I confess I made *no* effort. With all their grandchildren in the custody of the three ex-wives, little to no accommodation was made for them to spend any real time together. We reckoned all three probably figured Brett's oblivion came to him honestly, and I'm sure all three were acutely aware of Sis's fundamentalism. She broadcast it enough—they had to be. That may have been another factor in the estrangement. The two ex-wives (still living) minimize any past feelings they may have harbored at the time, but whatever kept them away, the Schlatter family was a house divided.

Sis never talked about Billy. He was as much as dead to her. From Bill, we learned that she even believed that if she'd have gotten him out of the house sooner, it would have been better for the other two.

With Jean and Mary-Alice livin' and workin' together, she just pretended they didn't exist. As long as she could ignore them, maybe her so-called friends at church wouldn't gossip too much about them. She was, after all, the biggest giver in the church. That bought her all the goodwill she needed, even with wayward children, to stay in good graces with the preacher and his adoring fans.

We would laugh together about this later, when Sis said, "I judged those Catholics for a lot of reasons, including how they would make an offering to have a mass said for some dead relative —trying to buy some soul out of purgatory. Here I was, funding the preacher's comfortable lifestyle, so I could stay in good graces and get into Heaven. Is there any difference?"

I replied, "Well, that preacher certainly put y'all in purgatory. I'm just glad we got you prayed out of it!"

With Brett, Sis didn't proclaim him dead to her or ignore him for the sake of the gossip mill. He was far enough away, and few had any clue as to what he was doing, or how often he was cycling through wives. Well, that's what she believed or, more accurately, convinced herself to believe. One thing about gossips—no one is sacred. There was plenty of talk around town about Brett and his divorces. Some of it exaggerated even beyond what it already was —as gossips so often do. I often wondered how in the hell they even found out about his marital shenanigans. All I can say on that is, the gossips have tentacles that reach well beyond what one would think possible. Besides that, Bill always told Ernesto what Brett was up to, and I don't know for sure, but I suspect Daddy told ol' man Cardona as well. From there, I'd guess, it got exaggerated as the news passed around town as such juicy news always does.

Bill never held back on sharing news on Brett, nor did he impose any vow of silence on anyone he happened to tell. I think he rather liked the idea of it getting back to the church crowd and driving a wedge between Sis and those so-called friends of hers.

Sis really had no idea what some of the Fort Davis gossips were spreading about the Schlatters around town. For a time, the family had quite a reputation even though anyone with any sense would say on any day, "That Bill Schlatter is the salt of the earth."

We all got a good laugh from Jaime when he shared with us what Chuy and Lupe told him about Bill and Sis soon after Jaime arrived in Fort Davis. Lupe started her take, "That Schlatter woman —now she's interesting."

Betsy uses that line on herself now —"That Schlatter woman ..."

I have to chuckle too that Lupe told Jaime Sis spoke in tongues. I guess that was what the Catholics thought was going on over there at Sis's church. I told Jaime, the only tongues that group spoke in those days were their "waggin' tongues" of gossip and castigatin' everybody to Hell!

In addition to Bill's problems with the dogma of Sis's church, he always considered the bunch to be poor stewards. While oblivious to the poor in the community, the little bit of money that didn't go to support the preacher, his pension and insurance, pay the mortgage and "keep the lights on," went to his Bible College and "special offerings" to the Gideons. Sadly, there were years Sis was known as the main critic of the food pantry, which her group considered an "enabler." "We have no poor in this community," they would say. Bill's two biggest secrets from Sis during her days in that church were his ongoing contact with Billy and his generous gifts to the food pantry.

Bill said to me once, "They think their calling is to buy Bibles for the 'sinners' in some Las Vegas hotel, but by damn, they won't buy a few pounds of hamburger for a poor old widow living on *nothin'* who they'll drive right by every Sunday!"

All it took for me to give to the pantry when they opened it was a memory of when we were stayin' in town. I saw an old woman that I knew didn't have any cats buyin' white bread and cat food. I don't know if that is what she lived on or not, but I never forgot lookin' at the grocery cart. I know Sis justified herself, thinking there was enough family support for each to "take care of their own." That's flawed logic, of course. You can only divide a hamburger so many ways before everyone is goin' hungry.

I hadn't shared this with anyone before, but I soon began measuring the years in SBL time—since Billy left. In 16 SBL, the snake oil salesman skipped town. The faithful said he retired. He did of a kind, as Jaime would say. Eventually, we knew more of the truth. His wife left him. I never met her. Bill described her as a pitiful, mousy creature under her husband's thumb. Sis described her as a virtuous wife who supported her husband in doing the "Lord's work."

Apparently, Bill's version was closer to the truth, but even the mousy woman had had enough. They never had any children of their own, which of course made it all the easier for the preacher to be able to tell mothers what perfect looked like when raised with his "family values."

One Sunday, her seat in the front pew on the outside aisle was empty. No prayer was offered for her well-being. When the faithful asked about her after the service, the answer given was, "She's gone to visit family." Two weeks later, he packed up and left with just a note in the parsonage (that the church owned) informing them he was retiring. The real scoop was, she'd filed for divorce. Neither was ever heard from again.

The faithful soon enough hired a young man fresh out of that Bible college, who, while plenty closed-minded already for a youngster, at least was softer around the edges. Fewer souls were castigated to Hell by default.

The most encouraging aspect of this change in leadership was the first sign that the faithful zealot, Sis, started ever so slowly to soften around the edges as well. She still would never talk about Billy. She will admit now, that she was beginning to long for a relationship with her own children that had been eluding her. Her blame for this in the past lay only with the Devil's power, but now it was occurring to her that she was so rigid she had failed to examine her own life. The pride she had grabbed hold of wouldn't let go easily, and more out of concern for her standing in the flock she called her friends than anything else, did she hang onto her fundamentalist ways. This softening was not visible to me, Bill or Momma and Daddy at the time. It was only in Sis relivin' this period that she admitted doubts began to creep into her rigid beliefs.

That Church of Self-Righteous Anger and Gossip was big on "professing the day and hour" you were "saved." If you couldn't name it, you'd be going to Hell if you happened to die suddenly. That seems like the most perverse kind of theology to me, but I know it is alive and well. If someone asked me "the day and hour" of when I first loved Momma and Daddy, I'd tell them the minute I drew my first breath—and maybe before that. You can't convince

111

me an innocent child, loved by their momma and daddy, isn't born into that love in a mutual exchange. Yet somehow, according to them, the great Creator of all that is, requires us to figure out on our own that we are inherently loved and therefore duty-bound (through free will, of course) to pinpoint exactly when we accepted that love.

Now, I'm not sayin' people don't have major epiphanies. Paul had his, and Jaime was "saved" the day Chuy and Lupe took him in. I don't know anything about Paul's momma and daddy, and so I can't speak to whether he knew he was loved or not. Jaime, I can say certainly, knew he was not, and thus needed a "conversion."

Suffice it to say, I never needed one. I am loved, have always been loved, and will always be loved. If that's not "saved," I don't know what is.

I just wanted to get that said before I get more into what came next with Momma and Daddy.

Now I can't tell you the day and hour when the momma I loved from that first breath knew she was going to die. And like unto it, I don't know when that realization aligned with my daddy. She certainly carried on as though all was well until she couldn't hide it anymore. She'd have an occasional nosebleed, and I could see she was losing weight—though she was always lean like me, so it wasn't all that easy to detect.

One Monday afternoon when Sis happened to be out at the ranch, Daddy pulled Sis, Bill and me aside for a talk out by the barn. "Anna says her time is runnin' out. I think she's right about that. We have to honor what she wants, which is to die in peace and at home. There'll be no long hospital stay up in Midland plugged into God knows what. I'd want the same thing, in case you don't already know that."

There wasn't anything to be said. He had confirmed what the three of us already knew, but had never talked about—she was dying.

We all went back in the house and Daddy declared, "Anna, the news has been delivered, and no one is callin' the sheriff on me for spousal abuse. Your wishes will be respected."

Crazy Daddy. Only he could put it that way. Momma smiled, and we huddled up for a good family hug.

We were still adjusting to that heavy news of Momma when a month in, it hit us hard. This time it was Daddy's death. He was getting up in years, but he still liked to help Bill and me at least a couple days a week. There was no reason he shouldn't have. Daddy was still strong as an ox, and he didn't have a single ailment I ever knew about. In fact, I'd begun to think he was going to need another horse, after all, as Starshine was gettin' up there. Not as old as Nellie would be one day, but gettin' close. It didn't look to me like Daddy had any plans to give up ridin' as long as he could get up in the saddle.

The three of us set out on a Monday morning to check the fence line on the far south ridge of the Geermann side of the ranch. We'd split up to check different parts. Bill and I could see each other in the distance as we rode along and got off long enough to do some little fix here and there as needed. Daddy was over a rise where we couldn't see him.

When I saw his horse come over the rise towards me, I knew right away Daddy was in trouble. I gave the loudest whistle I could muster to catch Bill's attention. I took off over the ridge with Bill in a full run behind me. There was no sign of Daddy, but his horse— who'd trotted back behind us—soon stopped and didn't move. We went over to where she was.

Daddy was just over a little drop-off with his head split open on a rock. He'd bled out quickly, we could see that. All we could ever figure was a mountain lion must have spooked his horse. Bill wrapped his shirt around Daddy's busted skull, and we got him laid up over his saddle. Momma, seeing us from the kitchen window, came walkin' out with her cane. She was already gettin' pretty weak. We told her the little we knew.

She mustered the strength to say, "Let's get him in the house so we can clean him up. As soon as we get him laid out, Bill, you call Betsy. Sallie, you call the funeral home in Alpine and see when they can get out here.

"I suppose the sheriff needs to be informed to be sure there was no foul play. Bill, if you could call him, I'd appreciate it."

Sis was there in no time. I don't think she ever drove through the mountains that fast in her life. Bill called the sheriff before I called the funeral home. He was there in short order and determined none of us were murder suspects.

Bill then called Jean and Brett while we were waiting on the undertaker. Sis called the minister at the Church of Christ where Momma and Daddy were members and arranged for the service the next day. Then Bill called Rogelio to come dig the hole with his backhoe. The undertaker got there about two hours after I had called him.

Momma made it clear what she wanted and what she didn't. "John wanted a pine box if you have one, and whatever is cheapest after that if you don't. He doesn't want to be embalmed. Other than the immediate family, he doesn't want to be on display. We're to bury him up on the south ridge, which oddly enough, is where he died.

"He didn't care about a church service—just a few words graveside—unless we felt otherwise. Betsy would really like to have a service at the church. You'll need to get the body to the Church of Christ in Fort Davis by ten tomorrow morning. He wants to be taken to the ridge in the ranch pickup, so we'll tend to everything once you've brought him to the church including digging the grave and covering it up.

"Girls, you're going to have to deal with getting a headstone for us. Just one, with both our names. Of course, your Daddy wants John Geermann on his, not Johannes Konrad. After I've joined him, I want you girls to plant two desert willows—one on each side of our headstone."

Momma was amazing. She and Daddy had worked out what to do, and she took charge doin' it. The desert willow was Momma's favorite tree. Sis, Bill and I love them too. We were sure to honor her request and have planted a couple at all the new houses on the ranch since then.

None of us had shed a tear at this point or gotten hysterical in any way. Hysteria doesn't come naturally to us, so that didn't surprise me, but I was a little surprised Momma and I weren't in tears. I guess that was just the shock of it, layered with what we knew needed to be done in that moment.

After the undertaker had left with Daddy's body, Sis and Momma stayed in the house, and Bill and I went outside and were gonna sit on the patio. Just as we started to sit, he looked over towards the barn. "Sallie, let's go talk out by the barn."

I didn't have to wonder why he wanted to talk there and not on the patio where we could be overheard easily. He wanted to talk about Billy. Sis still had no idea that any of us knew where he was. Billy loved his granddad. Now, what do we do? Whatever it was, we needed to decide quickly. The service was less than 24 hours away.

"He may not even be able to get away that quick," Bill reckoned. "I know he makes sale runs into El Paso sometimes. He could be on the road. With Betsy in the house, I can't even call up there without gettin' into our 17-year vow of silence on Billy's whereabouts. *Shit, damn and half a dozen other words!*"

I offered what I believed would be a comfort to him. "Bill, you need to call him, but you also need to be sure he understands he should only come if it's something he feels he *has* to do. Momma and Daddy told me on more than one occasion that their dying didn't mean Billy had to come back if he wasn't ready. Daddy even said, 'Billy knows my heart as well as anyone. Anna and I don't need him standing over our graves to know he loves us. When he comes home, it needs to be because he's comin' home for *good!*'"

"Good lord," Bill sighed. "God bless their souls!"

I added, "I'll persuade Sis that she and I need to run into town to make sure everything is shipshape at the church. Besides, she needs to call whoever she thinks needs to be at this church service of hers. You can call Billy then."

I did exactly that, and Bill left a message for Billy who was able to call him back before Sis and I got back to the ranch. I knew Momma would know what had transpired, so I just waited until Bill and Betsy went back into town for the evening to find out if Bill had been able to talk to Billy.

Momma filled me in and explained that when Bill relayed what Daddy had said about not comin' home until he was comin' home for good, Billy was quiet for a couple minutes. Bill knew he was cryin'. He was the first one of us to cry—no doubt, in part for the years of grief he was carrying already from being separated from his granddad. Finally he spoke, "Dad, you know I can't come home to stay.... Tomorrow, I'll go out on my favorite ridge on the Sierra Diablo ... and I'll honor him that way.... Give Grandma and Aunt Sallie my love."

And so the next day we buried John Geermann on that far ridge just as he'd prescribed, as Billy sat silently on Sal, with the morning sun shining brightly down upon them as they faced the Geermann ranch miles across the horizon, Billy alone in his grief—up there on his favorite ridge on the Sierra Diablo.

It would certainly be wrong to say that Momma gave up her will to live, but it was pretty clear she'd be content to go at any time. We knew well enough to duplicate for her what Daddy had requested for himself. Momma went downhill *real* fast. With the ever-more frequent nosebleeds, Sis and I suspected she had leukemia.

Men and women of a certain age were getting cancer more out in our part of the country, and Bill was persuaded it had to do with radiation drifting in this part of the world from the nuclear "testing" in New Mexico years before. As he pointed out, even if the government knew such was the case for those as far as we were from the testing sites, they'd never acknowledge it. I suspected he was right, and if the real fallout was assessed, they'd be paying compensation to half the country.

Vera was a big help during Momma's illness. She could attend to all the daily house and greenhouse chores, and I could attend to Momma with help from Sis. The last two weeks of her life, Momma could barely walk, and she stayed in bed most of the time. She liked to have Sis and me read poetry and the Psalms to her. With her eyes closed, I was never too sure what she heard and what she slept through, but I read on.

We couldn't imagine it going on much longer. While Momma still had her voice, she had a talk with Sis alone before Sis headed back to town one evening. Sis told me after Billy was home that Momma had scolded her that evening. "Daughter, you need to quit worrying about me and heal your family.... You have three children who don't even know the daughter your daddy and I raised.... They know some aberration.... They need to know you." She drifted off to sleep, and Sis came out of her room in tears, and left without sayin' a word.

Two evenings later, I was sitting with Momma when she seemed to awaken—eyes opened the least little bit for a second or two. I asked her if she wanted a few sips of water. She just barely moved her head that she didn't. It had been a couple days since she'd eaten anything. I held her weak, thin hand with one hand and petted it with the other.

"Momma, you and Daddy were the best parents any child could ever hope or pray for. I promise Momma, we'll get Billy home. We'll get *all* your grandchildren back home."

She opened her eyes just for a couple seconds and closed them again as she breathed her last. I sat with her for several minutes before leaving the room to tell Vera, and then called Sis and the funeral home.

We all knew the drill. Everything we'd done for Daddy, we now did for Momma. The next day we buried Anna Catherine Geermann on the far ridge next to her faithful, loving husband, while up on a ridge on the Sierra Diablo there was a young man on his horse grieving alone for a second time.

We all felt the lingering grief of Daddy and Momma's deaths, though it must be said Bill and I also felt the burden of being down one good hand. Daddy was a worker, and even though he'd sometime before passed on the overseeing to us, it didn't end his workin' days. We found ourselves more worn out than usual, and we were back lookin' for help more than we'd a liked. The spoken hope and constant prayers between us were for Billy to come home for good.

Starshine never recovered from the grief of Daddy's death. I contend she carried a load of guilt for havin' thrown Daddy. She pretty much quit eatin' and was dead within the month. We buried her up on the ridge not far from Daddy.

Jaime shared with me once the account of Daddy and Momma's death as told to him by Lupe—in which I said her tellin' was close, but not quite right as the news went around town. She'd told him Daddy's horse stumbled. Maybe she did, but Bill and I had to think a mountain lion spooking Starshine was a far more likely cause. It wouldn't have been like Daddy to be caught off guard by a simple stumble.

She was right in tellin' him Momma died two weeks later and "his horse" within the month, but what they didn't know was that we had expected Momma to die before Daddy.

Husband, wife and faithful horse entered their eternal rest, while those left behind felt like all our wind had been knocked out of us.

It wasn't too long after Daddy and Momma's death that Ernesto called the ranch wantin' to talk to Bill. Ol' man Cardona had hit some black ice on the road between Fort Davis and Alpine and was killed when his pickup rolled.

As long as I could remember, all I ever heard him called was ol' man Cardona even though he did a fair amount of work out at the ranch. That was all Daddy ever called him. Of course, the

Cardonas knew Daddy as ol' man Geermann. It wasn't until we all went to Mrs. Ol' Man Cardona's funeral a couple years earlier that I learned his name was Daniél. At his funeral I'd learn the full version, Daniél Rudolfo Antonio Cardona.

I don't think it took any persuasion, but Ernesto's *mamá* wanted him to sing at her funeral. Gettin' Ernesto to use that God-given talent never took any persuasion. He'd burst into song at the drop of a hat and was heard often enough singin' to himself in the grocery store. He'd stop to say hello to someone and pick up a bit further along in the song, as he was clearly still playin' it in his head while he talked.

He also sang at his *papá's* graveside. I don't think Catholics sing "Great Is Thy Faithfulness" in their churches, but that was his *mamá* and *papá's* favorite hymn, and so that's what he sang. There wasn't a dry eye to be seen including on this ol' tough cowgirl. Ernesto is such a character that when he uses that gift of his to comfort others, it just pulls the emotion right out of you.

I said to Bill afterward, I don't know why we didn't think to invite the Cardonas out to Daddy and Momma's burial—they were all at the church service—and Ernesto could have sung Momma's favorite, "Abide with Me."

He agreed, it did seem like an oversight on our part all the way around. It would have meant a lot for them to be included, and Ernesto would have been more than happy to honor them with his singin'. I guess we weren't thinkin' too clearly when Daddy died, and we didn't think to change anything for Momma's death.

It would be some time before the healing of the Schlatter family would finally begin in earnest. Gradualism had slowly consumed Sis's mind and hardened her heart against real love for her own children. The faithful husband grieved but never abandoned the woman who he knew dwelt beyond the hard shell. The delightful Geermann daughter he knew when he first arrived at the ranch was still in there *somewhere*. While we all, including Sis, credited Mr. Benson's book for knocking away that hard shell, as Sis and I went over this chapter of her life, she said Momma's deathbed scoldin' shook her up pretty badly. I guess we have to give Momma credit for strikin' the first blow that finally put a small fracture in the years-hardened heart. She had spent more than twenty years knowing inside and out and proclaiming loudly all she was against, and she had lost any perspective as to the one thing she should have been *for*—her own family.

One evening when Bill returned home from the ranch, Sis was deep in Mr. Benson's book. She hadn't started on any supper, and he could see she had been crying. He just left her be, made himself a peanut butter sandwich and sat quietly in the kitchen until she was ready to appear or until bedtime—whichever came first. Sis later helped fill in all the blanks for this tellin'.

An appearance came before bedtime. "Bill, I've been a fool, and I've ignored you, Momma, Daddy and Sis to my peril—and even worse to my children's peril. Please forgive me. We have *got* to find Billy and bring all our children home. *I've* driven them away; I just pray they will forgive me."

It was time for Bill's own confession. "About that, Mother, I happen to know that Billy will forgive you. I know where he is, and he has made it clear he would embrace you as soon as you were willing to embrace him as he is."

She said it again, *"Lord,* what a fool I've been! How could I measure my salvation by such faulty scales? I want to go see him.

"It's also time to build your dream house out on the ranch. I want some miles between me and the people I've defined as my friends all these years. Maybe my leaving their company will open a few other eyes to how *stupid* we've been.

"You need to get with Ernesto and get a house started. The sooner the better. I plan to let them know I'm parting company in short order."

Getting with Ernesto happened even sooner than Bill had planned. The next day he ran into Ernesto at the tractor dealer in Alpine where he met a young man the Cardonas had taken under their wing. That was when Jaime first came into our lives. By the time they left, Bill had negotiated the purchase of two tractors—one for the ranch and the other for Ernesto. They went straight to the ranch where Bill showed them where he wanted to set the house. Ernesto assured Bill that together they could come up with enough of a plan, and he didn't think they needed to hire an architect.

Jaime, who had never built a thing in his life or designed anything, stood on that ridge and imagined the possibility for a home and chapel as Bill described room by room what they had in mind. He stayed up the entire night drawing, and the rest, as they say, is history. Here I sit in that beautiful home that sits on this ridge like it has always been here and should always be. It is wholly beautiful in every loving detail, for it must be said, the crazy, badass Ernesto only builds one way, and that is the way of true craftsmanship and care. Love and a little beer go into every adobe and every rock laid.

It had been twenty years since his mother and I had seen Billy. I still pictured the boy as I knew him when he left. I didn't want to impose myself on their first meeting after so many years, but when Sis insisted I come along, there was no way I was going to turn down the invitation. Bill had arranged for Billy to meet us at the Mexican restaurant in Van Horn. I drove separate from them, as they were going on to El Paso to shop for cabinets.

I admit I was shocked, but I thought Sis was going to faint when Billy walked in. There was the reincarnation of John Geermann! In true Billy fashion, he didn't shake our hands or hug us individually. The first thing he said was, "All right—gather it up here. We need a big group hug!"

He could sure heal a heart in an instant! Sis broke into tears. Billy said, "Dad, I'm sure glad the body snatcher finally let loose of Momma! Aunt Sallie, I can't *believe* you couldn't wrestle her free sooner! Momma, I love you, let's just *get on* with life!"

We did wonder if he'd leave his job after being there for as long as he was and bein' a foreman for the last ten years. When Bill said he didn't suppose Billy would be able to come back and work for pinto beans on a two-bit ranch, Billy had one thing to say. "When the house is done, I'll be there!" I suggested he could've lived in the bunkhouse in the meantime, but he thought he owed it to the ranch who took him in at sixteen to give them more than ample notice. As he put it, "The time will fly, now that I know it has an end."

With the shake of a hand, Bill and Ernesto had the house deal sealed. Ernesto wanted Jaime to quit the tomato farm and work for him full time, which Jaime did. That crew wasted no time. While everyone benefited from Ernesto's talents and dedication to every job he took on, Bill, out of their long and odd friendship got a whole additional layer of effort. That crew of Ernesto's worked like no crew I'd ever seen. Sis had kidded them about being in by Christmas knowing there was no way, but Ernesto and Jaime had the fireplace built and a small fire burning for the Christmas luncheon in the partially built, but weather-tight home—complete even with a Christmas tree lit up. It was that first luncheon when Billy came to check on the progress.

Ernesto was as shocked as we had been—there was John Geermann standing in front of him, though as we all learned later, Ernesto pointed out to Jaime that Daddy didn't have the same hind end!

I didn't get to know Jaime that well while the house was being built. From time to time, I'd ride over to check on the progress and just quietly observe. You couldn't have derailed their work if you tried, but I had no desire to come between them and progress for gettin' Billy home. If Ernesto happened to be in one of his jovial moods while I was there, that was all to the good.

One time, I'd been sittin' there on Nellie for a good five minutes and hadn't said a word. Ernesto hollered over at me, "Hey, Sallie Faye! Come on over here, and I'll sing you a love song!"

I hollered back, "I'm not sure you could control yourself, and I can't be gettin' sideways with Rosalinda!"

"You can be sure I'll let her know tonight I rejected your unsolicited advances!" Crazy guy—he just laughed and launched into a love song anyway. I saw Jaime shake his head and smile.

They had the house ready by Easter, and Billy was home to stay. He and I rode to "Geermann Cemetery Ridge." I touched the top of the headstone shared by Momma and Daddy, and said, "Delivered home as promised, Momma. The boy is home to stay."

Billy added, "You two sure left a big hole. Aunt Sallie's got a lot of fillin' to do, but she's doing her best to fill it."

Then he asked, "I guess we'd better hug for their benefit, don't you think?"

He didn't have to ask me twice.

When the crew started workin' on the bunkhouse renovation, I told Bill I hadn't realized it had become quite so rough. Since Vera tended to the men that stayed there, I hadn't been in it for years. He confirmed in his mind, it was a ramshackle and long overdue for some care. We didn't seem to have a good answer as to why we'd ignored it for so long.

I'll say now it was to give fate its chance to do its work. Billy made regular stops there just about every day to check in. That was mostly because, as a boy, Ernesto had amused him, and he wanted to get to know him. In the course of getting to know Ernesto, he also saw, for the first time in his life, he might forge a friendship with someone his own age. Those first sixteen years of his life were spent with us on the ranch. He never got to know kids in town. Even the ones from school never really led to any kind of real friendship. His twenty years in Van Horn were *lonely* years for him. He was liked there well enough, but there wasn't anyone that he ever was close to in any way.

He did have some interestin' tales about visitors to the ranch—male and female—wanting him as their "cowboy conquest," but he never gave them the satisfaction.

Bill and Betsy already thought the world of Jaime and certainly encouraged Billy to get to know him. What came of that was what we all know as the best kind of friendship there is. Those two, from such polar opposite backgrounds, both of whom knew all too much of loneliness and estrangement, were never going to be lonely and estranged again. For Billy it was a renewal of the love he'd known as a boy. For Jaime—starting with the Cardonas—it was knowing love for the first time in his life.

124

I decided early on that Bill had his Ernesto and Jaime had his Billy. Bill and Jaime had their quiet natures in common. Both were good sports and easily amused by their crazy counterweights.

When I saw Billy and Jaime's friendship flourish, I found myself wondering for the first time *ever*, what my life might have been like if I'd made a life with someone like they had. I was never lonely, and they both had been lonely for *years*, so I don't think it's a fair comparison to align their lives along with my own. I'm not expressing any regret here. I'm just notin' how wonderful I thought it was that the two lived—are living—a life together, better than almost every marriage I've ever seen—certainly one that puts many a "family values" preacher or politician to shame.

Years ago, I read that Clarence Darrow had once said, "The first half of our lives are ruined by our parents and the second half by our children."

I knew as a child I was lucky to have the parents I had, but in my "formative years," it never occurred to me that I was *that* lucky. I didn't know of anyone that lived with a father that beat them or a mother that thought only of herself. I was observant enough to see there were a few I was glad I didn't belong to, but if they were truly bad parents, it was hidden from plain view.

Of course, that was me seeing the world around me through the eyes of innocence, with which, I believe, every child is born. Momma and Daddy both believed in original innocence and that the sin part comes willfully upon us when innocence isn't "exciting" enough. Having said that, I do believe that some children are born into hate, and the impact of that on innocence is profound. Too many never recover.

I would learn later that child abuse (and spousal abuse) did take place in the county, and the children of those homes, all too often, passed the abuse on to the next generation—generational sin, as Daddy called it.

When I began to learn Jaime's story, it hit me like a ton of bricks how true the first part of Darrow's depressing declaration was in Jaime's life. His divorced parents' toxicity (as he put it) towards each other was never ending. As the three children were bounced back and forth between the two, Jaime and his siblings never knew a minute of tenderness, kindness or love.

For Jaime, like so many, he carried that burden into his adult life. The one saving grace in his mind was that he had never married and inflicted his miserable life onto a wife or wives or children.

It is so hard to reconcile the Jaime we know now with the Jaime that first arrived in Fort Davis all those years ago—when the broke, desperate, depressed young man picked a dot on the map from a movie he'd seen to get as far away as possible from the life he'd known. The only thing important to him then was to leave that failed life behind in California. He didn't care about achieving some kind of material success. *All* he cared about was a fresh start, however humble, in a new place as different from the life he'd had as he could imagine.

His second day in town brought him his first great blessing — when on his first day as a laborer at the large hothouse tomato farm outside Fort Davis, his fellow worker, Chuy Cardona, offered Jaime use of a little ramshackle abode he and Lupe had next to their home. He could pay a little rent to stay there as long as he wished, and he could pay that little bit of rent when he got paid — no up-front payment required. That was lucky for Jaime who barely had enough gas money to get to Texas and was literally livin' on peanut butter sandwiches.

If there were two people in Fort Davis more suited to help Jaime heal than Chuy and Lupe, I can't imagine who they could have been. While never having children of their own, they didn't impose upon him their notion of who Jaime should be. He was quiet and withdrawn — understandably — in those early days. Chuy and Lupe gave him all the space to find himself and all the support to get from one day to the next.

As I learned of their journey together, my feelings for them as part of the Cardona *familia* moved from simple respect to the deepest admiration. I have to give credit to Ernesto's crazy side as well, which allowed Jaime to see how much fun and affection is possible within a family — somethin' he had never known existed except on TV or in the movies; an affection, he truly thought of as "make believe." As I had assumed all parents were basically kind and loving, with mine being exceptional, Jaime had assumed all were cruel and selfish as his had been, though he had a pretty good notion that his were worse than most.

I had seen Jaime on a couple of occasions at the grocery store, but other than a friendly nod and smile, we'd never spoken. I didn't know his name or anything about him. Three-plus years later when I would finally meet him — during the house build — I met a hard-working young man, roughly the same age as Billy, already healed and takin' each day as it came. He was a delight.

You could see his reverence for all the Cardonas—who had taken him in as their own, though as Rosalinda said to her husband, for reasons she did not understand herself, Jaime was on loan to Ernesto. His destiny would take him from his transitional life to something else. Chuy, Lupe, Ernesto and Rosalinda all shared this inexplicable understanding—one which Jaime wouldn't even have believed, if they ever had said as much to him. He was not on hold waitin' for some other new life to come along. He truly was takin' each day as it came, and that was enough.

It was the bunkhouse renovation that would finally reveal that new life to come. On his first "sleepover," which Ernesto never could stop teasin' Jaime about, the evening of making music and having dinner with Sis, Bill and Billy turned into a late evening chat. It was the late hour that precluded Billy from driving Jaime back into town as they had planned. Bill would have nothing of it. His discomfort with driving in the mountains late at night trumped their earlier plan.

One weekend turned into another and another, until Ernesto's laborer-on-loan found himself an apprentice ranch hand, and soon enough, a gen-u-ine cowboy. For purely practical reasons, with Billy now "foreman" of the Geermann-Schlatter ranch, I moved out of the house I'd lived in all my life. Vera took her well-earned retirement, and the boys moved in. Of course, I didn't move far; just the few miles across the cattle guards that defined the two halves of the ranch and into "Billy's quarters" in the new house.

I first pitched the idea of swappin' with Jaime, as I wanted to be sure he'd be okay with it before I got Billy all excited. There's no turnin' the boy back once he latches onto a plan he likes. I knew he'd jump at the chance. I remember being tickled about Jaime's concern about checkin with Billy first. I told him, "Whither you goest, he shall go." We both later decided it's better to acknowledge the way things really are—"Whither Billy goeth, we *all* shall go."

It's no secret I like quiet, and crowds are not my thing. I wouldn't even attend Christmas Eve services with the Schlatters at the Methodist Church after a while, as it seemed every Christian and heathen alike turned out to pack the place. Church never offered much for my soul, anyway. I feel "in communion" with the world just by being on the ranch. I've never been stingy about wanting to help someone in need, which it seems to me, is one of the chief directives of the Gospel. I guess just admittin' I help the needy means I've had "my reward" for puttin' it in writin' here. Well, that's okay. I have my reward every day I awaken to life on this ranch, as I hear the birds sing their morning invocation.

When Ernesto, Jaime and the rest of the crew finished Sis's little chapel, it became a daily space for her contemplation. It would be an understatement to say she loved the place. The beautiful rock wall that Ernesto and Jaime laid, and the beautiful iron gate that Bill and Billy fashioned enclosed a lovely and almost wild-looking rose garden. As you sit in the chapel, you can look over the wall to the mountains that seem close enough to touch. It is easy to find a rock, tree or yucca to fixate on and let loose of all the clutter that accumulates in one's mind. The space, and what it invokes, is wholly beautiful.

Sis felt it should be shared, and Jean and Mary-Alice had a notion as to how she could do that. The first Advent the house was finished, Jean and Mary-Alice invited their small church group in Marfa out for an Advent Quiet Day. Betsy put together a simple program where they would gather in silence as people arrived early on the first Saturday of December. Billy had fashioned a bell by cutting down an acetylene tank, and the bell was rung slowly three times, then three times more, and three times more.

Inside the chapel, there were short readings, simple chants and a closing prayer. It all took about fifteen minutes. People could stay and spend more time in contemplation, wander the grounds, or come into the house. A simple breakfast was served a bit later.

129

Then the bell would ring at ten, then noon, and again at two for the three other brief services in the chapel. After the noon service, another simple meal was offered. After the 2:00 service, all departed.

It was a Quiet Day, but not a silent day. No one was chastised or driven out for a little quiet conversation. Betsy made lanyards one could wear if they truly wanted complete silence. It was an easy way to see that the person wanted to spend the day devoid of any conversation. Except for the services, the chapel was a place of silence.

The first one was so well received, that it was tried again in January—and every month thereafter. Over the years, the numbers fluctuated as people got busy, moved, died or just lost interest. A few from Sis's old fundamentalist crowd even began attending when they, too, realized how rigid and burdensome they had unnecessarily made their lives.

All on the ranch attended. It certainly was more my cup of tea, and I always—well, almost always—wore the keep-silent lanyard with its line-drawing profile of a head holding up a single finger in front of the mouth to proclaim a silent, "Shhhh."

Early on, Jaime spent one Quiet Day pondering what he might say to his estranged siblings and parents. He had come to the point where he felt healed enough from the wounds his childhood had inflicted on him, to try to reach out for the first time since leaving California—and longer really, as he'd not had any contact for some time even while living nearby.

The letter he wrote that day was not a chastisement against any of them, nor did it contain any kind of pity-poor-me blame game. Billy read it. I never had. Jaime said, in the end, what it really ended up being was a love poem for lack of a better descriptor.

A couple years ago, he happened to mention the letter with some thought in his mind that I had read it at the time. When I said I hadn't, he printed me a copy of it. It is a love poem as much as anything.

Dear Cruz Family,

In 2000, I left behind my life of failures for what I hoped might be the start of a new life in a new place. While at the time, my choice of places made no logical sense, I envisioned it as radically different from what I had known as I could possibly conceive, and so it was that I ended up in the remote, west Texas desert mountains. From my first days, I experienced the only sense of hope I'd ever known. I felt the weight of all my failures begin to fall away—burdens I had carried even more than I realized. Many a deserving weight for the life I had lived, and many, needless burdens I didn't even realize that I was carrying, until they, too, were shed.

I hadn't recognized just how fragile I was, until I had nothing left but failure as my companion. I had lived my life as a singular leaf clinging to a rigid branch in a heavy storm.

We are the fragile leaves of the tree,
whose destiny is soaking up the sunlight.
But we are not the sunlight
or the branch or the trunk or the root.

Love is the root of the healthy tree;
compassion its trunk;
and cultural celebration the branches,
    reaching out,
in small twigs in all our diversity,
swaying with the winds of time.
    We, the leaves, come and go
in a season, to be replaced with
new life in the next season of growth.

No, we are not the root, the trunk
or the branches, yet it is only from these
    we know life.
I live my life now in the sunlight
    on a tree rooted in love
where I am in holistic union
with those who are now my family.

I had to awaken to reality—
I had made an idealized, artificial construct
where pride was my root, material success my trunk
and steel rods of iron-will the un-swaying branches
to which I had clung so desperately—even though,
I was not being fed, and instinctively knew
    I would soon wither and die.
When I finally fell to the ground
    to give myself over to the new soil
in which I had landed on this desert floor,
I was brought back to life through the roots,
up through the trunk and out onto the branches
    to spring forth as a new creation—
a green leaf, bright and shimmering in the morning dew and sunshine.
    I have found my new life, and my hope is that you, too, have found
yours.

Estrangement was our norm.
So much has separated us all these years.
Yet, the chasm isn't as wide
    as you might think.
My hand is here,
    reaching out,
if you ever want to reach across.

Peace to you,

Jaime

He sent the four letters off to the last known address he had for each. None came back as undeliverable, so he had to assume they had successfully made it to their intended. He figured it was a long shot that any would write back to him, and even wondered if they would bother to read the letter with any open mind as to what kind of life the son and brother had made in his new Texas home. He would welcome a letter from them, but he set no expectation in his mind that such would ever be the case. They were every bit, and in his parents' case, even more damaged than he was. While Jaime never blamed anyone else for his failures, his parents lived a life of blaming anyone and everyone for their unhappy lives—with the most hateful vitriol directed at each other. Jaime always wondered if there had ever been any love between them before the divorce. He couldn't recall a single tender moment, and was mystified as to what led them to marry at all—a question that has never been answered to this day.

It was a year from the mailing of the love poems that he finally received a response. His sister, Zoey, wrote a brief but tender letter in which she apologized for the long delay. She had read Jaime's letter and didn't know what to make of it. At first she wasn't even persuaded he had written it. She thought perhaps he'd copied it from something, but the more times she read it, she realized it was her brother in those words, and she credited them for beginning her own healing—a healing that coincided with her love for a man named Mark Mendoza, who aided her as well in the healing journey.

That note was followed by a long letter that laid out the past years of her life since seeing Jaime. Jaime let me read it, and all I could do was be amazed at what she'd been through, and how she came out the other side in no small part because of Jaime's letter.

She had been in an abusive marriage with a wealthy and wildly popular executive. She put up with him for far too long. For her own sanity, and knowing his influence with even their so-called marriage counselor and the flotilla of lawyers at his beck and call, she walked away from the marriage with nothing. Her delay in writing back to Jaime any sooner was the result of a recent cancer diagnosis. She didn't want to burden Jaime with that news until the prognosis was better known.

With the two siblings reconnected—more accurately, connected for the first time in any meaningful way—Zoey and Mark made their first trip to Texas, a Christmas trip, arriving in Alpine on the Sunset Limited. Then they made a second trip one summer and planned a third and longer trip for the following summer. By trips two and three, Noah was living on the ranch. While Noah and Jaime went off to Alpine to pick them up at the train depot for the extended stay, the "foreman" got the bright idea of extending a job offer to Zoey if they would move to the ranch. We all already knew they loved the place, but would they leave California to live here?

Billy's impromptu plan and sales pitch to Bill, Sis and me was that we needed to have an urbanite perspective to market our planned sale of grass-fed and grass-finished beef.

I have to chuckle that Billy thought they needed to hear from the "headman himself," so it was instead left to Bill with Sis and my endorsement of Billy's instant plan. They were certainly shocked, as were Jaime and Noah, but Mark and Zoey recognized what an extraordinary offer it was. Jaime wasn't about to derail an instant Geermann-inspired plan with no apparent flaws. So it came to be that Ernesto and crew were back on the ranch building another adobe designed by Jaime, with Zoey's insights quickly embraced and implemented.

Thus the GS Ranches brand was launched and included its own fair trade "Kick Butt" coffee blends—with Noah providing the graphic inspiration and drawing for the packaging and branding.

I suppose I need to take a break here to talk about that coffee. Some who read this will already know all about it, but for the sake of the others, I should offer some explanation.

Bill was very interested in Ernesto and Rosalinda's youngest son's work in El Salvador. Early on, Bill, who always referred to his oil revenues as his "ill-gotten gains," provided funds for the village where *Padre Jesús* lived so they could build a small medical clinic. That was followed later by providing funds (always by family vote) for fish ponds fed by the mountain streams and a small school, while at the same time Jean and Mary-Alice worked with Ernesto and Rosalinda's daughter, Conchita, to coordinate with the farmers in his parish to sell their coffee beans into the US through a fair trade agreement.

Only the bishops in El Paso and El Salvador and *Padre Jesús* ever knew where the funds came from for these projects. So far as we knew, young Chuy, as he'd been called at home—named after his uncle—never told any of his own family. Maybe he had, and they too had their own vow of silence.

Bill did not want the Geermann-Schlatters getting any attention from it. Much credit was given to Lupe's mother, Elma, our shared family treasure, for her constant prayers for "those poor people." None of the cash-giving benefactors would take exception to that. Some spirit moved Bill to look at the young priest with the greatest interest and concern. Plus, we would all agree, that anyone being the benefactor of Elma's faithful prayers was all to the good.

Once all was up and running, Bill, Sis and I made a trip to visit the humble *padre*. I loved all the colorful birds, and one spider monkey with a hind end about like Billy's, hung around my neck some part of every day. It was quite a trip—a beautiful place with the kindest people you can imagine, ruled by corruption at every turn. As the historian, Bill, rightly noted, "Any look into Central and South America, and you find our fingerprints on all manner of evils."

As I replay those words, I'm taken to an exchange where Bill said to Jaime that he reckoned if he marched downtown with a picket sign every time our government did something dumb or evil or both, he'd be labeled "unAmerican." When it comes to love of country, Bill Schlatter is a far better American than these *pendejos* that wrap themselves in the flag, and pledge their allegiance to the party and to the *cabrónes* on which it stands. "Cheap slogan jingoism," as Bill calls it.

Love of country and love of nationalism are two very different loves. The first, recognizes the care required for your own land and the far-off lands of others. The nationalist loves self *above* all others. Hubris is the word for that, and therein lies the problem.

That's enough of that. The only difference between Bill and the rest of family, in this regard, is the due diligence he has given to the task of understanding just how deep the lies are, and how blatantly they are perpetuated year upon year.

Ernesto and Rosalinda made frequent trips to see their son—the priest Ernesto's mother hoped Ernesto himself would be, but who didn't live long enough to see her grandson become one. We all laughed at any recollection by Chuy or Ernesto's telling of how their *mamá* said since her youngest wouldn't become the priest she wanted, she might just as well have had another girl rather than the dirty-mouthed little boy she got. It was that one line that inspired Ernesto to dress in drag every New Year's Eve. She'd hit him with her purse as she entered the house, and he'd say, "Oh, *Mamá*, you love me." Chuy always said his *mamá* and Ernesto did indeed have a very special bond—even if he was her potty-mouthed little boy. I'm sure that charismatic, beautiful baritone voice helped.

Circling back to Quiet Day—mercy, I do wander some in my tellin'—Bill, having witnessed Jaime's success of writin' his letter during Quiet Day, was inspired to try the same with Brett. Sadly, it would take a lot more than a letter to knock Brett from his state of oblivion.

I never thought it was coincidental that soon after Sal was laid to his rest in the horse cemetery, Billy got to thinking about some other kind of companion beyond just horses and Jaime. Sal had a good full life, and having the horse he'd acquired as a six-year-old boy along with him for his twenty years of exile was certainly a comfort—the inevitable death, a heartache. Had Sal died while still up at the Van Horn ranch, I think Billy would have tried to coax his dad into bringing him back to our ranch. Of course, no coaxing would have been required. Bill would have been up there within a couple hours. Fortunately, that was never necessary. Sal was given a good Geermann Christian burial with all in attendance.

So, first came the dogs, and then came the boy. When Billy got his notion that he and Jaime had to have a couple red heelers to help with the cattle, the plan rolled into high gear when Chuy, who had retired from the tomato farm and was volunteering at the animal shelter, knew of a couple pups for immediate adoption. So it was that Kola and Koala found themselves rescued. They arrived in a lot better shape than Nellie had come to us. Momma dog had taken good care of all her pups but found herself in the shelter with them. Chuy said they thought someone from Alpine had dumped 'em off. Billy would have adopted her and her whole litter, but by the time they inquired, only the two smallest were still available.

Billy, who had observed an older man at the Van Horn ranch train dogs for herdin', got to trainin' 'em in short order. They sure were cute dogs, and it was a delight to watch them work. Billy jokingly always said Koala, who'd slept with him, looked like Jaime, which Billy took as a sign that Jaime really wanted to sleep with him too. I'd chuckle at that, and Bill would give his customary, "Good lord," to anything Billy would say about such imaginings of his. Kola took over one of Jaime's pillows for her bed.

Watchin' them dogs work made me wonder why the generations before hadn't gotten and trained some dogs to help. They were better than some of the hands we hired and a whole lot cuter and more fun! I do remember Grandad and Daddy had a couple bigger dogs to stay with the sheep and goats that they had for quite a while "mowin'" scrub from around the ranch. Of course, they weren't house dogs, let alone bed companions. Kola and Koala got the best of both worlds—good daywork on the ranch, a comfy bed at night and no night-guard duties against the greater dangers of the night hours.

Just seeing them that one time raisin' hell with a rattlesnake suggested to me that if they had been expected to provide night protection, they would have given it their all. With their small size, that "all," against a pack of coyotes or a mountain lion would have also been their quick demise. I was never convinced that they had any killer instinct in 'em. They could put on a good show with each other, but never once did they ever draw any blood.

Billy had this notion, sometime earlier, that somehow Noah was going to land at the ranch. When he said it, we didn't see how that would ever come about. On that fateful day, when the sheriff arrived over at the new house (*Vista Grande*, as it would one day be called) to break the news of Noah's mother's murder, we were dumbfounded to say the least. By then Bill and Sis had already had their meltdown with Brett over his mortgage-backed securities' scheme that he'd tried to lure us into.

Well, for the record, I was the first to go into meltdown over it, not only for Brett's stupidity in tryin' to sell us the idea of sellin' up "for the good life," but even more so for what Sis rightly called, "sinning against the family." He tried to belittle Billy both as a person and as someone incapable of runnin' the ranch. To quote him directly, "You gonna let that fruitcake run it for you the rest of your lives?"

I didn't take too kindly to those words, and as Jaime's brother-in-law, Mark, described it, "The lioness knows how to tear apart anything trying to get at her adopted cub."

Hardly somethin' I could deny—then or now.

The point in mentionin' the meltdown now was the fact that Brett was in Phoenix by then, having given wife number four, Pamela, an ultimatum to move with him or divorce him. Pamela, with three children of her own from a previous marriage and sharing custody with her ex, couldn't just pack up and move. But Brett was in the height of his oblivion stage when he left El Paso, and hadn't given any consideration to Aiden and Noah who still lived there with two of his other ex-wives.

By the time of Olivia's murder, his scheme had collapsed. He was flat broke and hard to track down. The El Paso detective responding to the murder found a child support check Bill had sent on Brett's behalf, and so we knew before Brett what had happened. Poor little Noah was hiding upstairs under his bed when the police arrived.

After the murder, Noah coming to the ranch was not only the best option, but Bill made it clear to Brett it was the *only* option—at least until he got his life together. Brett, in his melt-down state, agreed, and for the first time in his adult life, he began to measure up the magnitude of his failures.

When Bill, Sis and Billy returned from El Paso with Noah, Jaime and Billy committed to taking him in. As soon as Noah entered the old ranch house for the first time in his life, he was greeted by two little red heelers who let the boy know they'd watch over him—no need to hide under the bed in fear anymore.

That night Billy and Jaime lost their bed companions for good and gained a boy to raise.

Pamela hadn't been Noah's stepmother for very long, but she felt strongly connected to Noah. She made a point to see him as much as she could after Brett went to Phoenix, even after their divorce. Noah credits her with helping him cope when his mother's attention had been completely consumed by her drug-dealing boyfriend.

Anytime that boyfriend came around, Noah would avoid him by staying in his room upstairs. He would process later how he believed the reason she was attracted to Brett and then such a loser, who Noah would avoid by staying in his room any time the man was around, was her need to cling to a man no matter who it was. Brett, who always liked the attention to be on *him*, was a natural for her "affections" until he was bored with her. Noah says as soon as Brett no longer was interested in her, she moved to the first man that showed her any attention.   We never knew where she'd dug him up.

He drove a Beemer, and so Noah guessed she figured he had money—which he did from his true ill-gotten gains in the drug trade.   Of course, he got a little greedy, which brought the higher ups in the trade lookin' for a big bag of cash.   A shoot-out ensued, and Olivia was caught in the line of fire—the only one to die that day.

I'll have a little more to say about this realization of his mother's need for attention later in Noah's story, but that would be gettin' well ahead of things.

In the "all to the good" department, that's how the two cowboys, the two cattle dogs and the boy would begin their journey together—one that would lead to the healing of not only Noah, but also Brett and all his children along with him.   They would *not* just survive but thrive.

Brett was ready to come home. As he ever so slowly dug out from the mess he'd put himself into, and as he clearly had awakened from his years in oblivion, Bill and Sis met with the realtor, Annie, in Fort Davis—who had handled the sale of the house in town after the move to the ranch, and whom we all had known many years before that. Annie was agreeable to their plan to help Brett start an office in Alpine as part of her brokerage.

Bill was still payin' all the child support for Brett to the ex-wives remaining. Brett was makin' slow but diligent progress towards payin' off his other debts. When Brett came back from Phoenix to live in Alpine, Noah made it clear to his dad that visits to Alpine were fine, but he did not want to leave the ranch. Brett, to his credit, recognized the young rancher-to-be and allowed for whatever relationship Noah was willing to have with him.

Brett's first two children, Jaxon and Quinn, were largely estranged from him as was the remaining son in El Paso, Aiden. With Bill paying the child support, the ex-wives seemed to be more open to the grandchildren spending some time on the ranch. Still, they were largely strangers to everyone, including Brett.

Brett's world wasn't done being rocked just yet, either. When Quinn's mother hung up on her during her freshman in college, Quinn called her daddy in tears to announce she was pregnant. All of us would have to confess that we did not take the news happily, but once it sunk in, we also knew we had to rally around Quinn and not give her a second to feel shame for her careless, drunken behavior with the frat boys. She was going to keep the baby, and that child didn't need the burden of a mother's regret and a family's imposed shame.

Quinn moved to Alpine to live with Brett, who also gave her a job in his office after the baby was born, where she could serve as receptionist while also tending to the beautiful Anna Catherine—named after her great-grandma. She later met and married Jay Ramirez who accepted Anna Catherine as his own.

After they'd been married a couple of years, I asked Jay if he and Quinn were hopin' to have other children. I found his answer quite remarkable.

"Sallie, I've made it known to Quinn that if she wants more children, I'll consider it, but I have some serious concerns about it."

He continued, "I know that neither Quinn nor I would ever look at our children who were biologically our own as somehow better than Anna, but I am worried that when some *pendejo* decides one or more of our children needs to know the circumstances of Quinn's pregnancy, it might cause great pain to Anna and to Quinn. We can't control how our children turn out, but I fear the biological child exposed to the gossip might feel superior and express it cruelly.

"I just can't live with that risk. You know enough people know how she ended up in Alpine and the gossip that circulated then. Some live to make sure superiority through gossip never dies."

I gave him a pat on the shoulder and said, "You're not wrong about those gossips. I think we'll keep you."

Quinn's mother, Josie, took a *long time* to come around—more afraid of her own family's judgment than she was concerned about growing distant from her children. Jaxon, the oldest, decided he might as well rock her world even more by announcing he was gay. He had moved to Alpine before Quinn and was enrolled in Industrial Technology at Sul Ross—living in the residence halls rather than with Brett. While there, he began dating a business major, Caleb Benton. The two boys were quickly spending time with Billy, Jaime and Noah at the ranch. Jaxon spent the summer of his sophomore year helpin' on the ranch. By their junior year, both boys were apprenticing with Ernesto.

After they graduated and with Bill's assistance, the boys bought out Ernesto's construction yard and equipment as Ernesto was ready to retire. He continued to work with them for a time to pass along what he could.

Billy was beside himself when gay marriage was legalized and let the boys know it—though at that point they were in no rush as they weighed how the community might respond.

Jaxon had, from the start, texted his mother photos of Anna Catherine as she grew. His most recent post had a picture of Quinn, Anna and Jay. A while later, in another attempt to keep her up to date and rock her world yet again, he texted her to announce that thanks to SCOTUS, he and Caleb planned to marry. She texted right back that she hoped her children were happy. That was the first time she'd responded to any of his texts. Jaxon immediately called Quinn and conferenced in their mother for a long talk. She soon made a trip to Alpine to see them, and their own healing journey began. Josie attended both weddings. Her parents and siblings did not. She no longer was willing to sacrifice her relationship with her children for their approval.

As soon as Aiden was "grown up enough" to ride the Sunset Limited on his own from El Paso, he began makin' more frequent trips to the ranch. Brett's brood, who were largely strangers to him and to each other and to all the Schlatters, became a real family. With Bill and I providing temporary ranch duties, Billy and Jaime took all the boys on a trip down to Big Bend National Park. Of course, Kola and Koala joined them on the trip.

I had to chuckle when Noah shared with me their sittin' out in the rain one afternoon. They saw a big cloud comin' towards 'em from over Emery Peak, and Noah thought maybe they ought to get in the tents and out of the rain. Billy would have nothing of it. Noah pointed out that Billy wouldn't be the one in the tent with "wet dog" smell, but Billy said a little wet dog never hurt anybody. So, they all just sat in the rain as the afternoon cloud burst passed over them.

I told Noah I thought maybe them dogs would've had enough sense to get in out of the rain, but then I added, "I guess if you were going to sit in the rain, so were they. Wither you goest, they will go, or I guess in this case, where you sit, they will stay."

After high school, Aiden stayed in El Paso, and though he made efforts to come to the ranch and Alpine, his life soon became too busy to do it with any frequency. He attended UTEP, where he would ultimately graduate with his business degree. Early on, he started seriously courting another freshman, Cynthia.

They married their junior year, and we all traveled to El Paso for a rather arduous day trip—Jaime and Mark staying behind to tend to things, as the rest of us attended the wedding. We'd only met her one time, but that was once more than we had met some of Brett's wives prior to marriage, and not much more often even after marriage. Ironically we see Pamela far more frequently now, since the divorce, than we ever did when she and Brett were married.

Aiden would do much better on that score than his father in staying connected. Ever since he spent time with Billy and Jaime, and all the boys made their trip to Big Bend, he felt very much a part of the family. I still haven't gotten to know him as much as I'd like. It's just a matter of miles. Certainly, none of us feel estranged from Aiden in any way.

He's followed in his father's footsteps professionally. He had no problem getting a job in one of the larger real estate firms, and he is quickly making a fine livin' sellin' houses. He made it clear he'd learned the lessons of his father and wasn't going to go off lookin' for greener pastures in the wife department or the job department.

Fertility in Brett's line didn't seem to be a problem. Of course, Quinn had gotten pregnant after one careless night. Soon after their marriage, Aiden and Cynthia were expecting their first.

Cynthia was Catholic and Aiden "converted." Thank the lord, Sis was past her prejudice against those of other faiths. That would have been one more lost soul by her earlier reckoning. Brett, Bill and Sis all went for baby Ryder Michael Schlatter's christening.

I'd have to say the first ten years of my life barely count in the work department as the same can be said for the last twelve. I certainly had my chores by the age of ten—more than the "foreman" these days assigns to me, though he still says I need to help Jaime and Noah on shoeing day. That puts my *real* workin' days right at sixty-two years. Fifty of those years included working alongside Bill, and here I am in my old age livin' with him. He can't escape!

Jaime once told us about the first time he talked to Chuy and Lupe about Bill and Sis. Chuy said Bill had "married into the land." That is certainly an accurate observation, and Bill is not alone in making such a vow of fidelity to this place—now or in the generations before him.

I don't think I need to elaborate more than I already have on how much I enjoyed workin' with Daddy, but I can't help but say a little more about the brother-in-law. Thanks to a marriage license, he is my brother "in the law," but we seem to have a knack in this family for taking in strays as our own. I can't imagine Momma and Daddy ever looking at Bill as anything but a son. He has always been both brother and friend to me. We've extended this familial integration to Jaime, Zoey, Mark and Pamela (who was an in-law once upon a time), each of whom I would now consider my nieces and nephews, though there is no "in-law" relationship to legalize it. Jaime says that just makes them family of a kind. Of course, he would put it that way, and it's as good a term as any, though hardly representative of how integral they are in our lives.

In case you are wondering what these others have to do with Bill, it must be said, no one, from day one, did more to welcome Jaime into the family and integrate him into the runnin' life of the ranch. I heard someone at the Slo Poke once ask Jaime if he felt like a fifth wheel out at the ranch. He didn't know I was still within earshot, as I was already halfway out the door.

He responded, "If you think such is *even* a possibility, you don't know Bill Schlatter."

I waited for him outside and gave him a big hug. Billy, who was ahead of me, turned to see me huggin' on Jaime, and shouted across the parking lot, "What the Sam Hill? Since when are hugs given around here without me bein' invited? I'm the one that usually says when it's time for a hug."

By then he was huggin' on the two of us, and asked, "What are we huggin' Jaime for?"

I answered, "Because of what he just told that nibby nose in there about your daddy."

"I didn't know you heard that," Jaime stated flatly.

"What the Sam Hill did he say?" Billy asked.

Jaime repeated the exchange. "He wanted to know if I felt like a fifth wheel out at the ranch, and I said, 'If you think such is even a possibility, you don't know Bill Schlatter.'"

"Damn straight!" Billy exclaimed, adding, "I don't even mind you leaving me out of it. Credit goes to the headman himself. I just follow orders. After all, it was he who said I needed to get your intentions all those years ago."

Jaime and I laughed and blurted out in unison, "Damn straight!"

Billy lassoed both us in his arms. "All right—let's bring it in here for one more big hug. Then we gotta get back to the ranch and get some work done, or the headman will be rethinkin' his plan."

I concluded, "Somehow I doubt that."

Bill has never had Daddy or Billy's gift for formulating the instant plan with no apparent flaws, but he can certainly recognize a good plan. Both are gifts, and I don't have either. One of the greatest gifts in life is to realize what is *not* your gift, and I have always known that any hasty notion of mine probably had more holes than value. Consequently, I defer to better planners than myself. I was always good at chores, so I was pretty good at "gettin' 'er done" for whatever I was supposed to do with their good plans.

What Bill lacked in instant plannin' was more than made up for in executin' on a plan with a great deal of common sense and no drama. He was one who made it all look effortless. If a plan had flaws or required regrouping, he always could see the next step forward. Daddy would agree—no one could keep a cooler head under pressure.

Years ago, when we had some ranch hands workin' new fence for several weeks, Bill made them take a whole day's work down and start over. I asked him, "You sure keep your cool—how do you do it?"

He smiled, "I get back on my horse, light a Kind Edward and take a Twinkie out of my saddle bag."

I chuckled and added, "I thought that was your coping mechanism for Sis's religious fervor."

He laughed then too. "I wouldn't broadcast this, but that church bullshit is likely to need two or three Kind Edwards and at least four Twinkies."

"Whatever works," I chuckled. "Whatever works."

As Bill would attest, once an oil lease is purchased and royalties set, one has no real say on what happens to the land. This was one of Bill's great consternations with his family's lease on the San Angelo ranch. He saw a fair ranch, which had supported a lot of fine cattle, give way to pump jacks, prickly pear and mesquite scrub. Daddy had some offers for oil and mineral rights, and even though he figured our location was far from prime land for any mining or drilling, he always turned them down. Bill was glad to be on a ranch where no one could "march in and take over."

At one point Bill said, "Those pump jacks are about petered out. I don't mind, though I know no one will ever do anything to clean it up and restore it. Oil companies leave a mess behind, and Texas looks the other way and lets them. So, there it will sit."

When we first heard about fracking, he wondered if they would be exploring the ranch for yet more oil. Sure enough, before long it was drill-baby-drill all over again. Soon, he was gettin' more of his "ill-gotten gains" than ever.

One thing he was not, was naive on any side of the equation. He understood the environmental damage firsthand as far back as some of the water tanks on the ranch that were contaminated when he was a boy. He also recognized that if the taps were turned off like many wanted to do, half the world would starve. The great plan executor saw the flaw in the rush to get off oil and gas, but didn't have a next step to solve it quickly enough for life to go without a great deal of suffering.

It was the same concern he expressed for plant-based-diet advocates that seem to think all it takes is a governmental decision to make it happen overnight as they remove the complex protein sources of meat and fish for supplements and processed-food replacements with no clue as to the inputs required.

Bill summed up his thinking, saying, "As Mao learned to his people's peril, dramatic changes in agriculture can starve a few million people in short order. Arable land, water and labor are all supposed to magically appear, I guess, and the next extinction can be all the ruminants if we don't beat 'em there first."

I suggested, "For the earth's sake, it might be better if we go extinct and leave the ruminants to thrive."

"Well, that they would do," Bill reckoned. "Nature's symbiosis back in balance as John Geermann would say. We always were the one species out of synch.

"I would add as well, I'm not sure in the end if anyone will be healthy or not from our new ways of eating. I'm hard-pressed to see that our government has ever advocated for health of the land and its people over profit and exploitation. They are endless advocates for the pharma and food industries and every other big money industry."

To that all I could say was, Too true—too true."

The main reason the natural-born rancher always called them his "ill-gotten gains" stemmed not only from the impact it had on the ranch of his childhood, but even more specifically from a "worthy cause" that suggested years ago that he invest it all in their environmental agenda. They told him, "You should put your ill-gotten gains to good use." Little did they know how much in contempt he held to their view of what makes for a healthy world.

He just told them, "No thank you. I'll use my ill-gotten gains as I see fit."

Of course, they had no idea how carefully Bill had managed that income all those years. I don't know anything about the group that came moneygrubbin' to him, but I'd venture to say, he has helped the poor and been the best kind of steward to all he's touched to a degree they couldn't even imagine.

He said to Daddy and me at the time, "My problem with 'causes' is way too much goes to the cause-managers of an unproven solution, and so they have to have more money for the next supposed solution and the next. I guess by the time their 'shift' is done, they have a nice retirement."

Every election cycle was also another opportunity to "make a difference." He was always bombarded by both parties grubbin' for money. He said Austin or the IRS must give 'em lists of upper-income filers, trolling for easy marks. He resisted the temptation citing Mark Twain, "There is no distinctly native American criminal class except Congress."

I was an old woman before I realized, thanks to Bill, just what kinda hell Twain raised against our government's injustices and wars. One of my favorite quotes from Twain was, "Sometimes I wonder whether the world is being run by smart people who are putting us on or by imbeciles who really mean it."

Bill commented, "You know what Jaime and Billy say, 'Shit-asses keep gettin' elected because dumbasses keep electin' them.'"

Well, I can't argue with that, and no doubt, Twain would have agreed.

I never have taken any kind of personality test. There seems to be a lot of options on how you can slice and dice people up into categories, and I've never been a slicer-dicer. When Jean and Mary-Alice told us about a woman who was comin' to Marfa as part of a weekend retreat, sponsored by the little Marfa church where they were still members of a kind, they asked if any of us wanted to attend. Our churchgoing, including Jean and Mary-Alice, was then, and is now, limited to Quiet Day once a month and our Sundays in the chapel on the ranch—*Capilla de la Rosa*, as Billy has dubbed it.

But back to the story, the woman taught the Enneagram. None of us knew anything about it, and I'm not sure we knew much more after Jean tried to explain it. She said it wasn't a personality test, but a spiritual tool. Merton called the false self that which we defend and try to project out to the world—driven by our ego. The nine Enneagram types suggest a sin or passion drives this false self in different ways according to our early life experiences. It looked like a pretty good list to me and certainly should cover everyone out there in one way or the other. From one to nine, the sins/passions are anger, pride, deceit, envy, greed, fear, gluttony, lust and sloth. That much we knew from Jean's brief introduction.

Sis and I decided we could stay at Jean and Mary-Alice's for the weekend and save havin' to drive back and forth. None of the rest thought they wanted to give up a weekend to be in Marfa, and "free beds" were limited at our Marfa hosts. I didn't really want to go myself, but when I could see that Sis was interested and Bill was not, I thought I'd keep her company.

It was a lot more interesting than I expected. The first thing our Enneagram master, Suzanne Stabile, instructed us to do was listen for what applies to us and not go labeling someone else with the "sins" of each of the nine numbers. This was "know your number" teaching where she went through each number's characteristics with the point of namin' the sin/passion attached to it as a way of understandin' some of why we do what we do. I wasn't guiltless in

151

hearin' some of the numbers with certain names comin' to mind. "Ah-huh, I got your number!"

The exploration number by number was quite interesting, and Suzanne was a hoot. When she got to "fives," who love to gather information and are all about order and security, I thought, "Good lord—is there a better descriptor for Jean?" When she got to "eights," who take their view of what is just very seriously—dominating and confrontational, I leaned over to Sis and whispered, "Any of this ringin' a bell from those fundamentalist days?"

She smiled and whispered back, "I can't imagine what you're talking about."

Early in the day, one man's face got beet red, and it looked like he was ready to explode. I could see where some descriptions might hit you like a ton of bricks. I guess they hit him. He departed at the next break and didn't come back.

I wasn't doin' too well on sizin' up my own number. A serious character flaw, no doubt.

After we'd been through all nine numbers at the end of the second day, when we were back at the girls' place, I said to them, "There must be a number ten she left out. I don't know where I fit."

Jean said, "I think that's just because you're on the healthy side of your number. We could pin 'eight' on Momma easily because of her unhealthy days with her old church crowd."

Sis agreed, adding, "I don't think you're that much of a mystery, and you *don't* need a number ten. Didn't you think 'fours' sounded a lot like you? Thanks to Momma and Daddy, you were never on the self-indulgent and temperamental side of that number."

I replied, "I did think I had more than a good chance of leanin' heavy into the temperamental."

"Hardly!" Mary-Alice exclaimed.

Sis continued, "According to my notes healthy fours are creative and connected, emotionally honest and get their inspiration from nature."

"Duh—inspiration from nature might have been a clue," Jean interjected.

Sis continued, "*Really*! And unlike an unhealthy four, you don't have to go around trying to be special so people will love you."

"I have been loved all my life and knew it. In that regard, four or not, I'm luckier than most."

"And that's the reason you are indeed special—just like a four," Jean said, adding, "You are special to our world."

Mary-Alice offered, "And you certainly know how to bear witness to pain—knowing when to speak and knowing when to stand beside in quiet support."

"Well, that would just be me lettin' Momma come through," I stated rather matter-of-factly.

Right then, I thought of what threw me off about "fours" when Suzanne first talked about them. "It was her sayin' fours have some early sense of abandonment, and I didn't see how I ever had any sense of that."

Sis had reflected on the same, and I suppose had an interestin' notion, "You were Momma's first child after two miscarriages. Don't you think she had some understandable detachment with her pregnancies—especially yours?"

"I'll grant, I would have," I acknowledged. "That makes sense. I was loved, but she'd gotten used to preparin' for another heartache."

Billy and Jaime wanted to know how the weekend went. I told them, "I don't think it probably would have helped Sis and Brett to know their Enneagram number back in their unhealthy years. Sis would have first needed to entertain the notion it wasn't the Devil's tool, which I doubt she could have done—and so does she. Brett couldn't have seen past his own oblivion. But I rejoice to report, we all seem to be moving ever-towards health of the soul."

Jaime replied, "I don't think you ever had much moving to do in that regard. I, on the other hand, must have been at the depth of pitiful of whatever number I am."

"But you're doin' all right now," Billy said.

Jaime acknowledged, "Yes, I'm doin' all right now."

Billy looked at me, saying, "I guess whatever number you are, I am too."

"For that not to be true, I'd say you'd have to start splitting atoms," Jaime responded.

I just chuckled at both of them. All I could say to that was, "I reckon you're right, Jaime. I reckon you're right."

We enjoyed Suzanne's teaching so much, Sis suggested we invite her back, and we'd host the weekend at the ranch. Her husband, Joe, came with her on the Marfa trip and joined her on this trip, as well. They returned several months later for a second teaching on the Enneagram, and they stayed in the bunkhouse.

After the last session on Sunday morning everyone departed, leavin' just us and the Stabiles, who were going to leave on Monday. We spent the afternoon with a couple bottles of wine, and sittin' at the large table on the front porch overlooking the north ridge. They expressed how much they loved the ranch. Joe, an ex-Catholic priest and now Methodist minister, had actually done some cowboyin' when he was young. He shared the story of how he and Suzanne met, and how love had changed both their lives—includin' the "good Catholics" excommunicating him and the Methodists takin' him in. After a couple hours of delightful conversation, we sat silently for a time just starin' out across the vast expanse.

Suzanne put her arm around her faithful husband and sighed, "Joe, just lay me out on this table when I die."

Over the years, we have done our civic duty as commonly practiced in this country. We vote when there is an election. We serve on juries when called to do so. Before every election, we have open discussions to talk about "the issues," without the hostility too many seem to find compelling. It won't be much of a revelation to know, we are far more of one mind than divided by party loyalty. Generally, the most depressing aspect of our discussions is the sorry asses that constitute our options. Any possible hope that comes from one candidate before the election, is soon enough squashed like a bug after the election, when the promise turns to the lie, once again.

And over the years, we've also begun to be just as disillusioned with state leadership as we are with our Washington "public servants." I think the bunch has some incurable brain infection that alters both reality and their judgment. We ignore them to our peril!

I marvel, along with my brother-in-law, whose due diligence in state and national affairs puts the rest of us to shame, how bizarrely easy it is to sell a lie as fact.

Bill found some fairly obscure book by Daniel Boorstin, *The Image: Or, What happened to the American Dream*. He thought a lot more people ought to be readin' it. He read me this line.

I describe the world of our making, how we have used our wealth, our literacy, our technology, and our progress to create the thicket of unreality which stands between us and the facts of life.

I told Bill, "You really know how to cheer me up. That's a truly depressing thought, as facing the hard truth generally is."

Bill fumbled through a stack of magazines and articles he keeps next to his "readin' chair" and pulled out what he was looking for. "Well, then you're sure to like this one by Hannah Arendt from her essay 'Lying in Politics.'"

The deliberate falsehood deals with contingent facts, that is, with matters which carry no inherent truth within themselves, no necessity to be as they are; factual truths are never compellingly true.

"Yeah, you're right. That cheers me *right* up!"

He added, "It should really cheer you up that Arendt wrote that back in 1971 and Boorstin's book was nearly a decade earlier than that."

"At least we're getting closer to perfectin' it all," I noted. "Think of the people thrilled with their success in foolin' millions."

Bill suggested, "I'd say billions."

"And like before, that cheers me right up."

I then asked, "How do you think we can get all these young people to sign up voluntarily to go off to some foreign land to fight and die? I mean, back in our day, they had to depend on the draft. Now, they have the 'all volunteer army.'"

"I can only offer a theory or two," Bill suggested. "We sell duty hard enough in this country that when you're eighteen it probably seems like your sacrifice will be appreciated. The truth is, we don't have anywhere near enough volunteers for all the places we're deploying these kids, so they get sent back again and again until we get them killed, badly wounded or deranged.

"Suicide, in and out of the service, and homelessness, addictions and mental illness of our vets is a huge problem, as you well know. It is remarkably ignored by politicians—our great patriots—and the public despite all the 'support the troops' bumper stickers.

"There are some poor kids who just don't know what else to do. They are not college material, or can't get the aid needed to go to college. I guess we have to factor in the growing push for 'Christian Nationalism,' too. And it must be said, plenty are adrenaline junkies. The noise, chaos and destruction of war is the ultimate high. Add on top of that, our new remote warfare where these young men and women bomb far-off lands from a joystick in the Nevada desert."

"I somehow knew I wouldn't fit in—tough as I am. An adrenaline junky, I am not," I replied. "The whole mess makes my heart sad."

Low crime rates and sparse population help minimize our civic duty when it comes to serving for jury duty. Though I suppose, with that sparse population our "number comes up," relatively speaking, as much or more than in major cities.

I've been on two juries plus I had to serve one six-month term on the county's grand jury. One of those cases was federal, and so I had to drive to the federal courthouse in Pecos.

The defendant couldn't afford his own lawyer, and he was appointed a federal public defender out of the Alpine office. I had to give credit to the young lady who defended her client. It was pretty obvious the judge presiding had about as much interest in justice as our politicians have in taking responsibility for the mess they create. He had one apparent goal—to clear the docket. It sure looked to me like the poor man snagged in the "war on drugs" was guilty whether innocent or not.

I wasn't too popular with my fellow jurists or the judge when I hung the jury. That was not how it was supposed to go. I sensed during jury selection, the prosecutor thought an old, tough cowgirl like me would be a shoo-in for a conviction. The federal defender, on the other hand, at least knew of me and perhaps held out some hope that one person on the jury would need to be persuaded by actual evidence, and not from what was purely circumstantial on its face. I certainly did my duty, as I was unpersuaded the man hadn't been set up to take the fall by some far more sinister character, still out there roamin' free. I had *more* than a reasonable doubt, and I was dismayed my eleven co-jurists could be so ready to convict.

It became pretty clear to me that most hadn't even paid much attention in court. They were just waitin' to render their verdict and get back to their life. Liberty and justice are fine, so long as one is not inconvenienced.

One man even said to me, "Just send the bastard to jail. What the *hell* do you care if he spends a few years behind bars?"

If my momma's fine raisin' of me hadn't predominated in that moment, I'd have said back to him, "I'm all for puttin' sorry bastards who serve on juries behind bars and throwin' away the key."

At any rate, I was largely unconvincing. I, and one other woman who was persuaded by my concerns, were the only holdouts.

As I understand it, the feds moved on, and they let the man go free rather than retry him. I guess they had their own doubts after all.

My six months of grand jury duty amounted to meeting one time to review three cases. Majority rules in these indictments. In two cases, the evidence was overwhelming and our votes were unanimous. Both involved theft. One was an embezzlement case, and the other was where someone had kicked in a grocery store door to get in after hours and steal some beer. In that latter case, the man had just barely gotten off parole from a previous conviction. I had to wonder if he simply wanted to get sent back to the big house. His actions didn't make much sense to me otherwise.

In the third case, I again found myself bucking most of my fellow jurists. Details of our deliberations are supposed to be confidential, so I'll not get too deep into the case. Suffice it to say, me and one man felt that people in the chain of events took a situation easily enough resolved, and escalated it to the point of no return. I'd have liked to have indicted one of those in that chain just for being a dumbass, but he was a "witness" rather than a defendant.

Bill says he lived the charmed life when it came to jury duty. Every single time he'd been "summoned" the case was settled out of court before it started. After my federal case he suggested, "It could be they pressured some poor guy into a guilty plea on a lesser charge, even if he was innocent, since the federal defender knew the odds going in against the man." He had been told by someone in that defender's office how frequent such deals are, and how hard it is to work within a system designed to brutalize.

Sis had a federal capital case up in Pecos where they were seeking the death penalty. That was during her fundamentalist days, and she laments now how ready she was to castigate him to Hell. I wasn't there to hear the evidence, but my confidence in bringing a just end in that court was left wanting from my earlier experience with that judge. It has been hard for Sis ever since, as she reflects on her role in sending that man to his death.

As she would put it, "I see now, what I was blind to then. Our justice system is flawed to the point that I couldn't send anyone to their death. Texas, *and* plenty of other states, have wrongly convicted and executed men proven innocent after they were already dead. Besides, in the end, it's just another form of bloodlust. The so-called closure it brings doesn't bring peace of mind."

While I think we are mostly live-and-let-live around these parts, I suspect more fellow neighbors than not would enshrine the death penalty in the constitution once and for all if they could, and would apply it to more crimes rather than fewer. Screw the Sermon on the Mount. In this "Christian country," an eye for an eye is alive and well. In some cases, it's more like a dozen eyes for an eye, it seems to me. And if you happen to be the wrong color, then "Katy bar the door!" The scales of justice are weighted heavily in favor of white, wealthy America. The only advantage poorer whites have, once it gets to court, is at least the jury of their peers is just that, more or less—poorer whites like themselves.

I don't know where we are headed, but I will say this, bumper stickers tell me enough to *really wonder* about my "fellow man."

For my eightieth birthday, those boys across the cattle guards decided I could use a new outfit. Despite the general impression of folks around here, I do have more than the one pair of nice black dress slacks and that one dark-red blouse, though that outfit was my favorite. Now, I had a new favorite, though I waited until Christmas Eve to show it off "in public." I did try it on for Billy, Jaime, Noah, Betsy and Bill, and I had to admit that for an ol' tough cowgirl like me, I looked pretty good. I even borrowed some clip-on earrings from Sis. It was the first time in my life I'd ever had earrings on.

Betsy took one look and said, I could almost pass for a frilly-girl. Bill just said I cleaned up real good. Billy thought he should probably drive me to a gay bar in El Paso and see if I could get lucky with a lesbian. Noah was all in on ridin' along, but Jaime assured me he would hide all their keys so there'd be no trippin' to El Paso. I suggested Jaime had the best plan.

Sis advised them on my sizes, feelin' she had to remind them I have "marbled up some" from my workin' days. Now, I got Billy's cheeks on my face and even a little more on my rear. All my marblin' seems to settle on those two places.

Noah, with the help of Sis, picked out a pair of dark blue slacks, a light blue silk blouse and a snazzy scarf to go with it. Billy said it was my dressin' up bandana and not a scarf, but it looked mighty fancy for a bandana. Billy got me a new pair of dressy cowgirl boots, and Jaime bought me a gorgeous new cowgirl hat. Just lookin' at it, I asked Jaime if he had to take out a mortgage to buy it. He assured me he didn't. They sure don't give those custom hats away.

Billy declared Jaime didn't have signature authority to put the family in debt, so he must have paid cash, adding, "Dad, we must be payin' Jaime too much."

Bill responded, "You never have paid him any wages, but he gets a good income from me for puttin' up with you. I can't risk losin' him."

"Well, I guess that's right," Billy reckoned. "I am his mess, not yours."

"Thank the lord," Bill muttered.

Jaime added, "Noah knows even better than I about unpaid wages. Isn't that right, Noah?"

"Too true—too true!" He chuckled.

I was dressed to the nines that Christmas Eve, and everyone had to get in on the act of gettin' a picture taken with me. I just smiled and said, "It's nice to be loved even if I'm gonna disappoint some old lesbian in El Paso."

On that Christmas Eve, I asked Jean and Mary-Alice if there was any reason in particular they still hadn't gotten married. It seemed to me for legal reasons, they ought to get "legit." Of course, they were close to all of us, comin' to the ranch pretty much every weekend, and callin' the bunkhouse their home away from home. They were also the official accountants for GS Ranches. In their very close-knit and extremely organized life, it just seemed kinda silly to me that they resisted gettin' that license.

We all knew children were not in their plan from the horrified look on their faces when the idea was floated that one of the options for Noah to come live "with us" was for Noah to live with them. Neither seems to have much of a maternal instinct any more than they have creative instincts.

That didn't diminish their fidelity in any way. It was obvious they were in it for the long haul. Mary-Alice said that as far as they were concerned, they had made their vows years ago, and a marriage license would only suggest somehow such vows were only recent.

Once they considered my question more, their practical nature finally swayed them to make it all legal at the courthouse. Mary-Alice's family mostly lived in what Caleb had referred to as his own parents' plausible deniability whenever they would see the "fine young man" Jaxon. That plausible deniability was crushed when the boys decided to marry.

I think this weighed on the girls more than anything else regarding actual marriage. Of course, Mary-Alice's family knew Jean and liked her very much, but the kind of relationship they had was *never* discussed. They couldn't imagine hidin' an actual marriage from them, but neither could they imagine informing them of such a decision.

Caleb, drawing from his own experience, told the girls, "They'll get over it."

I added, "If you look at Jaxon and Quinn's momma and Sis, you know the possibly is there. It's not guaranteed. It might introduce a whole new level of awkward, though you always have described your Burns family trips as time in purgatory, so I'm not too sure what you'd be sacrificing."

They made the decision to marry, and to do so in the chapel with Jaime officiating. He was still licensed, and as Billy pointed out, "He's experienced in gay weddings." Jaime didn't think there was a qualifier needed for that, but he did concede plenty of people still can't accept the notion of two people of the same sex making a life together. Some can look away as long as marriage isn't invoked — that is the step too far.

Mary-Alice's family was invited, and more came than didn't. None seemed to get all wound up about it. Some just didn't want to make the trip as they didn't feel that close to their sister anyway. Enough were comin' that we actually had to move the ceremony out onto the porch and ridge. The chapel was just too small.

Billy expressed the overflow as proof we'd all been waitin' for them to get their act together. After the ceremony, Mary-Alice's dad stood, lifting his champagne glass, and toasted, "Jean has been around us for so long we'd taken it for granted. Now, we get the chance to do something we should have done years ago. Jean, welcome to the family!"

It's fair to say, the only one more surprised than Jean to hear his words was Mary-Alice, who burst into tears.

Billy was sitting next to me and leaned over to whisper in my ear, "Here all these years, I didn't think a lesbian could cry. Shows what I know."

I gave a little whispered chuckle and added, "Lookin' at Jean, I still don't know if she can or not. She's the one you'd think would be in tears."

We had long recognized their "anniversary" which was the day when they first went on a date together. According to them, it was love at first sight. Since they had taken their jolly ol' time getting married, they decided to align the marriage to that anniversary date. As Jean noted, "We *don't* want two anniversaries."

They had their one big day, when all plausible deniability was put to rest once and for all. And in classic Jean and Mary-Alice fashion, they returned to their quiet accounting life in Marfa as though nothing in their world had changed—when in fact, in their minds and through their fidelity to each other, nothing had.

In Mark's remote support for computer systems, he is often working late at night doing system upgrades during his clients "off hours." Since such work has rather large gaps in the tasks needed as he waits for one thing to finish before he can go on to the next, he found himself spending that time looking at the night skies. He already knew, just from driving around the area, that many people had their own private observatories in addition to the large complex at McDonald. At 6,000 feet elevation, and with no city lights to illuminate the night skies, he and Zoey's homestead was a perfect fit for observation of the cosmos. He was inspired to get his own setup.

After quite a bit of research, he settled on an impressive astro-imaging computerized telescope, and at first, he just lugged it in and out whenever the weather and his schedule were aligned. Eventually, he had Jaxon and Caleb build an observatory to house this new toy.

We all benefited. For Christmas a couple years after he'd mastered its use, we all got a large framed print of different images from deep space. They are both amazing and beautiful. Daddy would have loved seeing the different "slices of the cosmos."

He shares its use with Noah, who from time to time, will spend a night exploring space. The foreman has made it clear to Noah that he'd better be "sharp and upright in the saddle" the next day or there *will* be consequences. So far, Noah has escaped any such consequences. What those might amount to is anyone's guess, and Billy won't say. Noah has said it might be Billy would dock his wages, but to do that he'd have to pay wages in the first place.

It's been a long runnin' joke between Jaime, Noah and Bill about Billy's wage payin'—or lack thereof. Billy contends if he paid wages, then it would only be right that Jaime and Noah pay rent, which given the quality of their accommodations and the splendid country in which they live, neither could ever afford—so clearly they are gettin' the better end of the deal.

As Bill is the payroll manager, technically Billy doesn't pay them any wages, but both are in fact taken care of well enough. Not surprisingly, we all go along with Billy's no wage payin' tale.

Here I go, wanderin' off the track into a Billy story.

Mark's new hobby inspired Zoey to take up her own. She was settled into her management of all the GS Ranches marketing and had her flock of chickens, which she tended, and from which we all got all of our eggs when they were layin'. Thanks to Jaime and Billy's anti-fox-and-coyote fencing, the birds were safe and sound.

Ready for another adventure of a kind, Zoey thought we "ranch girls" ought to take up knittin' as a joint hobby. You can see how wild we get with our adventures. I wasn't sure I'd make much of a knitter, but then I never thought I could quilt either, and it turned out, I had both the patience and interest to do that pretty well— maybe not quite to Lupe's high standard, but durn close. No one could hold a candle to her designs, but Sis has been "apprenticing" with her on the New Year's Day quilt projects.

We agreed we'd meet every Wednesday at Zoey and Mark's for our knitter's circle. None of us had ever knitted before, though Sis did some crochetin' years ago—making afghans. We would launch into this endeavor with a lot of trial and error, sometimes pulling out as much as we stitched together. At our first official meeting, we debated whether to invite the men of the ranch. We doubted any would want to bother, but we did think if Billy wasn't given an invitation, he'd have somethin' to say about it. We thought it might be worth the entertainment just to see what he would say and decided that was the route to take. We made sure Mark let the three "boys" know of our little weekly meetup.

After a month, we decided Billy was either plannin' somethin', or it had gone in one ear and out the other. On the fifth week, he and Jaime stopped by.

"I had to see exactly what you *conspirators* are up to over here," Billy started in. "You think because you're meeting over here at Zoey's, Jaime and I wouldn't notice you two were missing from the *Vista Grande* nursing home. You seem to have managed to get the headman to keep mum on the subject. He hasn't said a word about it."

I asked him, "Did you bring your knittin' needles? This ain't no gossip circle. If you're goin' to join us, you're expected to pull your weight."

"I don't think I'm gonna take up knittin', and I got Jaime *way* too busy for him to start."

"Tyranny abounds," Jaime muttered.

Billy continued as he handed us something Jaime had printed from a site off the Internet, "I'm here to give y'all purpose in life. Here's a group that accepts well-made stockin' hats and mittens for the needy. Now, if they are shippin' from this ranch, they'd better be top quality. If Neiman Marcus wouldn't sell it, you'd better pull it apart and start over."

Jaime added, "I know for a fact the foreman wants one of the hats for himself for the sake of 'QC'—quality control—before the first one gets shipped out."

"That's right!" Billy agreed, adding, "And for sure, Jaime and Noah need one too including who did which hat, so we can be sure we don't have one good knitter and two ringers. Aunt Sallie, you're good at a lot of things, but I gotta be convinced knittin' is a talent an ol' cowgirl can pick up at this late stage."

I showed him what I was workin' on. "Well, what do you think?"

He responded, "It looks pretty good—probably just needs a little more practice."

"Son, I think sending hats and mittens to the needy is a wonderful idea," Sis noted. "We'd talked about finding something like that to take on as a project, but our novice stitching didn't press us to get right on it."

Zoey added, "Billy, the foreman, never lacks for knowing what the next good job is to line up. We'll get organized and get our 'QC team' their three hats."

Billy continued, "One other thing, per the foreman's bylaws, we can't allow some closed society here. Could be Noah will still find a good man or a good woman to settle down with, and he or she might want to take up knittin' in their spare time. We'll leave you to it then," and he was out door.

We laughed and I said, "I didn't see that comin', but it was pure Billy."

The only thing left to do was get to work!

Now's a good time to circle back on some of Noah's story and his early years on the ranch. He was homeschooled after his momma was murdered and he moved to the ranch. He had five teachers. Bill, Sis and I stuck to an approved curriculum. Billy and Jaime provided OJT—on the job training—for ranch life, which included the never-ending chore of muckin' stables. He also apprenticed with me and Jaime on horseshoeing.

As he progressed in his studies, he was set on "graduating" early—graduation consisting of when we all believed he could pass the GED in his first run at it. After the GED was under his belt, he planned to work full time on the ranch and take a few courses he was interested in at Sul Ross. To his dismay, to get some of those courses he had to be a declared major, so he ended up in school a little more than he had planned. Still, once he took all the courses he had any real interest in, he quit.

Leadin' up to his GED graduation, Noah announced at the annual GS Ranches business meeting that he thought some consideration should be made—sooner rather than later—for his own house on the ranch. There was no rush, but he wanted to get it out there for consideration. We all realized the sense of what he was proposing, so long as it didn't involve an "early breeding program," as Billy put it. He assured us he was in no hurry to start a family. (He was only sixteen at the time.) Billy didn't see any point in waitin' to get started on a house, so Jaxon and Caleb got busy building a third adobe—this one nearest Geermann Cemetery Ridge.

Also, now is a good time to get back to the subject of Noah's realization of how dependent his mother had been on havin' a man's attention. While he was on campus at Sul Ross, he quickly found that another "Ag" student, a girl who shall remain unnamed, clung to him at every opportunity. At first, Noah rather liked the attention and pondered the possibility that perhaps he should take her advances seriously. Being an "Ag" student, she'd probably be okay bein' a ranch wife. However, as they began to date, he wondered if he was just following in his father's footsteps. Was he really attracted to her or just letting her attention toward him define their relationship?

The more she clung to him, the more he realized the hazards. She became possessive, and he felt like what he thought his dad must have felt with Olivia. He wanted space, and she wouldn't allow it. He broke it off early and as gently as he could.

At the same time, there was a boy who tended to sit next to Noah in their shared classes. They were friends of a kind and got along well enough. The boy was not a clinger, but when Noah broke up with the clinger, it became pretty clear this one wanted more than just a friendship. Noah respected the deep friendship that Billy and Jaime had forged in their life together, and he could imagine the same with this young man. When he laid out how his "uncles" lived, the boy said, "That sounds nice, but it's not for me."

Noah had even kidded with him, as Billy and Jaime had, on how some cold winter night or tent camping they might snuggle up and both enjoy it. It seemed the boy wanted both a nightly bed companion and some other life than bein' a cowboy. Any possible compromise on the first for Noah was forever thwarted by the second.

They remained friends, but the boy moved on for hopes of a different kind of relationship and a different kind of life from ranching.

Noah told us, "Uncle Billy sure lucked into the best kind of friendship. I don't seem to be having much luck so far in finding a wife or a friend who'd make a life with me."

He never did find one during his years of takin' classes.

We've laughed so many times at Billy's "lovin'" on Jaime in the Slo Poke Cafe and at their possibility of cuddlin' up on a cold night, I decided to ask Jaime something I'd kinda wanted to for a long time. I assured him that if they were in fact cuddlin' up on cold nights and just didn't want to say, I understood. If they weren't, I did wonder if they had seriously considered it.

He replied, "I'm glad to have shed most of my labels and just as glad to have quit trying to label others. I lost track of how many women I had sex with in my California days, which is pitiful in and of itself. A straight man can do that, and he's a 'real man.' Get intimate, even in a truly loving way with another man, and you're slapped with all manner of derogatory labels, judgment and abuse. But you know all that.

"Billy, the great lover, retains his 'purity'—which we've laughed about often enough—having kept himself, all those Van Horn years, from becoming someone's cowboy conquest.

"We both know if the sex meant something to one and not the other, we might well do irreparable harm to our friendship, and neither one of us is willing to risk it. Being playful in spirit is enough. A little measured restraint never killed anybody, and as Billy says, 'That's why God invented 'hot showers.'"

He laughed, "We have been known to hold hands on the couch even without an audience. That seems to be enough for us both. That and a good Billy hug—which we all need."

"Amen to that," I replied.

"And besides, we've made our vow until death us do part long ago. We couldn't have done that if our friendship wasn't already enough. It is enough. I wouldn't trade it for the world."

Mark was able to cut back on some of his remote database support while Noah was in school, so that he could help with chores on the ranch. He became a gen-u-ine cowboy-in-training, and he was a big help. By the time Noah was finished with his course work, Billy had the bright idea that he, Jaime and Noah needed to make a trip to El Salvador. They'd talked about it ever since Bill, Sis and I had made the trip, but it never seemed to be too serious a conversation. Bill was all for it, and it must be said, I could see he'd have liked to have gone along. He didn't want to impose himself on the boys and also couldn't see how Mark could handle things on his own without really dumping a lot on me.

I asked Bill about it, and he confirmed both his interest and why he didn't think he could go. I suggested we just look for some temporary help. Between Mark and I, we certainly knew the drill and could direct the hands as to what all needed doin'. I'd already told the boys I could stay over at Noah's, and let them dogs take care of me.

Finally, I planted the seed in Jaime's ear that I thought Bill would like to go with 'em. I knew he was the safe one of the three to tell rather than gettin' Billy and Noah all wound up. Jaime said he'd take care of extendin' the invitation. Bill and I always wanted reassurance from Jaime that whatever notion Billy had, Jaime was okay with it. That extended even to Bill having a conversation about takin' on Noah. Jaime had assured Bill then he was all in on raisin' the boy.

The invitation was extended, the date set and the backup hands lined up. Bill surprised us all when he floated the notion of stayin' for a month. Billy wasn't all that sure he wanted to go that long without a hot shower and eatin' mostly fish from the fish ponds the family had financed. They settled on three weeks, and set it for June, which also coincided with Noah's twentieth birthday.

I wish I'd have been along to see it firsthand. Bill's extended trip idea must have come from nature's symbiosis trying to set a plan in motion. *Padre Jesús* arranged for transportation from the airport to their mountain village through one of his parishioners, Antonio Vasquez, whose family owned a minivan. The Vasquezes had started a small "eco-tourism village" with half a dozen huts for guests to stay in. Restroom facilities were still shared, but to Billy's delight, they even had hot water. Billy announced, "We could have stayed a month after all, Dad."

The Vasquez enterprise also came with one other unexpected benefit—they had a twenty-one-year-old daughter named Mia. Bill, Billy and Jaime all said the same thing—it was love at first sight. Noah was smitten with Mia, and Mia was smitten with Noah. Billy told him he needed an older woman given how mature he was. Jaime didn't think one year was much of a difference, particularly as it was really only about six months—about the same difference in their own ages. Bill asserted age didn't matter one way or the other, but clearly their extended stay had its purpose.

Thanks in no small part to *Padre Jesús* and the Vasquez family's interest in starting the eco huts, the good *padre* had taught them all a good deal of English. Between my Spanish lessons with Noah and Jaime's bilingual past, the conversations fluctuated back and forth in their own version of "Texican" Spanish modified to fit the local dialect.

Now is as good a time as any to note where some of the financial assistance originally came from for the eco huts. Bill, the El Paso bishop and young Chuy—*Padre Jesús*—had set up a fund through the Franciscan order for grants and micro-loans to be distributed in the remote villages across El Salvador. The dual purpose of these funds was setting up businesses, and providing solar technologies for electricity and hot water for businesses and private dwellings. Young Chuy was the official trustee of these funds. The Geermann-Schlatters made annual donations to keep it going. When Ernesto and Rosalinda learned of the fund, they "shook down" (as Ernesto put it) all the Cardonas to add to it as well. Of course, the Vasquez family had no idea when Bill, Billy, Jaime and Noah arrived that they were hosting their benefactors.

Billy's hot water came from the grant funds for the solar hot water system as did the huts they themselves slept in.

It became pretty apparent during the first week that either GS Ranches was going to lose their intended future foreman, or the Vasquez enterprise was going to lose their oldest daughter to a Texas ranch. Before they arrived, *Padre Jesús* had certainly made it known to all the Vasquez family of the deep admiration the Cardonas had for the Schlatter family, and how despite their age difference, he and Bill had a special friendship. They had met Bill briefly on his previous visit, and the Schlatter family photo still hung in the medical clinic next to the Cardona family photo *Padre Jesús* had added. Underneath the pictures he had placed a note that didn't give away their roles as financial benefactors. It stated,

Nuestras familias de Texas que nos mantienen en sus oraciones

Translated, "Our Texas families who keep us in their prayers."

Bill made it clear to Noah that if the relationship turned into something serious, Noah and Mia's wishes would be respected. He shouldn't feel he had to forsake her for the sake of the ranch.

Billy added, "I'm not one to go against the wise counsel of my elders—and certainly not the headman, himself. He's right, of course, but that doesn't mean it would be easy for you or for us!"

The only thing settled before they left were plans for Mia and her mother to make a trip to Texas in about a month's time—a trip that would almost certainly determine if marriage was the next step or not, and where such a marriage might take root.

Kola, Koala and I had a good time together while the boys were gone. They were no spring chickens. Noah had dog beds for them as neither could easily pop up on his bed anymore. The three of us had all the ol'-ranch-lady kinks to work out in the morning. We were well matched. I told Noah when he got back that I thought they needed to come to the "rest home" with me so they could join me in retirement and we could grow old together. He said Kola and Koala had told him of my plan and that they didn't want to impose. Could be their bladders might get to leakin', and Grandma wouldn't want dog pee on her floors. The dogs were right about Sis not wanting dog pee in the house, so I decided I'd give up the idea, which I was never serious about in the first place. The boy and his dogs were not going to be separated. Billy couldn't have even persuaded the dogs to move back with him and Jaime.

When I heard all about Mia, I did wonder what we'd do if Noah moved to El Salvador. I wondered in equal measure what we'd do about the dogs. Movin' them to a foreign country seemed like a lot to ask of geriatric canines. I know it would be too much for this old geriatric. If Noah was gone, I was pretty sure they were going to feel abandoned, though I knew they'd be well cared for by their former masters. Funny all the things that run through your mind when it looks like change is going to be imposed upon you.

I recalled the wise words of my brother-in-law, who had noted, "I have heard it said that one of the most extraordinary aspects of our humanity is the capacity to learn, to grow and to change. To that I would add, it is certainly true that the most *common* aspect of our humanity is an *unwillingness* to learn, grow and change. Suffering often moves us to the extraordinary, while comfort—at least a tolerance of the status quo—leaves us mired in our unwillingness to allow for what can be."

I replayed those words, as I knew we needed to let the extraordinary happen even if it rocked our status quo. One thing was for certain, if Mia and Noah married, one family or the other was going to be forced into change—ready or not.

Soon, "ready or not" faced us on *another* front. Bill and the boys had only been home a week when Rosalinda called Jaime one morning to let us know Lupe had died. Like her mother, Elma, she died quietly sitting in her favorite chair—TV still on from whatever she'd been watching the night before. Rosalinda had made a habit every morning of calling her oldest in-law, and when Lupe didn't answer the phone, she went right over to check on her.

We all knew how hard her death would be for Jaime. Chuy and Lupe had literally been his lifelines from his very first days in Fort Davis. They would say, even after his moving to the ranch, "You're a Cardona." I believe in his heart, Jaime saw himself much more a Cardona than the Cruz he was. The Cardonas *were* a family in the best sense, while the name he bore was little more than a legal surname from a dysfunctional mess—something he could never rightly call a family, save for the one sibling with whom was able to forge a new life together—both *far* removed from the toxicity of their childhood.

The long-promised graveside music from Noah, Billy and Jaime was provided. Ernesto, who had never fully recovered from his hard bout of laryngitis, had recovered enough to get through "How Great Thou Art." According to him, he could muster about one song before his voice would give out again—even then only if the range wasn't too extreme.

Following the committal, we stepped away, leaving Jaime by the grave to bid a tearful farewell to the woman who'd been far more a mother to him than his own had *ever* been. Ernesto went over to Jaime and stood in silence with his arm around him. After a minute, Ernesto gave Jaime a big hug, let loose enough to take Jaime's head in his hands and kissed him on the forehead. We couldn't see that either ever spoke a word.

Bill whispered to me, "Is there anything that can move one to tears more than when somebody crazy like Ernesto or Billy knows when the only thing to be done is to stand quietly and embrace you?"

I didn't need to answer that and couldn't have if I'd wanted to. I couldn't have gotten out a single word right in that moment.

Mia and her mother, Maria, arrived for their own three-week visit just a month after the others were back from their trip. There was some debate as to the best accommodations for them, and it was decided, for the sake of their own privacy, to have them stay in the bunkhouse. Sis and I spruced it up, and we had it looking more homey than the old place had ever looked.

Mia's *papá* would have liked to have joined them but felt their fledging family business demanded he tend to matters at home. He gave his blessings to the trip and whatever its outcome.

Noah said to me, "Whither she goest, I will go, but I sure don't want to leave this ranch. I've got to be sure my heart is open to moving there if that's what it takes."

They knew from their time in El Salvador that Mia loved horses. Long rides were already in the plan—both group rides and rides for the young lovers. Billy suggested when it was time to ascertain intentions, there was no better spot than the big outcropping. As the second week was ending, Noah and Mia headed there to talk. They were gone a long time. Billy and Jaime were at *Vista Grande*, as we all eagerly awaited the young lovers' return.

After three hours, Billy said, "Either they've got a lot to talk about, or they may just be exploring their carnal desires. Jaime and I didn't take near so long to decide, but then I couldn't persuade him into explorin' any such pleasures."

"Good lord," Bill muttered. "It's a good thing Mother has Maria off with her prayin' in the chapel."

When they did finally make their way back to the house, we were all summoned to the dining room table where Sis quickly set out a few snacks and iced tea she had prepared for their return. Noah's very serious look was hard to decipher. Was it for the bad news that he'd be leaving the ranch, or the sad news that he'd be stealing the Vasquez daughter for life on a distant ranch in Texas. There could be no quick and frequent trips given the isolation of the mountain ranch and the mountain village, which even as the crow flies, is more than 1,500 miles. A multi-day driving trip which none us would be comfortable making—unless absolutely necessary—was also not practical. Even flying involved long drives on each end with at least two flight changes. One family or the other was going to deal with a lot of separation—made only a bit easier by the advances in recent years in communication technologies on both ends. Still, far from ideal for the closeness to which their family and ours was so accustomed to.

Mia sat with her mother to her left and Noah to her right. She held the hand of each. It was Mia who would announce their intentions.

There is no point adding any drama to the tellin'. I let the cat out of the bag when I first said it was Noah who came to me tellin' me to write my stories. All I'll add is that mother, daughter and son-in-law-to-be wept in the tellin', stood to embrace us all and sat back down to plan the wedding. Noah would travel there to be married by *Padre Jesús*. He would ask Jaxon and Aiden to be his "two best men;" both of whom made the trip. He hoped his dad, Bill and Sis would travel for the ceremony as well. Billy and Jaime had already worked out with Noah that if the wedding was in El Salvador, the two of them would stay behind to tend the ranch—stressing it was more important for his grandparents to be there, and me, if I wanted to go. I did go with the small Texas herd, even though I thought I was gettin' a little too long in years to make the trip. I survived, though my long-distance-travel days are now officially over. I *might* go as far as Alpine to the bookstore. That's about it!

No one saw any point in takin' any longer to get 'er done than travel arrangements would dictate, so our herd was there within three weeks. I suppose the good *Padre* broke the rules a bit by not making Noah "convert," though I'm not sure Franciscans get quite as hung up on "the rules" as some orders and certainly most priests.

After the wedding everyone came home but the newlyweds. Noah spent another month with the Vasquez family before uprooting Mia and transplanting her onto the Geermann-Schlatter ranch.

As it turned out, it was an unforeseen Geermann instant plan in action after the fact. The world was suddenly hit with something called Covid, and went into lockdown. Once settled in Texas, Mia couldn't have gone home even if she'd wanted to. Still, we linger under the shadow of that pandemic. For how much longer is anyone's guess.

With all the runnin' of the roads and the tourists that come out here, we knew it was only a matter of when, and not if, the virus would get here. We determined at the outset, that only a prideful fool would pretend they were somehow immune. And I never did like being sick. Dyin' in a hospital on a ventilator ain't my idea of the way to go. We exercised caution from the get-go.

Of course, not runnin' to town never was a problem for me. Billy and Jaime would still go in twice a month to work at the food pantry and have lunch with Ernesto and Rosalinda at the Slo Poke Cafe, but even they decided that needed to take a back seat for a while. Poor Sara and the Slo Poke owners are suffering in the short run as the tourism has dropped off.

In comparison to the cities, things are pretty tame here, but people are catchin' it, and some are not comin' out the other side. Rogelio Cardona is dead from it, and only the immediate family attended his burial. Ernesto and Rosalinda both had it—probably caught it from him—and were miserably sick for a good three weeks, but it looks like they're gonna make it.

Ernesto told Bill on the phone, "It was one *helluva* ride! I wouldn't wish it on anyone. Well, maybe a *cabrón* or two come to mind."

Several are still touch and go. So far, all the Schlatter crew has been lucky.

Sis's old church group never has been able to pay a minister much of anything since Sis and the other main benefactors, Ava and Dew, quit going. The young minister hired right after the snake oil salesman left town "heard a new calling" when the budget dropped. Their latest preacher was "raised up" from within the congregation and works as a plumber when he's not in the pulpit. He has persuaded the group that Covid is a hoax. Well, the hoax has caught up with him, and I hear he is in Midland on a ventilator

—not likely to make it. Maybe that'll wake that group up, but I doubt it.

Noah and Mia have faired okay despite the pandemic. So far, her family hasn't been impacted by the virus—health-wise. We'll hope those in *Padre Jesús's* parish make it through it all. El Salvador doesn't seem to be as hard hit as some in their neck of the woods. For that we are thankful. Of course, it isn't helping business at the eco huts, but if there is one trait those villagers share, it is resilience. They possess that in spades—takin' each day as it comes.

Noah, who promised the family back when his house was first built that he wouldn't start any early breeding program, quickly settled into his changing world, with a wife whose world was changing so much more than his. And with the two of them, the two dogs—by Noah's side since the day he arrived nearly twelve years ago.

Noah and Mia's first year of marriage was a year of sorrows and joys. Mia adjusted well enough to her new surroundings—her new life. Once a week, they would "Facetime" with her family all thanks to the solar power and satellite connection at the eco huts. Covid barred any possible travel between the families, but "lockdown" otherwise didn't affect much of the day-to-day life on the ranch.

I guess the dogs knew their work for the boy's welfare was done. Kola developed an inoperable schwannoma, which finally rendered her unable to lift her hind end, as it was between her two back legs. The vet in Fort Davis had to put her down. She was no sooner buried than Koala started losing weight and getting very weak. The vet diagnosed liver failure, which she said was quite common in an old dog. Koala soon quit eating, and before her organs began to shut down completely, she too was put down to spare her any suffering.

It took no persuasion for Noah to convince us that we needed to bury the dogs up on Geermann Cemetery Ridge. We left plenty of room around Nellie's grave for any horse that made it to the ridge rather than the horse cemetery, and the boys roped off a little patch to the east of the family graves for the dogs and any other pets that might end up there.

Lord, have mercy—we all sure were attached to them dogs. Of all the creatures in our lives, only Nellie's death was harder for me, and for Noah, Billy and Jaime their deaths were harder than for any horse they'd buried before. To lay those sweet little faces in the ground and cover them up was *damn hard*.

At Kola's Christian burial, Bill rightly spoke for us all, while Koala stood by Noah's side. "When it comes to unconditional love, the dogs taught us what poor role models we are." Looking at Koala he added, "And when it comes to intuition of a young boy's needs, they bonded with the boy in an instant."

It had been less than six months from diagnosis to their burial. As Noah had observed those years ago when Elma died, the big hole could now only be filled little by little with memories of the dogs—of which there were many.

Noah said, "I'm not sure I'll know how to eat popcorn without two dogs to catch what I toss their way."

Jaime recalled, "There was that time when they were just pups, and before we had sense enough to throw rawhides all over the house, they chewed up Billy's dress cowboy boots. Oh, he was mad then!"

Billy replied, "Them damn boots were too fancy anyhow, and the dogs knew they needed to go in the burn barrel!"

Jaime added, "One look at those faces, and you just couldn't stay mad at 'em."

Billy chuckled. "That's an understatement."

Mia reflected, "I hardly had any time to spend with Kola and Koala, and they had to size me up before even letting me pet them. Seeing how this family buries its pets tells me all I need to know. Noah's roots are deep. I'm glad to grow alongside him."

I smiled and said, "I think we'll keep you!"

Billy added, "That's right. We specialize in keepers. No throwaways in this bunch!"

Noah surprised us when he then announced, "Speaking of keepers, there's a little Vasquez-Schlatter on the way!"

Over the years, Noah, Billy and Jaime had continued their Holy Saturday egg dying with Lupe which they had done ever since Elma's death—the artistic Easter eggs that were such a part of Lupe and Elma's lifelong symbol of devotion to those they loved. Lupe had suggested in later years that they cut down the quantity but never the quality of their annual creations. The big Easter family gathering had diminished over the years, and the younger kids comin' along were far more interested in candy than the gift of beautiful eggs from the long tradition.

As the second Easter after Lupe's death approached, Noah gathered those of us living at the ranch for a consult. He thought the tradition of the elaborate egg decoration needed to continue along with Elma's deviled eggs. Lupe had shared the recipe with Jaime who had already assumed the role as our chief deviled egg maker.

Noah said, "Now, Jaime doesn't ever want to do the decorating, but he is the master boiler and water dumper. We need to decide how many we are going to do and where they will all go."

Bill replied, "For sure we need to have big baskets ready for the Schlatter diaspora in Marfa, Alpine and Fort Davis, and maybe Aiden and Pamela's bunch too if they happen to wander over here during Easter."

"That's gonna mean quite a few eggs since I plan to take some to Ernesto and Rosalinda, some to the other Cardonas and some to the volunteers at the food pantry," Noah added.

"If we're going to do some for the pantry volunteers maybe we should do at least a half-dozen basket full for each household," Billy suggested.

Jaime, who was our longest-serving food pantry volunteer, rightly noted, "That would be a lot of eggs. We'd even exceed what Elma and Lupe did in their heyday, but we potentially have more help than they ever had."

I interjected, "With this virus, if we can pull it off, it would be kinda an article of faith—offer the families that little bit of hope we all could use right now."

Zoey responded, "I don't know about Mark, but I'm all in. It sounds like a wonderful idea and a tradition worth preserving."

"I'm sure I can do something even if it's just collecting sprigs of things and dead bugs—those I seem to recall are elements of the design," Mark noted.

Jaime added, "Lupe once told me how as a little girl Elma would work in anything she collected from the yard—so yes, we need some dead bugs!"

Sis exclaimed, "I do believe we have just taken on a new family tradition! I'm delighted. Noah, where are we going to organize the Easter bunny's workshop?"

Billy suggested, "We'll do it at our place. We don't want the mess in this house or the other two newer houses. Best to keep it at *Casa Vieja*. Besides, we've got the biggest kitchen to work in."

"Of course, I should have consulted with the foreman. What was I thinking, asking Noah?" his mother asked.

Noah joked, "Really Grandma! What *were* you thinking?!"

Billy said, "I did just kinda jump in there, didn't I? I was just trying to volunteer Jaime before he could weasel out of it."

Jaime laughed, "I know you were worried about me slackin' off, if we did it somewhere else."

I just added, "Jaime, as I've heard you say before, tyranny abounds! I guess I'd better get to collectin,' if I'm gonna stay on the good side of the foreman."

One of Lupe's lasting gifts were her meticulous quilts. She had still made one for every child born in Fort Davis. Ever since Billy and Jaime launched their New Year's Day movie marathon and Lupe joined Sis, Jean and me in starting the quilt for Anna Catherine on New Year's Day (and whatever days it took to finish after that), we cranked out quilts for everyone in the family. This included Jaxon and Caleb; Quinn and Jay; Aiden and Cynthia and their son, Ryder; and Pamela and her three children, Alina, Josiah and Colton. We also did one for Zoey and Mark. On the cold winter nights, all were kept warm by one of Lupe's creations.

Lupe had assured us quilting neophytes early on, "I had to pull out the few stitches Chuy made, and I told him he probably had better things to do outside. I'm not going to pull any of yours out unless you're as clumsy as he was with a needle."

She had always looked forward to when she could make a quilt for any children Noah might have. She would not live to make the quilt for the baby due around Christmas, but we would be sure to spend our New Year's doing so with the same love and care she put into every stitch.

Year one of Covid ended with new life in the Schlatter family. Aiden and Cynthia had the birth of their second, a daughter, Sophia Isabella Schlatter, on Christmas Day.

The Christmas Day birth reminded Jaime of where the notion came from that Ernesto should be a priest. He too was born on Christmas, and his *mamá* took his Christmas birth as a sign he should be a priest.

Billy announced that he hoped Sophia would look like Sophia Loren when she grew up as he always thought the actress was "the cat's meow."

Bill smiled at Billy's comments regarding Ms. Loren, adding his own. "Now, if she'd have wandered across my path those many years ago, you might have a different mother, though if I'd been open to an older woman, Lena Horne could have given her some competition."

Sis exclaimed, "I had no idea I was so far down the list!"

Noah and Mia celebrated the birth of Emilio Jesús Schlatter on December 31st. It would seem the possibility for life on this old ranch might make it another generation—if not in its present form, maybe of a kind, a lifetime from now. We can't know the future, and no one in this family was going to impose their notion of what Emilio's life should be or the life of whatever other siblings come along after him.

With his first look at the child, Bill stated, "I'm not going to brag, but I think that child looks a lot like my baby pictures, except he's got his momma's gorgeous complexion and bright dark eyes. I guess those eyes could be the Geermann *or* the Vasquez in him—probably both."

Billy took a good look and said, "Yea, those eyes could be Geermann, and he's got my fat cheeks. But I'm still the only one with a real hind end."

Noah replied, "Uncle Billy, you're a mess!"

To which Jaime added, "Noah, now he's not just our mess, but little Emilio's too."

Bill muttered, "Well, there's plenty o' mess to go 'round."

It was during "lockdown" when early in the new year, Bill received a very unexpected and rather long letter. It was from his youngest niece, Becka, whom he had never heard from before. She had waited a long time to marry, but soon had three children, as the husband's main objective seemed to be to produce a son, but alas, could only spawn daughters. Not unlike Zoey's experience with her ex (the wildly popular executive), this husband was obviously every bit the abusive narcissist Zoey had endured.

Becka explained her reasons for contacting Bill as coming from her recollection of how, when she was a small child, Bill had reminded her of her grandfather, whom she had admired a great deal. Then, she used a word that rather surprised him regarding her own father—Bill's only brother. "My father lived in a general state of oblivion. I couldn't talk to him about anything serious when he was alive, and Mom is not much better."

If it was all right with Bill, she would like to email him from time to time just to have someone older and wiser to talk to. She included her email address, and she noted that she did not want to correspond by mail that her husband could intercept. She felt her email was much more secure. Bill quickly responded—including his phone number, if she ever wanted or needed to call. He also made it clear that she could come to the ranch anytime, and if things got worse with her husband, he would do whatever she thought would be helpful to their situation.

He let Sis and me read the letter. He noted, "I guess the Schlatter side owns Brett's years of oblivion. Here I tried to blame it on the Geermanns. It appears it runs in my family."

Sis's immediate reaction at reading the letter was, "Those poor girls."

I shook my head in general disgust, saying, "A complete control freak. Another abusive man. When will the cycle end?"

"I dare say, the way she spells it out so thoroughly, his abuse rises to the level of toxicity as Jaime would put it," Bill added.

"Too true—too true," I said.

Sis noted, "As to your claim on Schlatter oblivion, I was oblivious for more than two decades so apparently it is a common flaw in our gene pool on both sides."

"It permeates the species," I suggested.

"There is plenty of evidence to that effect, I'll grant," Bill agreed.

The day after the letter arrived and our subsequent discussion of it, we were sitting in the living room when we heard a cracklin' sound coming from the porch side of the room. We looked to see the outside pane of one of the patio doors shattering, as tempered glass does, but without a single piece of glass falling out.

Bill said, "One little strain too many on some weak spot, I guess. A good gust and that glass will be all over the porch." He went on the porch to knock it out, swept up the pile of fragments and called a glass company in Fort Stockton to come and measure the replacement needed.

As he worked on the cleanup, clearly, his mind was turning. He came back in, sat down in his chair without sayin' a word, and began to scribble in his notebook. When he finished, he put the pen down and said, "I'm calling this 'Tempered Glass.' If you think it's all right, I'll send it to her."

I am a sheet of tempered glass.
The blows I take do not break me.
Yet I know that the smallest stress,
in the weakest place, may well send me
into a thousand pieces.

This is the life I live now.
It cannot be walked away from
without great risk to those I love—
those I have brought into this world.
It is only for them I stay.

When they are old enough
to understand—to help in the choice—
then we will escape the oppression

of the present time for hope
of brighter days and years.

The day cannot come soon enough,
yet that day often seems too far away
to hold out the hope that is needed.
If time flies, there are times it
does not fly fast enough.

My life, at present, plods endlessly on.
I am luckier than some.
The blows I take are verbal, emotional
though a battered body, by law,
could bring a quicker end.

The hardened shell now
slowly enveloping my life
is not the answer to my prayers,
but until those prayers are answered
it must do to get me through.

I put my hands in the soil
to plant flowers that will
remind me the good seed
will flourish if nourished.
They bring beauty to my day.

I cook with love for the
nourishment and joy it will
bring my children who must
know all is not well in
the abode in which they dwell.

I take them into the sunshine,
and together we delight in our
momentary freedom from
the dark that now envelops
our days, our nights, our dreams.

Sis spoke first. "Bill, she will know how carefully you read her letter and how much care you wish to convey to her in her situation. Yes, I think you should email it to her."

All I added was, "I'm with Sis."

We were of one mind. If she ever needs to come here with her daughters for a respite or a new life, we shall welcome her.

When I started to hear about cryptocurrency, I went to the one source I thought might be able to explain it to me—Bill.   As I suspected, he had read up on it, and he came away as baffled as I was.

"Somebody well beyond my pay grade will have to explain if it is actually anything more than a legalized-gambling-shell game," he replied.   "I suspect it is little more than another greed-driven market to be manipulated. I suppose its creators, with a bit of an anarchist spirit, may have envisioned upsetting the global financial system, but it doesn't take long for greed to imagine the possibilities."

Noah was visitin' with us at the time and asked, "Since all the money moves around the world in digital transactions anyway, wouldn't it be better to just have one world currency?"

"We have enough of that now with the trading in dollars," Bill explained. "Lesser economies on the Euro suffered more during the economic meltdown due, in no small part, to their inability to compete with the German industrial powerhouse which could weather the storm and dictated the Euro monetary policy.   They were clobbered with 'austerity measures' as they called it.   Of course, that means passin' the buck to the people for the mess created by the powerful—be they bankers, politicians or both.

"We use our sanctions and the power of the all-mighty dollar to grind countries into desperation.

"No doubt, the richest would love one world currency, so long as they alone could control it—just like one billionaire would like to dictate agricultural policy for the entire world.

"I think we need more currencies not fewer—some have even tried local currencies at the city level just to keep the money in the community. I suppose if these were set up as crypto exchanges somehow, that might work, but local currencies I don't guess will ever win much of a following.   People like to move around too much, but it has merits in my book.

"I'll grant that money being the root of all evil, there is not now, never was and never shall be a greed-proof, just and egalitarian financial system. The best you can do is regulate it to protect the weakest. Something this country has never excelled at, and it has only degraded further over the past thirty-plus years."

"To our peril," I added.

I was reflecting on this conversation when I was taken back to Bill's comments on the starvation in China after Mao implemented radical changes in a perfect storm aligned with natural disasters. You cannot approach life without risks. However, risks on a small scale are always better than risks on a global scale.

Somehow, we seem to overlook that detail just a little bit too conveniently. After all, it is the "big risk takers" that reap the "big rewards." If they happen to have the "good fortune" of lax laws and generous governments to bail out their asses, then the big risk takers' only real risk is to keep their game just inside the legal lines to stay out of jail when it all goes to hell in a handbasket. They don't even have to worry about failure. Their friends in government will bail them out for "our sake." "Too big to fail," they call it.

I rather like the laudable ethic—"first do no harm." I'm not at all sure that the large medical industry these days lives within its inherent constraint. There is certainly evidence to the contrary in my book. Not only do I wish that doctors and hospitals would live up to it, but I truly wish it applied to land, forest and water management as well as to laws and government programs. I'm hard pressed to think of where such an ethic would *not* apply. Sis's preacher could have saved this family a *lot* of heartache had *he* applied it!

There are too many in this world, for reasons I can't understand, who find it necessary to first do harm even in their own families and casually, carelessly—deliberately—against the world around them as they turn everything they touch into toxic excrement. Let's just call a spade a spade. They are louts, and louts abound.

On the small family scale of this problem, how can I *not* think of Jaime and Zoey. It's been a few years now since they wrote their last letter to their long-split-up parents. Having never received even a short note, let alone a kind letter or phone call, they resigned themselves to move on and stop trying to connect with them.

Mark still diligently looks for death notices in their local online news where it is presumed each still lives. As far as we know, they live on, and given their lack of response, are probably as miserable as ever. I've decided "lout" is as good a descriptor for them as any. It is remarkable to me that they wallow in their sins, and it is equally remarkable to me how a little love pulled my now niece (Zoey) and nephew (Jaime) of a kind, out of that mess to reveal the absolute gems they are. They are true testaments to the power of love.

Jaime said to me once about his parents, "What might their lives have been, if somewhere in their early marriage, a Chuy and Lupe had given them a nudge in the right direction. I can't imagine how different things might have been."

"You are right, of course, but this family would be down three good souls," I stated rather selfishly. "We are the beneficiaries of their poor choices."

"Mark had none of the baggage to unload that Zoey and I had," Jaime replied. "He, in fact, was as instrumental in her healing as the Cardonas and the Geermann-Schlatters were in my own.

"I know she would say the same—I can't imagine another life now, apart from the one I have. 'Grace upon grace,' as Betsy would say."

Remembering his working days with Ernesto, he added, "Ernesto liked to tease me, saying once that if I ever started acting like my parents he would 'fire my ass.' I told him, if I ever did, to take me to the vet and have me put down—put me out of my and everyone else's misery. He said that would cost him too much to put down a bull my size—he'd just back over me with his John Deere. Then he could take the backhoe and bury the evidence right away."

I chuckled and said, "I guess he never had to put that plan o' his into action."

Jaime smiled, "I have resisted imitating my parents in any way, shape or form since arriving in Fort Davis. May thus it be for all my remaining days!"

May thus it be.... I wish I had the assurance that our now-healed family could forever be immune to fracturing again. Life has its own heavy measure of grief and loss without all the too common self-inflicted harm. It is pure naiveté to even entertain the notion that we are now immune to such fracturing and estrangement. Harm can come in an instant or by gradualism. I can't imagine it *ever* coming again to any of Sis' children and our "family of a kind." But in my dark moments, I have deep concern for Brett's grandchildren and those who will be his great-grandchildren, if and when they come along—and for all the children of the world, it must be said. The wrong crowd, the zealots—religious, political and social—mental illness, addiction, the lure of fame and fortune, and a whole host of other influences, are like the barbarians at the gates waitin' to drag off some poor, vulnerable soul.

One can only pray that with a little humility and gratitude for all that abounds in this world, the generations to come will keep the barbarians out, and our world leaders don't destroy all that is. They sure as hell seem determined to do so.

I begin each year in hope that we shall awaken to *some kind* of a new history. It is hardly an assurance of a "happy new year," but like all years preceding, I find joy in the simple moments through the inherent beauty that still thrives around me—this world of beauty which is ours to cherish, and not ours to destroy.

One night at dinner, Momma shared the news of a man from their church who had "blown his brains out."

Daddy was saddened by the news but not surprised, noting, "Life, as defined by him, had been a series of unfortunate events unencumbered by any responsibility for his own history. He also suffered from his apparent inability to move beyond his feelings. Feelings for him—and for too many, it must be said—were his validation that something was true."

Daddy didn't lack for wise words. Whether those were his own or the words of some other wise soul, I cannot say. However, those words in particular stuck with me as I pondered the depth of them over and over. I still ponder them.

I have certainly tried to live in the full awareness of my own history and that of our ranch, our county, our state and our nation. To the degree possible, I have tried to safeguard against claiming any possession of absolute truth derived from my mood and feelings. Nature's symbiosis and plenty of contemplation have persuaded me that if the preacher, politician or press proclaims truth—beware! They define the "straight and narrow" to our peril. Thanks to Daddy, I've learned that if what they say seems contradictory to the great cosmos, the cosmos is not wrong—they are. Facing that one fact could have vindicated many a "heretic."

And thanks to Momma, I have the Sermon on the Mount as my ethical guide—yet to be improved upon by any who have followed the carpenter from Nazareth.

Then, there is the symbiosis between land and the local economy that seems to me is too often ignored. The price of land bears no correlation to its economic viability these days. We could certainly cash out, and let someone with more money than they know what to do with own this ranch. I doubt they would ever live out here. They might show up to show it off to others once or twice a year—or a few times a decade until they lost all interest. More likely, we'd just become some "high-end" huntin' ranch for those escapees from the big Texas cities—our houses decked out with a bunch of stuffed heads of dead animals, a few cowhide rugs and a cowhide chair or two. No doubt some deer hide footstool. Maybe they could stuff me, and stand me in a corner as some relic of the bygone era of family ranchin'. I'd probably look pretty good—if they kept me dusted. We get a lot of dust in the air here on those windy days in the spring. Dusted or not, then they'll wonder why everyone thinks the place is haunted—'cause I will haunt them if I have any power to do so. Well, maybe not. I might find hauntin' duties pretty boring.

Some people just have to own as much of anything and everything as possible. Braggin' rights for ownin' a large west Texas ranch seems to be in vogue at the moment. I suppose there are worse outcomes for remote land like ours, but I just happen to be of a mind that we either need to use our land wisely for agricultural means where possible, or get serious about depopulating remote regions like this and let nature take it all back. The mix of moving people in and cattle out doesn't make sense to me, but I am just an ol' cowgirl. What do I know?

The global population they say will hit ten billion by 2100. That's four billion more mouths to feed over just one century. Growing the population and shrinking agricultural land sounds like a recipe for disaster, but I guess the "smart people" will know just what to do. They are doin' just a fine job already!

I can't say I've ever felt my life was defined as following one path—let alone, a straight and narrow path, that's for sure! I might be limpin' toward the valley of the shadow of death, but I shall fear no evil, though evil abounds. From my birth, this ranch has defined my life. I can't know what new paths lie ahead. It must be said, I never could see past the end of my nose with any reliability. Yet lookin' back, I find it all quite extraordinary. The people who now define our family here—from the strays we've rounded up for the past two-plus decades—and this beautiful world, and the delight of all its creatures will see me out, whatever paths, now unseen, lie ahead.

One of the few men that came to Quiet Day was a fine calligrapher, James, who was one of the brothers that bought Bill and Sis's old house in town. I asked him to "pen me" a quote I had, which I then bought a frame to fit. I keep it hangin' behind my desk in "Jaime's room." Actually, the first inspired a second—both of which still hang there.

The first was a quote by Oscar Wilde. "To live is the rarest thing in the world. Most people exist, that is all."

The other was said to be a favorite of Mr. Lincoln. "This too shall pass."

Wilde's quote certainly represents what lies deep inside me, as I have sought to live and not just exist. The second reminds me that joy can turn to sorrow in an instant, and that however wonderful my life is, it will pass. I have only "now" to be who I was born to be in the fullness of creation.

When Noah instructed me to get on with it, I thought laying out memories would be a slow and tedious task to keep me occupied for the next two or three years. In reality, every day I got out of bed, I knew the next story or two of what I wanted to write out. This has taken me rather by surprise, and I suppose what I'm passin' on is a *Cliff'sNotes* version of my life. I've tried reading some other autobiographies and biographies, and my own "memoirs" don't stack up to those that dig deep into every nook and cranny of one's life.

I said to Bill once, "I'm givin' up on these. I thought I'd really like 'em. I'll have to leave 'em to you historians, as I don't need to know what pen they used or what underwear they wore on some particular day."

It seemed to me some get just a little too granular in their tellin', as though every detail is life or death. And save for only their greatness has the world gone on. In those memoirs, I knew enough before startin' out that they had no repentance for the things they should have been repentant for. If they had been a little sorry for their sins, their account might have settled with me better.

You'll have to pardon my own story where you think I was too general, or where for the sake of my reliving of an event, I might have gotten too detailed myself. I have enough sense to acknowledge that, if I had never lived, the world in all its beauty would have gone on without me. The fact that I could experience that beauty and the love that keeps it going is the greatest joy of my life.

I never did keep a journal or even a diary as a young girl. My memories are a collection of loose artifacts, not given easily to sequential documentation. I assume the boys know me well enough to have some idea of the kind of stories I would convey. I hope this at least halfway measures up to what they had in mind. Surely, they may have hoped for more in the old family histories, but I just don't have much more I could say on that. We had so much ahead of us to work for and delight in, looking back just never occurred to us.

As Noah rightly observed, I'd been doing a lot of readin' since I settled here in *Vista Grande*. Those memoirs and biographies I thought would be so interesting quickly bored me. I've taken to reading anything and everything written by Wendell Berry—any good agrarian's kindred soul. Thanks to Bill's influence, I've taken to reading a lot more poetry, which, of course, Berry has plenty of, but I enjoy a number of poets. One of those I've grown quite fond of is Mary Oliver, who I'd never heard of but stumbled upon while in the Alpine bookstore. A few lines of her poem, "When Death Comes," stick with me.

... I look upon time as no more than an idea
and I consider eternity as another possibility
... I think of each life as a flower
... each body a lion of courage, and something
precious to the earth
I don't want to end up simply having visited this world

Mercy! That pretty well sums it up for me.

Billy is a true believer that if we were "doin' life right" we would have heaven on this earth instead of the hell that dominates in too many desecrated places. Indeed, Berry is right when he says, "There are no sacred and un-sacred places. There are only sacred and desecrated places."

His notion carries me to my own long-held belief that there is no distinction between spiritual and secular. Too many religious try to corner the word spiritual for their own narrow use. Too many nonreligious don't want spirituality polluting their notion that there is no soul. I'm content to say everything is spiritual just as everything is sacred. Until someone can explain all the mysteries of the cosmos and, in doing so, disprove the soul, then I shall stand by my view that whatever it is the soul might be, we all have one. And I don't limit souls to Homo sapiens. I'll put Nellie, Kola and Koala right in that mix along with every creature that draws breath.

When Nellie was dying, as I looked into her eyes, it was as though I saw and felt her soul leave her body through those eyes— flyin' right past my head! And that is no exaggeration. One second they were filled with life—even as she lay dying—and the next frozen, glassy and lifeless. I can't explain it, and I can't forget the moment either.

In the soul department, I'm not too sure about fish, but maybe they qualify too. I never got to know one. One look at a video with a dolphin or whale tells me if I've got one, they *must* have one, so fish probably shouldn't be dismissed for my lack of acquaintance with them.

I feel much the same about the existence of God. I can't deny "him," which I don't believe is a "him," but we are inclined to reduce any complexity to our anthropomorphic selves. Sometimes the faith required seems an intellectual step too far, but then people a lot smarter than I have maintained their belief. I hold there is *some* amazing cosmic force of love—call it what you will, and ignore it to your peril.

Jaime loaned us his books by the monk, Thomas Merton. Bill was surprised to read how forcefully he spoke out against the war in Vietnam and our militarism, wryly commenting, "No wonder he died of electrocution. I'm sure it was an accident just like they say."

We learned he died in 1968. The same year as MLK, Jr. and RFK. Tough year for anyone speaking out for peace.

Jaime had said much of Merton's writin' went over his head in terms of Catholic theology, but he still plowed through it. I found myself in the same boat. I did find this little treatise on God something I had to ponder, and I decided it fits my view pretty well.

Your brightness is my darkness. I know nothing of You and, by myself, I cannot even imagine how to go about knowing You. If I imagine You, I am mistaken. If I understand You, I am deluded. If I am conscious and certain I know You, I am crazy. The darkness is enough.

After I'd pondered his words for several days, I read it to Sis saying Merton and I were of one mind in this regard. She responded, "In my 'funny' days, I'd have read that and said it was proof positive Merton wasn't a born again Christian—being used by the Devil to lead others astray."

I chuckled, "I've long suspected the Devil has been bitin' on my tail. I guess I haven't managed to shake him loose if I'm agreein' with Merton."

Of course, I had to tell Jaime of our conversation. He replied, "You and me and Merton—what's to be done with us but send us to the eternal flames. Betsy's old church crowd gets all giddy just thinkin' about it!"

I wonder what twists and turns are tangled up in the mind of these Christians, whose purpose, when not castigating others to Hell, is to egg on any and all towards what they believe is a fulfillment of prophecy ushering in a literal Armageddon—sweepin' 'em up in a cloud and leavin' the rest of us to endure all manner of calamities while *the* antichrist dukes it out with God's holy army. To spare themselves from these calamities, they have to go cherry-pickin' the letter to the Thessalonians to be sure they are swept up just as the trumpet blows—missin' all the fun their lust for the end-time theology demands.

I digress here of a kind, but I'm pretty sure the long war in Revelations, as described, is the repetitive cycle of every century of every millennium since the first weapon was dreamed up. The four horsemen of the apocalypse: conquest, war, famine, and death—yeah, when have we ever seen those align?

I'm not going to pick apart the imagery of the mystic, Paul, who is credited as the author of Thessalonians. Paul essentially admits he is a trouble-twisted soul, but he certainly had his beautiful thoughts. None are finer to me than that recitation of his on those gifts of the spirit (I'll repeat 'em as we can't ponder them too much —love, joy, peace, patience, kindness, generosity, faithfulness, gentleness, self-control) and his discourse in the thirteenth chapter of First Corinthians on faith, hope and love—as well as many other inspiring words from his letters. He wouldn't have known what John of Patmos was going to write later, but such contexts bear no problem for the cherry-pickers whose entire theology is dependent on *their* (superior) understanding of "God's word." In my book, the word *hubris* comes to mind regarding most theological "certainties."

John Geermann said he couldn't align his thoughts on Heaven with those of John of Patmos. I never did think to ask him what he thought about John of Patmos' other visions, though his words implied an equal measure of nonalignment. I studied them to the degree I could find any interest in them, which is to concede, it wasn't much of a study. Our certified spiritual "heathen," Jaime, wondered how it was these zealots were so sure we'd fall under the influence of one great "antichrist" when world leaders are working against Christ as a never-ending act throughout history.

Billy added, "And we even reelect the *cabrones!*"

I'm hard-pressed to put it any better than they have. I'm with Billy on his notion that all this "heaven-heaven-heaven/hell-hell-hell" talk only keeps us from working toward heaven in the here and now. John of Patmos, like most the prophets before him and since, had a vision of it all ending in glorious peace and perfection.

That would be wonderful, but in my lifetime, we are no closer to that as best I can discern. And as for the cloud takin' the faithful up in a flash, they may just get their wish. Our nuclear weapons might take up the "saved" *and* the "lost" in a few hundred or thousand nuclear mushroom clouds across the earth. The one thing John of Patmos couldn't envision in his day, was man's own capacity to incinerate himself and turn all that is to dust at the touch of a button. Such is the progress of our humanity—just in my lifetime.

Everyone is being extra careful these days not to infect us senior citizens over here at the *Vista Grande* "rest home". I'll be glad when this crazy pandemic is over—if it ever is. Somehow pandemic or not, wars can go right on. Bill had been readin' about the ongoin' mess in Yemen. As he noted, "We manufacture wars to sell weapons. It has nothing to do with defense.

"It was called the war department in the early days. At least that was truth in advertising. Now, we throw out the phrase 'for our national security' as the catchall for why we need to ratchet up spending year after year—no matter how diabolical the end result will be. Enough is never enough."

He is right, of course, but thinking about the pandemic and wars just made me lonely for normality. Last evening, I was particularly lonesome for the boys. I called to warn them I was comin' over. I'd be wearin' my mask, so they weren't to shoot me as some robber comin' to kill and plunder. I also informed them that all three of us aged had gotten our first shot that day, and so far we were all still standin'.

When I got over there, they were on the patio reclining in their new chaise lounges having finally worn out the old set that Momma and Daddy had purchased *years* ago. Billy had spot welded them until there were more welds than original steel. (That might be a little exaggerated. Suffice it to say, they looked pretty rough in their old age.) First thing I asked was, "Are they as comfortable as that last set? We sure got our money's worth out of them."

Jaime responded, "They could use a little thicker pad, but then Billy doesn't need it. Bill and I would benefit from a bit more padding."

I settled into one and agreed with Jaime. "Not as good as the old ones, but they'll do."

Jaime asked, "Were there many up gettin' their shots when you were in town?"

"I'm glad you brought that up. We walked right in. I know you young'uns aren't officially approved by the government for your shot yet, but they said they had enough vaccine and you should come on in. Just go to the fire station. You'll be in and out in five minutes. We can get the second jab in a month or so."

"I guess we'll do that *mañana*," Jaime reckoned.

"Get 'er done," Billy responded.

Then he asked, "So how you comin' on with that writin'?"

"That's the first you've even acknowledged you knew I was working on it," I answered. "It's hardly like you to not come nosin' around to check on my progress."

"Livin' with Jaime and Noah, I learned *long ago* not to interrupt the creative process. I figured when you were ready to talk about it, you'd wander over here."

"And here I am," I said. "Probably ahead of schedule from what you expected."

"Does that mean you're done?" Jaime asked.

"All done but finishin'," I clarified.

Billy said, "You didn't even know you had all that bottled up in there, did ya?"

I chuckled, "You have no idea!"

"Well, when we gonna get to read it?" Billy inquired.

I told him, "You already know all of it."

"Yea, but I need to make sure you didn't skip over anything or forget to mention me."

"Yyeeaaa," I drew out slowly. "I know you thought I'd leave you out of the tellin' of my life."

"You didn't leave out them dogs did ya, or Nellie? Nellie will come back to haunt you if you did."

I assured him, "Dogs, Nellie and the boy are all covered."

"And what about Jaime? Just because his last name is Cruz doesn't mean he should be left out."

"Billy, I think you know that Jaime and Zoey made the cut. I've included all the strays we've rounded up including our family of a kind."

"Well, that's good. Sounds like you've done your due diligence," Billy stated flatly.

I added, "By the time little Emilio is ready to get up on a horse, if he doesn't go to screamin' like Brett, I'll not be riding with him. It's up to you boys to pass along my life to him."

Jaime reassured me, "In that regard, you've got every niece, nephew, great-niece, great-nephew and the odd family member of a kind like me and Zoey to be sure they know who their Aunt Sallie was."

Billy interjected, "Don't be puttin' her up on that ridge just yet! She's got another good ten years at least."

I didn't deny it. "I might live that long, but I'm content to go any time."

Billy noted, "We haven't gotten over buryin' them dogs yet."

"That's for sure," Jaime added. "I can't believe how much we miss 'em."

Billy added, "I've got the word out at the shelter that if they get a couple Aussie Shepherds we want 'em."

"No red heelers this time?" I asked.

Jaime responded. "We don't want to project Kola and Koala onto two innocent pups. We thought we start with another breed— see what they amount to."

"That's sorta been the pattern going from horse to horse here, hasn't it?" I reflected.

Billy answered, "That's right. Start fresh."

The three of us just sat there silent for a long time. The sun had set, the pastel colors fadin' into night. It was going to be a clear moonless sky. I knew if we sat there long enough, the Milky Way would soon be appearing. We did just sit there; all content and each lost in our own thoughts.

Billy finally broke the silence to ask, "Does your story have a theme—one that stands out maybe more than the rest?"

I thought about it a few seconds before answering. "I suppose that would be Daddy teaching me about nature's symbiosis and saying, 'Ignore it to your peril.'"

Jaime responded, "I'm not sure I knew he'd said that, but I can attest to how deeply it is instilled in this family."

I thought Billy would say something, but he seemed content to return to silence.

When the Milky Way was up there in all its glory, I said, "Something else Daddy said, Jaime, that you might not have ever heard. He loved to sit out on this very patio and do what we are doing right now. He'd say, 'Look at that little slice of the cosmos. Somethin,' isn't it?'"

"It sure is," Jaime replied.

"Boys, I might be limpin' toward the valley of shadow, and will soon enough lie down in green pastures—I don't even mind that the grass is brown and gray half the year. Any good stand of grass is all to the good. My life on this ranch has been nothin' but all to the good—all to the good."

Billy replied, "Well, Aunt Sallie, when it comes to being all to the good in someone's life, you're our example."

"Don't get carried away," I replied. "But I know the love that spoke those words comes from that place none of us can fully understand. We just live into it."

Jaime muttered, as to record those words, "We just live into it."

This ends my tellin'. When Billy is comin' up on my age, he should probably add his own stories to the family record. I have tried to honor Noah's directive, "We don't want some glorified version that makes everybody look like saints." That was easy enough, and I know Billy wouldn't know how to even write such a glorified version—not that I ever could have either.

It has certainly been a mix of joy and sorrow and amazement, as I brought all these memories back to what occupies my days now. What a journey my life has been, even though most of my days, for virtually all of my life, I've not moved more than a few miles across this ranch! And even my last journey will only take me back across the two cattle guards to the cemetery ridge where we now go for our final rest, while my soul drifts to wherever souls drift, in this amazing cosmos.

As I ponder what others will make of my stories, I am reminded of another Twain quote. "If you don't read the newspaper, you're uninformed. If you read the newspaper, you're misinformed." Most won't ever read these stories, and they will be uninformed as to what defined this family in this unique place. For those who do read my stories, I trust I've kept things on a level of unvarnished truth, so as not to misinform others as to my life or the lives of those who occupy my mind—and hold dear.

If those who read them can make any sense from all my meanderin', well, then I guess I've done my due diligence in tellin' my stories. Hopefully, even if it isn't *all* to the good, enough is to the good to register as havin' been worthwhile gettin' to know what makes this ol' cowgirl tick.

All my love,

Sallie Geermann